August 2013

Dear Friends,

Welcome to the second installment in the Rose Harbor Inn series. Jo Marie is eager to update you on what's been happening at the inn. The inn is booked solid this visit and you'll enjoy meeting Kent and Julie Shivers, who are celebrating their fiftieth wedding anniversary—the only problem is they can't seem to get along. Their granddaughter is refereeing them and dealing with the boy next door, who was nothing but a pest . . . except now he can't take his eyes off her. And then there's Mary Smith . . .

But wait, I'm getting ahead of myself. This happens with novel writers. We fall in love with our stories and characters and have trouble not blurting out the entire plotline.

What I really want is for you to make yourself at home at the inn. Jo Marie is baking cookies for this big shindig she regrets . . . oops, I'm getting ahead of myself again. And of course there's the handyman Mark, who . . . okay, that's it. I'm not saying one more word. I'll leave it to you to turn the page and get started reading.

Now, please, sit back and relax. I promise I won't give anything else away. Everyone at Cedar Cove is eager to update you on what's been going on, and, as always, that seems to be quite a lot.

Something else writers like . . . feedback. I'd love to hear what you think. You can reach me in a variety of ways. My website at DebbieMacomber.com is one, Facebook is another, and then of course you can always write me at P.O. Box 1458, Port Orchard, WA 98366. I'd love to hear from you.

Warmest regards,

Debbie Macomber

BALLANTINE BOOKS BY DEBBIE MACOMBER

Rose Harbor in Bloom
Starting Now
Angels at the Table
The Inn at Rose Harbor

For a complete list of books by Debbie Macomber,
visit her website at www.debbiemacomber.com.

ROSE HARBOR
IN BLOOM

BALLANTINE BOOKS

NEW YORK

DEBBIE MACOMBER

Rose Harbor in Bloom

A Novel

Rose Harbor in Bloom is a work of fiction. Names, characters, places, and incidents are the products of the author's imagination or are used fictitiously. Any resemblance to actual events, locales, or persons, living or dead, is entirely coincidental.

Copyright © 2013 by Debbie Macomber

Published in the United States by Ballantine Books, an imprint of The Random House Publishing Group, a division of Random House, Inc., New York.

BALLANTINE and the HOUSE colophon are registered trademarks of Random House, Inc.

LIBRARY OF CONGRESS CATALOGING-IN-PUBLICATION DATA
Macomber, Debbie.
Rose Harbor in bloom : a novel / Debbie Macomber.
pages cm
ISBN 978-0-345-52893-3 (hardcover : acid-free paper) —
ISBN 978-0-345-54332-5 (ebook)
1. Hotelkeepers—Fiction. 2. Life change events—Fiction.
3. Domestic fiction. I. Title.
PS3563.A2364R67 2013
813'.54—dc23   2013010607

Printed in the United States of America on acid-free paper

www.ballantinebooks.com

2 4 6 8 9 7 5 3 1

FIRST EDITION

Book design by Dana Leigh Blanchette

To

Peter and Maureen Kleinknecht,

our fun Florida friends

Here's to wine, golf, yarn, and friendship.

ROSE HARBOR
IN BLOOM

Chapter 1

Rose Harbor was in bloom. Purple rhododendrons and red azaleas dotted the property. I stood on the porch, leaning against the thick white post, and looked over the property for my bed-and-breakfast. *The Inn at Rose Harbor* was beautifully scripted on the wooden sign and was prominently displayed in the front of the yard along with my name, *Jo Marie Rose,* as proprietor.

I never planned on owning or operating a bed-and-breakfast. But then I never expected to be a widow in my thirties, either. If I'd learned anything in this road called life it's that it often takes unexpected turns, rerouting us from the very path that had once seemed so right. My friends advised me against purchasing the inn. They felt the move was too drastic: it meant more than just moving and leaving my job; it would mean an entire life change. Many thought

I should wait at least a year after losing Paul. But my friends were wrong. I'd found peace at the inn, and somewhat to my surprise, a certain contentment.

Until I purchased the inn, I'd lived in a condo in the heart of downtown Seattle. Because of my job and other responsibilities, I hadn't had pets, well, other than as a youngster. But shortly after I moved to Cedar Cove I got Rover. In only a few short months, I'd grown especially fond of him; he'd become my shadow, my constant companion.

Rover was a rescue dog I'd gotten through Grace Harding, the Cedar Cove librarian. Grace volunteered at the local animal shelter, and she'd recommended I adopt a dog. I thought I wanted a German shepherd. Instead I'd come home with this indiscriminate mixed-breed short-haired mutt. The shelter had dubbed him Rover because it was clear he'd been on his own, roaming about for a good long time.

My musings were interrupted by mutterings from the area where I planned to plant a rose garden and eventually add a gazebo. The sound came from Mark Taylor, the handyman I'd hired to construct the sign that stood in the front yard.

Mark was an interesting character. I'd given him plenty of work, but I had yet to figure out if he considered me a friend. He acted like my friend most of the time, but then every so often he turned into a grumpy, unlikable, cantankerous, unreasonable . . . the list went on.

"What's up?" I called out.

"Nothing," he barked back.

Apparently, the ill-tempered monster had returned.

Months ago I'd asked Mark to dig up a large portion of the yard for a rose garden. He'd told me this project would be low on his priority list. He seemed to work on it when the mood struck him, which unfortunately wasn't often, but still I thought a month or two would be adequate in between the other projects he'd done for me. To be fair to Mark, though, it'd been a harsh winter. Still, my expectations hadn't been met. I'd wanted the rosebushes planted by now. I'd so hoped to have the garden in full bloom in time for the open house I planned to host for the Cedar Cove Chamber of Commerce. The problem, or at least one of them, was the fact that Mark was a perfectionist. He must have taken a week simply to measure the yard. String and chalk markings crisscrossed from one end of the freshly mowed lawn to the other. Yes, Mark had insisted on mowing it first before he measured.

Normally, I'm not this impatient, but enough was enough. Mark was a skilled handyman. I had yet to find anything he *couldn't* do. He was an all-purpose kind of guy, and most of the time I felt lucky to have him around. It seemed as time progressed I found more and more small jobs that required his attention.

New to this business and not so handy myself, I needed someone I could rely on to make minor repairs. As a result, the plans for the rose garden had basically been ignored until the very last minute. At the rate Mark worked, I'd resigned myself to the fact that it wasn't possible for it to be ready before Sunday afternoon.

I watched as he straightened and wiped his forearm across his brow. Looking up, he seemed to notice I was still watching him from the porch. "You going to complain again?" he demanded.

"I didn't say a word." Reading his mood, I forced myself to bite my tongue before I said something to set him off. All Mark needed was one derogatory word from me as an excuse to leave for the day.

"You didn't need to say anything," Mark grumbled. "I can read frowns, too."

Rover raised his head at Mark's less-than-happy tone and then looked back at me as though he expected me to return the verbal volley. I couldn't help being disappointed, and it would have been easy to follow through with a few well-chosen words. Instead, I smiled ever so sweetly, determined to hold my tongue. All I could say was that it was a good thing Mark charged by the job and not by the hour.

"Just say what's on your mind," he insisted.

"I thought I'd told you I wanted the rose garden planted before I held the open house," I said, doing my level best not to show my frustration.

"You might have mentioned this earlier, then," he snapped.

"I did."

"Clearly it slipped my mind."

"Well, don't get your dander up." It wasn't worth fighting about at this late date. The invitations were mailed, and the event, ready or not, was scheduled for this very weekend. It would be nothing short of a miracle if Mark finished before then. No need to get upset about it now.

Actually, I was as much at fault for this delay as Mark. Often before he ever started work, I'd invite him in for coffee. I'd discovered that he was as interesting as he was prickly. Perhaps most surprising of all was that he'd become one of my closest friends in Cedar Cove, so naturally I wanted to find out what I could about him. The problem was he wasn't much of a talker. I'd learned more about him while playing Scrabble than in conversation. He was smart and competitive, and he had a huge vocabulary.

Even now, after five months, he avoided questions and never talked about anything personal. I didn't know if he'd ever been married or if he had family in the area. Despite all our conversations, most of what I knew about him I'd deduced on my own. He lived alone. He didn't like talking on the phone, and he had a sweet tooth. He tended to be a perfectionist, and he took his own sweet time on a project. That was the sum total of everything I'd learned about a man I saw on average four or five times a week. He seemed to enjoy our chats, but I wasn't fooled. It wasn't my wit and charm that interested him—it was the cookies that often accompanied our visits. If I hadn't been so curious about him he probably would have gone straight to work. Well, from this point forward I would be too busy for what I called our coffee break.

Grumbling under his breath, Mark returned to digging up the grass and stacking squares of it around the edges of the cleared space. He cut away each section as if he was serving up precise portions of wedding cake.

Despite my frustration with the delay and his persnickety ways, I continued to lean against the porch column and watch him work. The day was bright and sunny. I wasn't about to let all that sunshine go to waste. Window washing, especially the outside ones, was one of my least favorite tasks, but it needed to be done. I figured there was no time like the present.

The hot water had turned lukewarm by the time I dipped the sponge into the plastic bucket. Glancing up at the taller windows, I exhaled and dragged the ladder closer to the side of the house. If Paul were alive, I realized, he'd be the one climbing the ladder. I shook my head to remind myself that if Paul were alive I wouldn't own this inn or be living in Cedar Cove in the first place.

Sometimes I wondered if Paul would even recognize the woman I'd become in the last year. I wore my thick, dark hair much longer these days. Most of the time I tied it at the base of my neck with a scrunchie. My hair, which had always been professionally groomed for the office, had grown to the point that when I let it hang free, the tendrils bounced against the top of my shoulders.

Mark, who rarely commented on anything, made a point of letting me know I looked like I was still a teenager. I took it as a compliment, although I was fairly certain that wasn't his intent. I doubt Mark has spent much time around women, because he could make the rudest comments and hardly seem aware of what he'd said.

My hairstyle wasn't the only change in my appearance. Gone

were the crisp business suits, pencil skirts, and fitted jackets that were the customary uniform for my position at the bank. These days it was mostly jeans and a sweater beneath a bib apron. One of the surprises of owning the inn was how much I enjoyed cooking and baking. I often spent the mornings in my kitchen whipping up a batch of this or that. Until I purchased the inn there hadn't been much opportunity to create elaborate meals. These days I found I could read a recipe book with the same rapture as a *New York Times* bestseller. Baking distracts me and provides afternoon treats for my guests and wonderful muffins and breads I take such pride in serving for the breakfasts. I'd put on a few pounds, too, no thanks to all the baking I did, but I was working on losing weight. Thankfully, my favorite jeans still fit.

Some days I paused, wondering if Paul would know the new me—mainly because I didn't recognize myself any longer. I'd changed, which I suppose was only natural. My entire world had been set upside down.

After dipping the sponge in the soapy water, I headed up the first three steps of the ladder, ready to wash off several months' accumulation of dirt and grime. I wrinkled my nose at the pungent scent of vinegar, which my mother had recommended for cleaning windows. Unfortunately, I failed to write down the proportions. Seeing that it was a big bucket, I emptied half a bottle into the hot water. At this point, my bucket smelled more like a pickle barrel.

"What are you doing?" Mark shouted from across the yard.

"What does it look like I'm doing?" I asked, refusing to let his bad mood rile me. Being Mark's friend required more than a fair share of patience.

He stabbed the pitchfork into the grass and marched across the lawn toward me like a soldier heading into battle. A thick dark frown marred his face. "Get down from there."

I remained frozen on the third step. "Excuse me?" This had to be some kind of joke.

"You heard me."

I stared at him in disbelief. No way was I going to let Mark dictate what I could and couldn't do on my own property.

"Ladders are dangerous," he said, his fists digging into his hip bones.

I simply ignored him, climbed up one additional step, and started to wash the window.

"Don't you know sixty percent of all home accidents involve someone falling off a ladder?"

"I hadn't heard that, but I do know sixty percent of all statistics are made up on the spot." I thought my retort would amuse him. It didn't. If anything, his frown grew deeper and darker.

"You shouldn't be on that ladder. For the love of heaven, Jo Marie, be sensible."

"Me?" If anyone was being unreasonable, it was Mark.

"It's dangerous up there."

"Do you suggest a safety net?" He made it sound as if I was walking along a window ledge on the fifty-ninth floor of a sixty-story building instead of on a stepladder.

Mark didn't answer my question. He pinched his lips into a taut line. "I don't want to argue about this."

"Good, let's not. I'm washing windows, so you can go back to planting my rose garden."

"No," he insisted.

"No?"

"I'm staying right here until you give up this foolishness and come down from there."

I heaved an expressive sigh. Mark was treating me like I was in kindergarten instead of like a woman who was fully able of taking care of herself. "I suppose I should be grateful you're concerned."

"Don't be ridiculous," he said. "For all I care you could break your fool neck, but I just don't want to be around to see it happen."

"How kind of you," I muttered, unable to keep the sarcasm out of my voice. His attitude as much as his words irritated me, so I ignored him and continued washing the windows. When I was satisfied the top two were clean, I carefully backed down the rungs just to prove I was capable of being cautious. Mark had his hands braced on the ladder, holding it steady.

"Are you still here?" I asked. I knew darn good and well he was.

Again he ignored the question.

"I'm not paying you to stand around and watch me work," I reminded him.

He narrowed his eyes into slits. "Fine, then. I quit."

I didn't believe him. "No, you don't."

Within seconds he was off the porch and stalking across the yard, every step punctuated with irritation.

I jumped down the last two rungs and followed him. I don't usually lose my temper, but he was pushing all the wrong buttons with me. I'm far too independent to have anyone, especially a man, dictate what I could and couldn't do.

"You can't quit," I told him. "And you certainly can't leave my yard torn up like this."

Mark acted as though he hadn't heard a word I'd said. Instead he gathered his pitchfork and other tools, most of which he'd left in the grass.

"We have a contract," I reminded him.

"So sue me."

"Fine, I will . . . I'll have my attorney contact you first thing in the morning." I didn't have an attorney, but I hoped the threat of one would shake Mark up enough to realize how foolish he was behaving. I should have known better; Mark didn't so much as blink.

Rover followed me across the lawn and remained at my side. I couldn't believe Mark. After all these months he was ready to walk away over something completely asinine. It made no sense.

With his pitchfork and shovel in one hand and his toolbox in the other he started to leave, then seemed to change his mind, because he abruptly turned back.

I moved one step forward, grateful he'd come to his senses.

"Give your lawyer my cell phone number."

"Yeah, right. You forget to carry it half the time, and if you do, the battery is low."

"Whatever. Give your attorney the number to my business line, seeing that you're so hot to sue me."

"I'll do that." My back went rigid as Mark stalked off the property. I looked down at Rover, who'd cocked his head to one side as if he, too, found it difficult to understand what had just happened and why. He wasn't the only one.

"He isn't worth the angst," I advised my dog, and then, because I was half afraid Rover might be tempted to run after Mark, I squatted down and patted his head. "Everything takes ten times longer than he estimates, anyway." Raising my voice in the hopes that Mark would hear me, I added, "Good riddance."

I stood back up and remained in the middle of my yard until Mark was completely out of view. Then and only then did I allow my shoulders to sag with defeat.

This was nuts. Barely an hour earlier we'd been sipping coffee and tea on the porch, and now I was threatening Mark with a lawsuit. And the way I felt right then, he deserved it.

Returning to my window washing, I was so agitated that I scrubbed and washed the glass until the shine nearly blinded me. I finished in record time, the muscles in my upper arms aching from the vigorous scrubbing I'd done. For half a second I was tempted to contact Mark and let him know I'd survived this dangerous feat but then thought better of it. He would have to apologize to me because he'd been way off base, treating me like I was a child.

My apologizing to him simply wasn't going to happen. But I

knew him well enough to realize how stubborn he could be. If he said he wasn't coming back, then I had to believe he meant it.

My anger carried me all the way into the evening. I didn't want to admit it, but the truth was I would miss Mark. I'd sort of grown accustomed to having him stop by every so often, if for no other reason than coffee. He offered great feedback on the cookies and other items I baked. We'd grown comfortable with each other. He was a friend, nothing more, and I appreciated that we could be simply that: friends.

In an effort to distract myself, I emptied the dirty wash water from the bucket in the laundry-room sink, rinsed out the sponge, and set it out to dry, and then went into my small office.

I had guests arriving this weekend, which was the good news and the bad news. The first name I saw on the list was for the mysterious Mary Smith. I took the reservation shortly after taking over the inn, and it had stayed in my mind. Mary had sounded unsure, hesitant, as if she wasn't sure she was doing the right thing booking this room.

A party had booked the inn as well. The original call had come in from Kent Shivers, who hadn't sounded the least bit excited about all this hoopla his family had planned for him. Kent and his wife, Julie, were about to celebrate their fiftieth wedding anniversary by renewing their vows. Other room reservations had been added at later dates, all from family members. Seven of my eight rooms were booked for Saturday.

Only one of the guests would be here through Sunday evening, though, and that was Mary Smith. Remembering her hesitation, I'd half wondered if she'd cancel at the last minute, but to this point I hadn't heard otherwise. Her room was made up and ready.

I didn't have much of an appetite for dinner and ate chips and salsa, which wasn't anything I'd normally choose. Because I was restless and at loose ends I decided to bake peanut-butter cookies, one of my favorites. It wasn't until they were cooling on the countertop that I remembered they were Mark's favorite, too.

Rover curled up on the rug in front of the refrigerator, one of his favorite spots. He seemed content, but I was restless, pacing the kitchen, and then a short while later moving from one room to another. Once in my private quarters, I tried to knit, but I ended up making one mistake after another and finally stuffed the project back into the basket. Television didn't hold my interest, either. A book I'd found fascinating just the night before bored me now.

I might as well admit it. All this fidgeting was due to my argument with Mark. In retrospect I wished I'd handled the situation differently. But really, what could I have done? Mark seemed bound and determined to argue with me. He was the one who'd gone completely off his rocker. Oh, great, now I was thinking in clichés, but it was true—our clash of wills was all due to his being high-handed and completely unreasonable.

Really, who else would go ballistic over something so ridiculous as washing windows because I chose to stand on a stepladder? He'd been rude, demanding, and utterly irrational. I wasn't putting up with that. Not from him; not from anyone.

Still, it saddened me that it had come to this.

Rover lifted his head from his spot in front of the fireplace and then rested his chin on his paws.

"Just think of all the money I'll save in flour and sugar," I said in a weak attempt at making a joke.

It felt flat even to my own ears.

Okay, I'd admit it. I was going to miss Mark.

Chapter 2

I didn't sleep well, which wasn't surprising after my tiff with Mark. I did feel bad about our disagreement, but I couldn't allow him, or anyone else, to dictate to me what I could and couldn't do in my own home.

If he was intent on breaking the contract, then so be it. The threat of a lawsuit hadn't fazed him in the least. I'd spoken in the heat of the moment and regretted that. I'd leave matters as they were for the time being until we'd both cooled down.

With no guests to prepare breakfast for, I took my time, luxuriating in not having any demands placed on me first thing in the morning, although Mary Smith would be arriving sometime before lunch. Rover followed me into the kitchen, where I brewed myself a cup of coffee. I walked out on the front porch, leaning against the round column, holding my mug while Rover did his business, watering the front lawn. When he finished, he leaped up the porch steps, bounding with such energy that I couldn't keep from smiling.

The sky was overcast and gray, threatening rain. My hope was the sun would burn off the clouds and eventually shine. Sipping my coffee, I looked over my torn-up yard where I'd hoped to have roses in bloom and slowly exhaled, feeling frustrated and irritated.

I had some baking I wanted to do that morning, muffins this time. I made a mental note to contact either Grace Harding at the library or Peggy and Bob Beldon, who owned another Cedar Cove B&B, about who I might hire to finish planting the roses and building the gazebo. One thing I could guarantee: whoever took on the job would complete it long before Mark ever would have, had he not quit.

I went inside and fed Rover, and as I was putting his food back in the pantry, I heard a car door close. Checking my watch, I saw it was early yet, barely seven-thirty. The side door opened, and I heard Hailey call my name.

"I'm in here," I shouted back, and Rover hurried over to greet her.

Hailey Tremont was the high school senior I'd hired, recommended by Grace Harding. Hailey came in twice a week to help me with housekeeping chores and anything else I needed done.

She rounded the corner, leading into the kitchen. "Morning," she said, and bent over to pet Rover. She was a pretty girl, petite and sweet-natured. She was small for her age, and looking at her, I found it hard to believe she was eighteen years old.

A few weeks back Grace had asked if I could use help. Apparently, Hailey's family owned property next to Grace and her husband's ranch in the Olalla area. Grace told me Hailey hoped for a career in the hospitality business and needed a part-time job. It would give the teenager experience and a little nest egg before she headed off to college in the fall.

"I wanted to see if you needed me Saturday or Sunday," she asked.

I knew the high school graduation ceremony was scheduled for this weekend. "What day is your graduation?"

"Sunday. I could work if you felt you needed me." She looked down. "My grandparents will be in town and my aunt Melanie, too, but I could stop by."

I could use the help on Sunday, but I wouldn't ask her to come in on the day of her graduation. "Why don't you come after school today and tomorrow?" I glanced up. "Does that upset your schedule?"

"No, that's perfect." Her eyes brightened when she realized she was free on Sunday.

I wished I had more hours to give her, but my business was just getting off the ground.

"I'll be here this afternoon."

"Perfect," I told her.

Hailey glanced at her wrist. "I better get to school. It seems a little silly to attend classes when all our assignments are in and we've already gotten our grades. I think most of us go simply because we know these are the last days we'll be together."

I remembered my own graduation. It seemed like a lifetime ago. I'd drifted away from most of my high school friends, but stayed in contact with my two best friends. Diane had moved to Texas, was married with two children, and Katie lived in north Seattle. Katie was married with three children. We kept in touch on Facebook and by email, although it'd been far too long since we'd last gotten together. I promised myself I'd make the effort to have Katie over to Cedar Cove soon. She'd seen the inn after I'd first bought it and loved it as much as I did.

"I better head off to class, or non-class," Hailey said, and added a short laugh. "I'll see you later this afternoon."

"Great." I got out the mixing bowl and the other ingredients I'd need for the muffins.

I had the cookbook open in front of me and brought out the necessary ingredients when I heard a noise outside. I paused, but I didn't investigate right away. I had a sneaky suspicion it was Mark.

When I peeked out the foyer window, I saw that I was right. Mark stood looking down on the grass he'd dug up in order to plant the rose garden. My guess was he felt as bad about our disagreement as I did and wanted to set matters straight. Most likely he'd just begin working again and pretend yesterday had never happened.

I wouldn't ask for an apology, although I felt he owed me one. For that matter, I probably owed him one, too. My shoulders relaxed, and I hesitated. I didn't realize how tense our disagreement had made me, nor did I want to admit how glad I was to see him.

I decided to play it cool. I'd wait a few minutes, pour him a cup of coffee, and tell him I intended on baking muffins and see how he reacted. I watched the clock, and after five very slow minutes I brought down a coffee mug, filled it, and carried it outside. I hesitated on the top step.

Mark was nowhere in sight.

I couldn't imagine where he'd gone but then noticed the door to the large tool shed was cracked open. I walked down the steps to the shed, opened the door, and turned on the light. Mark wasn't there. In that short amount of time, just minutes, Mark had come and gone, taking with him the few items he'd stored at my place.

It looked like he was serious about breaking the contract. He'd had all night to think matters over. If he felt the same in the light of a new day, that told me he didn't have any regrets. Well, so much for that.

I heard the phone ring in the distance and hurried back into the house. I dumped the coffee on the lawn, rather than risk spilling it in my rush to get to the phone.

"Rose Harbor Inn," I said, hoping I didn't sound as breathless as I felt.

"Good morning," a cheerful male voice greeted me.

"Morning," I replied.

"I'm calling to see if you have any more rooms available starting tomorrow and through the weekend."

I didn't need to check my reservation book to know that I did. "I only have one room left."

"Great; book it. I'll be driving Kent and Julie Shivers from Portland. My name is Sutton, Oliver Sutton, and I'm a longtime family friend. I'll be in town for their anniversary party."

"Yes, yes, I have their reservation right here," I said, glancing down at the book. The family would be gathering in Cedar Cove. I had to wonder why they would choose to come all the way from Oregon to our sleepy town, but I figured I'd find out soon enough.

"Would it be possible to give the Shivers a room on the bottom floor?" he asked. "I'm assuming there are stairs from the photo of the inn I viewed online?"

"Actually, the inn has guest rooms on three floors, but fortunately I do have a room on the main level." It was my favorite one, larger than the other rooms, with a love seat and fireplace. It had a beautiful view of the cove, and when the weather was clear the Olympic Mountains shone as a backdrop. Some days they were so breathtakingly beautiful it was all I could do not to simply stare at them.

"Is it available?" Oliver asked.

"Yes."

"Wonderful. I'm afraid stairs are a bit much for Kent these days, although he'd never admit it."

"I can switch rooms without a problem, but there's a slight price difference." It was only fair that I tell him that.

"No problem. Just add that to my bill, if you would."

"Okay. Do you have a preference when it comes to your room?" I asked.

He hesitated. "Annie Newton has also booked a room at the inn, is that right?"

"Yes, as a matter of fact, she has." I'd met Annie a couple of times, although only briefly. She was the Shivers's granddaughter and the reason I knew that the Shivers were celebrating their fiftieth wedding anniversary. Annie lived in the Seattle area and had stopped by to check out the inn and make other arrangements for the family gathering. I'd learned she was a party planner by profession, and had taken on organizing the event.

"If possible, I'd like a room on the same floor as Annie's."

"I can do that." That meant shifting Mary Smith to another room, but that wouldn't be a problem.

"Perfect. I'll see you tomorrow, then, with the Shivers. I plan to arrive around noon."

I took his credit card information and paused as I looked down. I'd taken the reservation for Mary Smith the same day that Kent Shivers had phoned. Both conversations had stayed in my mind, which was unusual.

By mid-morning, the scent of the carrot-and-pineapple muffins filled my kitchen. The recipe was a new one, and I was anxious to try it out. The ingredient list called for walnuts, raisins, and flaxseed. Filled with fruit, nuts, and seeds, they were healthy, and if the heavenly scent coming from the oven was anything to go by, they would be delicious, too. I also planned to bake cookies, if time allowed.

Hailey arrived around two, when the kitchen countertops were lined with cookies and the muffins rested on top of the stove.

"Where would you like me to start?" she asked, after setting her backpack inside my office.

I gave her a detailed list that I'd made up earlier. She read it over, asked me a couple of questions, and then set about completing the tasks. While she was busy I worked in the kitchen. I finished loading the dishwasher, and after placing the cookies for the open house in an air-tight storage container, I wiped down the countertops.

I planned to serve the muffins with breakfast over the weekend. My baking for the open house was just getting started. I had several cookbooks spread out across the table when I heard the sound of a car approaching.

I looked out the window as the driver parked the car, climbed out, and then came around to the other side of the vehicle and opened the passenger door. A woman I could only assume was Mary Smith slid out and paused as she viewed the inn. She was an elegantly dressed businesswoman.

I removed my apron, and with Rover at my heels met her on the walkway leading to the front door.

"Hello and welcome," I said. "I'm Jo Marie Rose. Welcome to Rose Harbor Inn."

"Thank you," she returned with a faint New York accent.

I recognized the high-end designer suit immediately and realized it was slightly too big for her. It wasn't until then that I noticed the scarf on her head cleverly disguised the fact that she had lost her hair. Mary Smith appeared to have recently undergone chemotherapy. She had cancer, and I could only speculate what would bring her all the way from New York to Cedar Cove and Rose Harbor Inn.

Chapter 3

Exhausted from the long flight out of Newark, Mary Smith lay down on the bed and closed her eyes. The desire to visit Cedar Cove had come after she'd been diagnosed with breast cancer. It'd been an impulse motivated by fear, she realized. The truth was she never actually expected to make the trip. She wasn't an impulsive woman. She lived a purposeful life. Flying all the way across the country on a whim was completely unlike her, and yet . . . yet here she was.

Mary had intentionally booked a nonstop flight into Seattle so she wouldn't have to change planes. She feared the necessity of rushing from one gate to another might have completely worn her out physically. As it was, the six-hour flight between the east and west coasts had utterly drained her. Yet tired as she was, she found it impossible to nap. Her mind raced, tumbling back through the years . . . to the decisions she'd made and the man she'd once loved.

For all she knew George might still live in Seattle. The last she'd heard, nineteen years ago—oh, had it really been that long?—he'd married. Mary wanted him to be happy, which was one reason she didn't plan on contacting him. She'd stayed completely out of his life and that wasn't going to change.

The app on her phone displayed the weather forecast for the next five days, including the weekend. What she remembered, having lived in the Seattle area for almost a year, was that it had rained almost continually. As if to contradict her, the app showed nearly five days of sunshine, which came as an unexpected bonus. What she was surprised to learn, once she'd left Seattle for a position on the East Coast, was that New York City received a higher annual rainfall than Seattle. But then Seattle had the drizzle factor and more days in which the skies were gray and overcast.

The song that said the bluest skies they'd ever seen were in Seattle had it right, though. Despite the weather, whatever it might be, Seattle would always hold a special place in her heart. It was here that she'd fallen in love, truly, deeply in love, for the one and only time in her life.

It seemed ridiculous to stay indoors and attempt to sleep when the sun was out. She had packed light, and it didn't take her long to place the few items in the dresser drawer.

Once she'd finished, she left the room and slowly climbed down the stairs. The proprietor stepped out of the kitchen when she reached the bottom step.

"I hope everything in your room is satisfactory?" Jo Marie asked, and then with a look of concern added, "Are you going to be all right with the stairs?"

"It's fine."

"There is one room on the main level, but unfortunately I've already promised that to an older couple. Had I known . . ." She hesitated.

Mary held up her hand, stopping her. "It's fine. I'm getting stronger every day."

"Is there anything more I can do to make you more comfortable?"

"Nothing, thank you," Mary assured her.

The proprietor didn't look convinced. "Can I get you a cup of tea?"

"That would be lovely." Mary didn't much feel like chatting. "Would it be all right if I drank it on the porch?"

"Of course. I'll bring it out to you. Would you like sugar or milk?"

"Just plain."

The Adirondack chair offered her a view of the Olympic mountain range as a backdrop to the smooth waters of the cove in the forefront. The shipyard was across the way, with an aircraft carrier and a number of other vessels docked there. The waters of the cove were a deep green, with a lighthouse at a point in the distance. This was a lovely area. Ideal, really.

The door leading off the porch opened, and a teenage girl stepped out carrying a tray with a teapot and china cup and a couple of cookies on a matching plate. She set it down on the table next to Mary's chair.

"Hello," Mary said, smiling up at the girl.

"Hello. Jo Marie asked me to bring this out to you."

"Thank you."

"Would you like me to pour?"

Mary hesitated. She was perfectly capable of pouring her own tea, but she welcomed the girl's company. "Please."

The girl lifted the teapot and, holding onto the lid, tipped it ever so carefully as she filled the delicate cup. Steam rose, and the scent of chamomile wafted toward Mary.

"What's your name?" Mary asked.

"Hailey."

"Do you live in the area?"

"I do." Hailey straightened and stepped back. "It can get a bit chilly out here, especially if the sun goes behind a cloud. Would you like me to get you an afghan?"

"Please; how thoughtful."

The teenager left and returned a couple of minutes later with a hand-knit afghan in warm pastel colors. She laid it across Mary's lap and then added a pillow.

"Do you attend school here?" Mary asked.

"I do," Hailey said. "I'm graduating on Sunday."

"Congratulations."

"Thank you."

"Any plans for the future?"

Hailey nodded with enthusiasm. "I want to go into hospitality and work in the hotel industry."

"Wonderful."

"It's going to be hard to leave Cedar Cove, my family, and all my friends, but this is what growing up is all about, right? It's time I tested my wings. That's what my grandmother said."

"She's right."

"Mom would like it better if I attended community college for a couple of years, but I got a scholarship for Washington State University."

"Congratulations. How big is your graduating class?"

"Big. Six hundred."

"That's huge."

Hailey agreed.

"My own graduating class was around that size. I was fortunate enough to be the valedictorian."

"Really? One of my best friends, Mandy Palmer, is our class valedictorian. She's so smart. Were you like that?"

Mary smiled. "I'd like to think so, but the ability to get good grades doesn't necessarily translate into living a successful life."

"Mandy will. She's got it all together."

"I'm sure you do, too," Mary said.

"I wish," she said, and folded her hands in front of her. "Is there anything more I can do for you?"

"It's all good. It's been a long day, and I'm feeling tired."

"Then I'll leave you. If you need anything, please don't hesitate to ask. I'll be heading out soon, but Jo Marie is here. It was a pleasure meeting you, Ms. Smith."

"You, too, Hailey."

The teenager left, and, feeling better than she had since she'd stepped off the plane, Mary closed her eyes. It'd been a foolish decision to travel all the way across the country. Her oncologist had advised her against the trip. She needed time to rest, to give her body a chance to heal.

To her surprise, Mary felt her body relax and surrender to the warm bath of sunshine. Almost before she realized it she felt herself drifting into a light sleep. It was only natural, she supposed, that thoughts of George would fill her head.

No man had ever loved her the way George had. There'd been men before and since her affair with him, but no one had ever cared as deeply as the young attorney in Seattle almost twenty years ago.

She remembered the first time they'd met. It'd been a Saturday afternoon, summertime. June, wasn't it? Yes, June. Her friend Louise had suggested lunch at the Seattle Center and made reservations at the Space Needle. They were to meet at the base of the Needle. Mary waited outside, but her friend hadn't shown up.

Growing restless, Mary had paced the area, checking her watch every few minutes. She'd been so intent on looking at her wrist that she'd inadvertently bumped into a man on the sidewalk. That man had been George.

After apologizing profusely, she'd been pleasantly surprised when he said he'd been stood up for lunch himself and wondered if she'd be willing to join him. Seeing that she already had a reservation and it was a shame to let it go to waste, they'd taken the elevator to the restaurant. Rarely had she clicked with anyone the way she did with George. Their attraction was strong and immediate. They enjoyed a three-hour lunch. Later, he confessed that he'd told her a fib. He hadn't been meeting anyone, but had instantly felt drawn to her.

Later, Mary learned that her friend had gotten an emergency phone call. Her father had suffered a heart attack. These were the days before personal cell phones, and Louise didn't have any way of letting her know what had happened.

Seeing how well her afternoon had turned out, Mary wasn't complaining. George asked to see her again, and they met the next day and then the day after that. Inside of a month they were lovers. They were wild for each other, crazy in love, feverish. It had never been like that for Mary. Not before George, and not after him, either.

Mary worked for a brokerage firm, struggling in a man's world, and was making a name for herself. She hadn't wanted to move to Seattle, although it'd proved to be beneficial on a number of different levels. Her work often led her to travel to New York, and she had her eye on a key position with the firm there.

When they first met, George had just made partner in an up-and-coming law firm. They both worked long hours, and the week-long separations were hard. Yet they found ways to be together as much as possible. Three months after their first date, George proposed.

Even now, all these years later, Mary still remembered the disappointed look that came over him when she turned him down. Every instinct told her she was going to be offered the position in New York. George was a law partner, and she wouldn't ask him to give that up. Her gentle refusal hadn't discouraged him, though. If George was anything, it was persistent. Mary lost count of the number of times he'd argued his point. He loved her. She loved him. Even if it meant traveling back and forth between coasts, they could make it work. Their love would carry them, and everything else was small stuff. They'd find a way.

Mary wanted to believe that was true, but after six months flying from one coast to the other, she could see what it was doing to them both. This was no way to live and certainly no way to raise a family. George wanted children; he loved kids, and he deserved to be a father. Frankly, she wasn't good mother material. She didn't have a maternal bone in her body. Motherhood simply didn't interest her. And so Mary had done the only thing she could, and that was to end their relationship. Once she was offered the position in the New York office, she accepted, sold her Seattle condo, and kissed George good-bye one last time. It'd broken her heart and his, but it was necessary.

He'd been stunned, shocked into silence, and unbelievably hurt. She'd hated to do that to him, but really there was no other way.

The cut was clean. Painful, terribly painful for them both, but quick. Two years later, George mailed Mary an invitation to his wedding. It was the one way he had of getting back at her, she supposed, of letting her know he had found someone else to love. Someone who was willing to give him all the things in life he wanted that she wouldn't. Mary had wept twice in her adult life. She cried the day she got his wedding invitation, addressed personally to her in his own hand, and the other . . . well, that was the reason she was in Cedar Cove.

George had moved on, and for that she would always be grateful. Mary had loved George; she supposed she always would. She'd never considered marriage, but if she had, there could be only one man, and that was George. Wonderful, sweet, caring George.

Raising her hand to her forehead, she felt the stubble from her hair, which was just now starting to grow back, following radiation and chemotherapy. Mary sighed and reached for her tea.

Cancer.

The diagnosis had turned her life upside down. One minute she was at the pinnacle of her career. The next moment, following a suspicious mammogram report, she was looking stage-four breast cancer in the face and it had metastasized. Overnight her world changed. Instead of heading board meetings, making decisions, commanding attention, she was sitting in a chair at an oncology center and having medical professionals tell her how best to beat this disease. Instead of giving advice, she was on the listening end.

All her life, Mary had been a woman in charge. Nothing had stood in her way. She was smart, savvy, and sophisticated. She'd stood up to financial institutions, the federal government, and attorneys without batting an eyelash.

She'd risen higher than any woman in the firm to take over as vice president of one of the country's largest New York brokerage firms. She was wealthy beyond her expectations. But money meant little when it came to cancer. She couldn't intimidate cancer, couldn't overwhelm it with the strength of her personality, couldn't pay it off or hand it over to one of her personal assistants.

Nor could she ignore it.

Cancer was there, front and center, staring her in the face, leaving her with no options.

She was sick, and she could get much sicker. Everything that was possible had already been done. What was left was a period of waiting, of resting. In twenty years, Mary hadn't sat still; her life had revolved around her career. Forced now to analyze her past, she was troubled by a series of decisions she'd made . . . decisions that involved George.

It was time to be honest. She'd been a straight shooter with others and was amazed she hadn't dealt with herself the same way.

The excuses for traveling across the country slid off her tongue with ease.

Lies. All lies.

The time had come to own up to the truth. She was in Cedar Cove because of George.

"Mary?"

Mary's eyes flew open and she saw Jo Marie standing in front of her. Gone were the apron and the comfortable jeans and sweater. Now she wore black slacks and a white silk blouse with a pink rose pin secured at the top button. "I need to run a couple of errands."

Mary blinked, unsure why Jo Marie found it necessary to tell her this.

"Don't worry about answering the phone."

For the love of heaven, why would she do that?

"I'm having an open house on Sunday, and . . . ?"

"Okay," she mumbled, but she still couldn't figure out why any of this was her business.

"I won't be gone long, but Hailey is here if you need anything."

· "You don't need to report to me, Ms. Rose. This is your home, and you can do what you like."

"I realize that, but I felt you should know in case anyone arrives."

"Are you expecting anyone?"

"Not really. But I was hoping . . ." She let the rest fade. "If you need anything—"

"I won't," she said, cutting her off. She regretted having chosen a bed-and-breakfast now. She'd heard they could be warm and welcoming. An online search had led Mary to the website for the Inn at Rose Harbor. She'd been wooed by the simple elegance and beauty of the inn. Looking at the online photo of the view had convinced Mary this was where she wanted to be, and she'd booked it.

"Don't fuss over me," she said, perhaps a bit too bluntly. Mary didn't want allowances made for her. Not because she had cancer. Not for any reason.

Jo Marie nodded and left. Her shoes made clicking sounds against the wooden steps.

Mary closed her eyes once again, intent on returning to her thoughts. For years she'd felt bad for the way she'd treated George, especially toward the end of their relationship. She'd been cruel, thinking she'd been doing them both a kindness. And now, sitting in the warm sunshine, with him possibly just across Puget Sound in Seattle, she felt an incredibly strong desire to see him again for what possibly would be the very last time.

She couldn't. Wouldn't, though. George was married. To disrupt his life now would be doubly wrong. She'd made her choice, and now she had no option but to live with it.

Chapter 4

I was on my way out the door when the phone rang. For a moment I was tempted to simply let it go and be about my business. I couldn't, though; I was in business, and this inn was my livelihood.

"Rose Harbor Inn," I said automatically.

"Jo Marie."

I recognized the voice immediately, and my back went rigid.

"This is Lieutenant Colonel Milford."

My hand tightened around the telephone receiver. The last time I'd seen Lieutenant Colonel Milford was at the memorial service held for Paul at Fort Lewis. From the moment I'd learned Paul had gone down on a mountainside in Afghanistan the lieutenant colonel had been wonderful. He'd patiently answered my questions; he'd offered me words of comfort. He'd promised he would do everything within his power to retrieve my husband's remains. He'd been Paul's commanding officer. Paul had thought highly of him, and the respect had been mutual.

"I'm calling because of a promise I made to you and the other families who lost loved ones last April."

"Yes." I was barely able to get the word out from the constriction that tightened my throat.

"I told you at the memorial service that we would make every effort to retrieve Paul's remains so you could give him a proper burial."

"I remember," I whispered. I was sure he was about to tell me Paul's remains had been retrieved. Part of me wanted to hear it, needed to hear it, and at the same time I wanted to place my hands over my ears and shout for him to stop. If they'd located the crash site, that would be the final confirmation that my husband was dead. Despite everything I'd been told, all the assurances that Paul couldn't have survived the crash, I couldn't help holding on to the belief that he had somehow found his way out and he was alive.

"Jo Marie?"

Apparently, the lieutenant colonel had said something and I hadn't picked up on it.

"Sorry."

"The terrain where the helicopter went down was deep in the mountains and inaccessible, but with recent changes we are now able to operate within the area."

He didn't mention what those changes were, but it didn't take much for me to speculate what had happened. Paul and his team had been sent deep into al-Qaeda-held territory. The mountain landscape had made it even more difficult to retrieve the bodies.

"Recent changes?" I repeated. I swallowed hard and bit into my lower lip. "Are you telling me I can bury my husband?" I asked, and my voice trembled as I spoke.

"Yes and no. As I explained, we now have access to the crash site. A team has been assigned to go in and investigate. Once they do and the bodies have been retrieved, we will, of course, need to test for DNA."

"Of course."

"I promised to keep all the families updated."

"Yes, thank you."

"Can I do anything more for you, Jo Marie?"

I wanted to shout at him to bring my husband back to me alive. I wanted him to return to me all that I'd lost on that mountain half a world away. But I knew that request was both impossible and unreasonable. Sooner or later I would need to give up this crazy notion that Paul was still alive. As long as Paul's remains stayed up on that mountainside, I could pretend. I'd clung to that slender thread of hope because that was all I had left to hold on to.

"Paul Rose was a good soldier and a fine officer."

Lieutenant Colonel Milford didn't need to tell me what I already knew.

"Please let me know if there's anything more I can do for you." He hesitated and added, "Is there, Jo Marie?"

"Not just yet . . . Thank you for the call."

"I'll be in touch as soon as I have more information."

"Yes, please," I managed to squeak out, struggling to hide the tears in my voice. "It was good of you to call."

"Remember, I'm here if you have any questions."

"I'll remember." My hand shook as I hung up the phone. When it came to anything having to do with Paul, I couldn't hide my emotions. My life, my dreams were all tied up around my husband, and he'd been taken away from me. I didn't know if I'd ever grow accustomed to this unexpected and tragic turn my life had taken. Meeting him, falling in love, and creating our future together had been some of the happiest days of my life. I'd given up on ever finding the right man. And then there he was when I'd least expected it.

I couldn't understand why God would bring Paul and me together only to snatch him away. But then I'd done plenty of crying out to the Lord since I got the news of the helicopter crash.

Drawing in a deep breath, I was determined to hold myself together. I had one guest, and more would be arriving soon. Because my knees felt weak, I slumped down into a chair and braced my elbows against the table.

Rover came to me, as though sensing I was in need of consolation. He braced his front paws against the side of my thigh and rested his chin there. I placed my hand on his head and sat, drawing in deep breaths until the trembling had stopped.

I'd barely had time to compose myself when Hailey came down the stairs.

"I'm going out for a few minutes," I told her. "Mary Smith is on the porch and seems to want her privacy, but if she needs anything, will you see that she's made comfortable?"

Hailey's eyes brightened. To this point I'd never left her to look after the inn or guests while I was away. I could see that being given this new responsibility pleased her.

"I'll be happy to," she said with real enthusiasm.

"I doubt I'll be gone long." Rover strained at his leash, eager to be on our way.

"I'll look after the inn," Hailey promised as I headed toward the door with the plate of cookies in one hand and the leash in the other. Hailey hurried down the remaining steps and opened the front door for me. "Have a good walk," she said.

"Thanks, I will, and help yourself to a cookie or two if you want."

"Okay. Peanut butter are my favorite, and by the way, where's Mark?" she asked. "I thought for sure he'd be here today."

Rather than explain to the teenager that the two of us were on the outs, I shrugged. "He's probably busy with something else."

"He knows about the open house, doesn't he?"

"He knows," I said, and tried to hide my frustration and disappointment in him.

I never had been one to hold on to my anger for long. As angry as Mark had made me, as the afternoon progressed I began to regret my heated exchange with him more and more. While I didn't appreciate Mark's attitude, I had to admit the crux of our disagreement was based on the fact he didn't want to see me get hurt. Despite what he thought, I knew I hadn't been in any real danger.

I could see I wasn't going to rest until we settled this awkwardness between us. In addition, I'd been shaken by the call and needed a friend. Mark was a good listener. He didn't say much, but when he did I was taken by his wisdom and insights. Maybe the plate of cookies would be the peace offering we both needed.

Whether Mark agreed to return to the job or not was of little consequence, although I hoped he would. Either way, it was our friendship that mattered. We'd both behaved foolishly. One of us was going to need to take the first step, and while I wasn't willing to say I was in the wrong, I was willing to suggest we put this difference of opinion behind us. I hoped he felt the same.

It seemed Rover knew exactly where I intended to go, because he automatically headed in the right direction. Mark's home and place of business were only a couple of blocks away from the inn, and we'd made the walk several times in the last few months, but always for business purposes.

Unsure if Mark would even be home, I debated what I'd do if he wasn't. His workshop was in the back of the house. If he was away, I decided to leave the cookies in the shop and hope Mark would find them. That would make the next move up to Mark, which was far more comfortable for me. It was hard enough on my ego to be the one to take the first step. Swallowing my pride wasn't an easy thing.

As I neared the workshop, I heard the radio. Mark was apparently in his shop listening to some talk show. Rover barked and I shushed him, preferring not to announce our arrival. I hadn't really thought about what I wanted to say and wished I'd come better prepared.

I squared my shoulders and opened the door. Mark barely glanced up. He was sanding a cradle, one I'd seen him working on before. It was a stunning piece of craftsmanship. It wasn't a commissioned piece but one he worked on in his spare time.

Mark's hands stilled when he saw it was me. After the briefest hesitation he went back to sanding.

"Hi," I said. My mouth felt dry, and I stood awkwardly just inside the door of his workshop.

"Hi."

He certainly wasn't making this easy.

"I baked cookies this morning."

"Peanut butter?" he asked, and continued sanding, his hands working the wood, smoothing away the rough edges.

"Your favorite. I brought you a plate."

Mark glanced up as if noticing it for the first time.

"It's a peace offering," I explained.

He moved to the other end of the cradle but continued to face me. "Is this because you want me to come back and work on the rose garden?"

"No . . . not exactly."

"Then why?"

"Because I consider you a friend," I said, "and I don't want to leave matters the way they were yesterday."

"You were being foolish."

"You were being unreasonable," I returned just as adamantly. "It might be best if we can simply agree to disagree. Do you think we can do that?"

Mark shrugged as if it was of no concern to him one way or the other but I detected a hint of a smile that told me our disagreement hadn't set well with him, either.

"Do you want me to leave the cookies?"

He glanced up and laughed outright. "I'm not stupid. Yeah, I want the cookies."

I waited for a moment, expecting him to say something more. He didn't. Disappointed, I set the plate down and turned to leave. Rover had curled up on the floor and didn't seem to want to budge. I tugged at his leash. Most times he was the one dragging me. His reluctance was unexpected.

"I'll go, then," I said, disappointment heavy on my shoulders.

Just as I was heading out the door, dragging Rover, who staunchly refused to move, Mark spoke: "No need to rush off. Besides, we should talk about the rose garden." He moved away from the crib and tucked his hands in his back pockets, his elbows jutting out at his sides.

"What about it?"

He walked around to the front of the cradle. "Do you want me working on it or not?"

I shrugged in the same nonchalant way he had earlier, as if it was of little concern to me. "That's completely up to you. You're the one who decided to quit."

"Yeah, I guess I did." He moved to where he kept a coffeepot and poured himself a mug and then gestured toward me with the glass pot, offering me a cup, too.

I wasn't much in the mood for coffee but I could see this was his way of saying he was willing to let bygones be bygones, so I nodded.

"Quitting wasn't one of my brighter ideas. I was looking forward to working on that project."

I smiled, and he returned the smile, and the burden of regret I'd been carrying lifted from between my shoulder blades.

He handed me the coffee, which had a distinct burned scent as though it'd been sitting on the burner far too long. "Is this fresh?" I asked.

Mark nodded. "Made it myself yesterday."

I laughed. "You're joking, right?"

He smiled again but didn't answer me, which led me to believe he wasn't kidding.

"It'll put hair on your chest," he said, taking a sip.

"Just what I need." I tasted it, grimaced, and set the mug aside.

Mark pulled out a stool, which I took as an invitation for me to sit. Once I was seated, he peeled off the plastic wrap from the plate and reached for a cookie. "Want one?" he asked.

Seeing that I'd been baking a good portion of the day, I wasn't interested. It was difficult enough losing weight being around the kitchen so much of the time. "No, thanks."

Mark grabbed a second stool and sat down across from me. He studied me for a moment and then frowned. "We're square, right?"

"I hope so." I hesitated and then asked, "About the rose garden? You're coming back?"

"If that's what you want, but don't expect any miracles. It won't be done in time for your open house."

"I guessed as much."

Mark munched down on the cookie. "Your best to date," he mumbled, with crumbs at the side of his mouth. He was a lanky guy, and from what I could see he was probably one of those people who could eat whatever he liked without ever needing to worry about his weight.

"If we're square, then what's troubling you?" he pressed, as he reached for a second cookie.

"What makes you think anything is?" I asked, surprised he could read me so easily, and unsure I liked that.

He frowned slightly, and I bristled a bit under his scrutiny. He pointed his finger at the middle point between his eyes. "You get these funny little lines right here when you're concerned about something."

"I don't, either."

"You do."

I didn't want to argue with him. I knew he was right. "I had a disturbing phone call just before I left the house."

"Oh?" He cocked his eyebrows and took another swallow of the coffee. How he could drink the bitter liquid I didn't know.

"Paul's commanding officer contacted me."

Mark set his coffee aside. "About?"

"The site where the helicopter went down is now accessible." I clenched my hands in my lap and looked down, avoiding eye contact. I was grateful to have someone to talk to about this latest development. "Lieutenant Colonel Milford let me know that the army has sent in a team to retrieve the bodies."

Mark brushed cookie crumbs from his knee as he assimilated what I told him. "I would think you'd want to bury Paul's body."

"I do," I whispered, and was surprised by the slight tremble in my voice. "Of course I do. I don't want my husband left on some mountain on the other side of the world. Paul and the other men who were with him deserve a proper burial."

"Then why did you say you had a *disturbing* phone call?"

"I said that?" All I remembered saying was that I'd gotten a phone call. The *disturbing* part must have slipped out unnoticed.

"Clearly you're upset about it. Is it because anything having to do with Paul is like opening a healing wound?"

The question was a valid one, and I suppose that was part of it. "Perhaps."

"But there's more?"

I nodded and swallowed against the hard lump that had formed in my throat. Mark's gaze went to my hands, which I'd clenched in my lap, and I noticed they had started to shake. I wanted to tuck them under my arms, hide my reaction, but I didn't want to be obvious about it.

He didn't say anything for an uncomfortable moment, nor did I. It was as if neither one of us knew what to say.

I was the one who broke the silence. "If Paul's body is located, then I'll need to give up the fantasy that he might still be alive."

"Is there a possibility of that?"

I shook my head. It went without saying that the life insurance money wouldn't have been released if there was the slightest chance Paul could have survived the helicopter crash. I'd long suspected Paul's commanding officer had stepped in to facilitate the dispersal of insurance monies to family members.

"It's time, don't you think?" Mark asked.

"No," I said with conviction. "Not yet. I can't." We'd never discussed Paul before, and I realized that although I considered Mark a friend he couldn't possibly understand the emotions I was dealing with in regard to this latest upheaval concerning my soldier husband. I shouldn't have mentioned the phone call. Eager to leave now, I slid off the stool. Rover reluctantly came to his feet.

"I need to get back," I announced, my words sounding stiff and formal. "Come on, Rover." I tugged at his leash and he responded right away, straining in his rush to get out the workshop door.

"Thanks for the cookies," Mark said, walking me to the doorway.

"Sure . . . any time." I lifted my hand in farewell.

He responded by raising his own hand. "I appreciate that you're willing to admit you were in the wrong."

I almost started to argue with him before I realized that last bit was intended as a joke. "Very funny," I muttered.

Mark chuckled. I could see that he wanted to help but didn't know how. It was too soon to talk about what I'd learned, not when I had yet to properly digest this news myself.

"See ya," he said as he held open the workshop door.

I nodded. This was Mark's way of letting me know he'd be around again soon.

I could tell that Rover would have liked a much longer walk, but I felt the need to get back to the inn. I didn't want to leave Hailey alone for long.

"We'll take a longer walk another day," I promised Rover. He continued to strain against the leash until he could see that it would do no good and then gave in and reluctantly headed back to the inn.

Mark remained standing in the doorway. I felt his gaze, and when I looked over my shoulder I found him leaning against the jamb, watching me. How long he remained there, I didn't know.

Chapter 5

Hailey met me at the door when I returned to the inn.

"Everything okay?" I asked.

Nodding, Hailey handed me a pink message slip. "Annie Newton called and left her phone number. She said she'd call back in a few minutes."

"Great, thanks," I said, and collected the slip. Hailey left for the day with a promise to return the following afternoon.

I'd no sooner put Rover's leash away when the phone rang. I still had to get to the Chamber of Commerce meeting. "Rose Harbor Inn," I said, and glanced at the clock on the office wall, hoping this wouldn't take long.

"Hello, this is Annie Newton, Kent and Julie Shivers's granddaughter."

I found it interesting that Annie felt the need to introduce herself every time we spoke. In the last six months Annie had been over to the inn twice, making preparations for her grandparents' fiftieth-wedding-anniversary celebration. At one time she'd considered holding the entire affair at the inn itself, but it soon became apparent that the inn wouldn't be large enough for the two-hundred-plus invitations she planned to mail out to family and friends.

"I'm calling to see if it would be possible to come over to the inn this afternoon rather than tomorrow morning the way I'd originally planned." Her voice trembled with the request. If we hadn't spoken previously, I might not have noticed, but I certainly did now.

"Is everything all right?" I asked.

"Yes, yes, of course, well, actually, no, I'm a bit shaken at the moment. I think I might have mentioned that I broke off my engagement six months ago."

She hadn't, but I wanted to encourage her to continue. "I'm sorry, Annie. It must have been a huge disappointment for you."

"Yes, it was . . . It is. Lenny called today, and we argued, and I thought it might do me good to get away."

"If you want to come over early, that won't be a problem."

"Great."

I could hear the relief in her voice.

"That would work nicely. My grandparents will arrive tomorrow morning sometime, and I want to be sure and be there to greet them. I thought it might be a good idea to review all the events I have planned with them beforehand."

"I spoke with a family friend of yours, I believe," I told her. It seemed I wasn't the only one who'd been upset by a phone call that day.

"A family friend?" Annie repeated.

"He phoned earlier today to book a room. Apparently, he's driving your grandparents from Oregon."

Annie hesitated. "This . . . family friend didn't happen to mention his name, did he?"

"Well, yes, I've got it written down here on the reservation. It will take me just a moment to bring up the file."

"Never mind. It doesn't matter," she said, and sighed heavily as though this was another piece of unwelcome news.

From everything she said, Annie wasn't having a good day. "Your room is ready, so if you want to come this evening, that's fine. Only . . ."

"Yes?" she asked with more than a hint of anxiety.

"I planned to be away for part of the afternoon. What time were you figuring to arrive?"

"Oh, take your time . . . I could easily kill a couple of hours."

"You're welcome to arrive anytime, Annie," I assured her. Seeing that I already had her credit card information, I added, "Tell you what; I'll put your room key on the kitchen countertop, so if you arrive before I return, you can go right up to your room."

"Are you sure that won't be a problem?"

"None whatsoever, although I should let you know that I have another guest, so if you meet up with her, just explain who you are."

"Will do."

I noticed, right away, how much lighter her voice was now. I didn't need to be Sherlock Holmes to figure out the discussion with her ex had upset her. Annie had enough to deal with taking care of the details with her grandparents' anniversary. If she had mentioned the broken engagement earlier, then it had slipped my mind, although this wasn't a detail I was likely to forget. Knowing this about Annie helped explain why she'd thrown herself into the project with such enthusiasm. I'd come to like the other woman and respected her organizational talents. She'd seen to every detail of this family gathering, working with local caterers, the florist, and the city for permission for the renewal-of-vows ceremony to be held at the gazebo on the waterfront. She'd told me repeatedly how she wanted everything perfect for her grandparents. Now I knew that she'd also needed a distraction.

If it wasn't for the Chamber meeting, I might have taken a few extra minutes to chat. I was later than I wanted to be already, having gone to deliver the cookies to Mark.

We said our good-byes and I grabbed my purse and petted Rover's ears on my way to the front door. He didn't like it when I left the house without him. The moment he saw me getting ready to go, he'd raise his head, and when he didn't see the leash, a sad woe-is-me look would come over him and he'd rest his chin on his paws and mope. But then by the time I returned home, he'd be over it and greet me as though I'd been away far too long and been terribly, terribly missed.

"I'll be back before you know it," I promised my faithful friend.

As I came out onto the porch, I saw Mark busy at work in the garden once again. Hesitating on the top step, I paused and smiled, grateful that I'd made the effort to settle our differences even if I'd been the one to make the first move.

Mark must have heard the screen door close, because he looked up, and when he saw it was me, he leaned against the pitchfork. "Where you headed off to?" he asked.

"Chamber meet and greet," I said. Thanks to Peggy Beldon's advice, I'd joined as soon as I moved to Cedar Cove, and attended every meeting. I enjoyed the camaraderie among the business owners. We encouraged and supported one another. Come to think of it, I'd never seen Mark at any of the get-togethers. He had his own business and would benefit from the association.

"How come you're not a Chamber member?" I asked.

"Who says I'm not?"

Good point. "I've never seen you at the meetings."

"I don't go."

"Why not?" In my humble opinion, it would do him good to be a bit more sociable.

He shrugged. "For one thing, I got more than enough work to keep me busy as it is. For another, I don't go for chitchat and exchanging business cards. If these people would spend half as much time working on building up their businesses as they do on schmoozing with one another, they wouldn't have time for all these social niceties."

"You're just Mr. Personality, aren't you?"

He grinned and nodded. "I don't have time for all that stuff. You want me to work on your garden or head off to some cheese-and-crackers get-together?"

"Work on the garden."

"My point exactly."

Mark grinned again. Twice in one day; this was amazing.

"I won't be long," I promised him. "Another guest might show up in the next hour or so. I left her room key on the kitchen countertop."

"What about the woman sunning herself on the side porch? What's her story?"

"Mary Smith? I don't know."

"She okay?" He frowned, looking toward my guest.

"She's under the weather," I told him. "So if she gets a bit prickly, ignore her. I think the flight must have drained her. She seems to need the rest, so don't take it wrong if she snaps at you."

"Not to worry, I'll snap right back."

"Mark," I warned, "be nice."

"I will," he promised, and I was off.

Because most everything is a convenient distance from the inn, I chose to walk to the Chamber meeting. The office building was right off Harbor Street. It wasn't really a formal meeting as such; those were held once a month at noon at a local restaurant. The Chamber of Commerce had recently changed locations, and this was an invitation to come and view their new digs. I supposed this was a casual open house of their own.

By the time I arrived, the building was already crowded. The first person I saw was Grace Harding, the local librarian. She'd become a friend and a great source of information for me. Having lived in Cedar Cove her entire life, it seemed she knew just about everyone in town. In addition, she'd been a widow for several years before remarrying, and because of that she'd sort of taken me under her wing. I appreciated both her friendship and her advice.

It'd been a while since we'd last talked, although I saw her often enough at the library, but lately that was only in passing.

"Jo Marie," she said, walking toward me. She held out both hands in greeting.

"Grace, it's so good to see you."

"You, too. How's Rover?"

"Loyal as ever," I supplied.

"I'm glad you decided to keep his name. It suits him."

I'd gone back and forth with the idea of giving him a more dignified, catchy name. First off, Rover was such a plain, rather overused dog name. I wanted to be more original, clever. A name like Buttercup. Grace and her husband, Cliff, had donated a fenced area for the rescue dogs to run, in memory of their beloved golden retriever who had become Grace's faithful companion after her first husband's death.

Buttercup.

What a wonderful name for a pet. By comparison, Rover seemed dull and unimpressive. The fact that he'd been roving around was another reason I continued to toy with the idea of renaming him. Rover had a home now. I, too, had been a rover of sorts in my own right, and like my dog, I'd found a safe harbor.

"Rover is doing well? No problems with him toward the guests?"

"None whatsoever."

Her face relaxed. "Wonderful."

Digging the remaining invitations out of my purse, I handed her two. "I'm hoping you can come and bring Judge Griffin with you. Here's a couple more if you can think of anyone else I should invite."

Grace looked over the invitation. "I'd love to see what you've done with the inn. I know Olivia would as well."

"Then come. I'd enjoy showing you around." I hesitated to mention the rose garden. Despite the fact that Mark and I had patched up our differences, I was sorely disappointed that the rose garden remained unfinished.

"I'll look forward to it," Grace said, and tucked the invite into the side pocket of her large handbag.

"Grace," Sheriff Troy Davis called out to her. He spoke with another man I didn't recognize and looked over to the librarian.

"If you'll excuse me," Grace said.

"Of course."

By the time I left the meet and greet I'd handed out all the remaining invitations and had several business owners assure me they would be stopping by Sunday afternoon. Both Peggy Beldon and her friend Corrie McAfee offered to help with anything I needed done. I thanked them, but at this point, I had everything under control—or so I hoped. I promised to call them if it became necessary.

The first thing I noticed when I got back to the inn was that Mark had left and Annie Newton had arrived. Her car was parked in the driveway. Mary was no longer on the porch, and I had to assume it'd become too chilly for her and she'd moved inside.

My faithful Rover was waiting at the door when I came into the inn. And after the usual I'm-so-glad-you're-back routine in which he jumped and yelped and raced two or three circles around me, he hurried into the living room area to make sure I knew an additional guest was in the house.

I found her sitting on the sofa in front of the unlit fireplace, staring into the empty pit.

"Hello, Annie."

She glanced up with a surprised look on her face. Apparently, all the racket Rover made hadn't alerted her to the fact that I'd returned. When she saw it was me, she smiled. "Thanks for letting me arrive early."

"It wasn't a problem in the least." I set my purse inside my office and returned. "Did you meet my other guest?"

"Mary Smith, right?"

"Right."

"She said she was feeling tired and went up to bed. I hope she's okay."

"Did she mention anything about dinner?" I asked. If she wanted, I could order a meal and have it delivered. For that matter, I could cook for her myself.

"No. I don't think she's up to eating just yet."

"Probably not. She's still on East Coast time, and the flight must have tired her out.

"I was about to brew some tea. Would you care to join me?"

Annie paused for just a moment and then nodded. "I would. Thanks."

Annie was a lovely young woman with auburn-colored hair and deep green eyes. I envied her long, thick hair that fell halfway down the middle of her back. If she wanted to, she would probably qualify for one of those shampoo commercials, with cascading hair down her backside. She followed me into the kitchen, and as she sat on a stool I noticed she had a wadded-up tissue in her hand. It was apparent the phone call with her ex-fiancé continued to trouble her. I understood far too well how she felt.

I made busywork around the kitchen, assembling a pot of tea. "I'm a good listener if you want to talk, Annie," I said casually. I didn't want her to think I was pressuring her, but we'd developed a good rapport over the last six months.

"I'm over him," she said. "I really am. If I'm sad, it's because of what we might have had together. My mom said I was in love with being in love, and I think she might be right."

"Moms are like that, aren't they?" I said as I slid onto the stool on the opposite side of the counter from where Annie sat. "They seem to know us better than we do ourselves."

Annie studied the marble countertop as if finding sense in the meaningless wandering pattern of the veins there. "Lenny remains under the misconception that I'll change my mind. I did once before, but I won't again." She said this with the same determination I'd heard earlier.

I poured us each a mug of hot tea and waited for Annie to continue, if she wanted to. Although I couldn't help being curious, I wouldn't badger her with questions.

After a moment, she reached for the mug and cradled it in her hands as if she needed its warmth. "It's for the best."

I sipped my tea while I continued to give her my attention.

"I love . . . loved Lenny. Funny, isn't it? I loved him enough to want to be his wife. Then I learned while we were dating that he'd been with another woman. As soon as I heard about what he called his 'little slip,' I broke off the relationship entirely. Over time he managed to convince me to give him another chance."

"And you did?"

She nodded. "Then, six months ago, it happened again. That was it. We were through. I broke the engagement. The first time around I didn't tell my parents. My family liked Lenny. He's fun and personable, and, looking at him, he seems to be the perfect guy."

"Except for this one flaw."

Annie raised the tea to her lips. "A pretty major flaw, don't you think? Unfortunately, Lenny hasn't been able to accept the fact I refuse to marry him."

It sounded to me like she'd made a wise choice and was well rid of him.

"What I can't understand, what's been so hard," she said, looking down at the mug, "is that despite everything, I miss being with him." She snorted a laugh. "That's absolutely ridiculous, isn't it?"

"Not in the least," I told her, and leaning my elbows against the countertop, I held my tea mug close to my lips. "The two of you must have spent a lot of time together. Being with Lenny is simply habit."

Annie stared at me for a long, heart-stopping moment as she considered what I'd said. "You're right. I saw him every day; we did practically everything together . . . or so I assumed." This last part was added with a smirk.

"I think you're better off now than making this discovery after you're married."

"My thoughts exactly. He swears it meant nothing . . ." Closing her eyes, Annie shook her head. "He actually claimed the other woman seduced him just so she could ruin any chance he had of finding happiness with me."

"Do you believe that?"

She motioned with one hand. "I don't think it matters if I do or not. If she intentionally seduced him, no matter what her reasons, Lenny had a choice, and he chose to . . . to betray me."

"It hurts terribly now, but it does get better." I'd learned that life after a loss wasn't easy, but gradually one learns to live with that pain.

"I refuse to marry a man I can't trust."

Again, I agreed with her.

"Lenny seems to think if he pesters me enough I'll eventually change my mind. It's been six months and he still believes there's a chance for the two of us, despite everything I've done and said."

In order to escape Lenny, Annie had decided to arrive a day early. She was looking to escape her ex-fiancé or perhaps the fear that she might change her mind yet again. Although it was clearly a painful decision, it appeared to be the right one. I just hoped that being at the inn would help her heal, the way it had me. At least now being in Cedar Cove would give Annie the space and strength she needed.

Chapter 6

In an effort to distract herself from the broken engagement, Annie had worked hard on this anniversary celebration for her grandparents. Everything had been set into place. The special invitations she'd designed as scrolls had gone out in small tubes. She'd received RSVPs from more than a hundred and fifty family and friends. In addition, she'd met with the local priest and arranged for a renewal-of-vows ceremony to take place on the waterfront. The reception, buffet dinner, and dance to follow should go off without a hitch. The dinner menu was set, and a three-piece band that had come highly recommended had been hired. Two of the band's original members had been playing in the area fifty years ago, and now their children had stepped into their roles. There was every likelihood that Annie's grandparents had danced to the band's music when they were young.

What Annie hadn't anticipated was how determined Lenny would be to win her back. The problem, she realized, was that she'd 'forgiven' him the first time. Now he seemed to assume that because he'd been able to change her mind once, all it would take was time and that she'd be willing to look past this second indiscretion. Well, that wasn't going to happen. In an effort to distract herself from the painful breakup, she'd put all her effort into making this anniversary party one the family would never forget.

As if on cue, her cell phone rang. Annie reached for it and glanced at caller ID, although it wasn't necessary. It was Lenny, just as she suspected.

At first she toyed with ignoring the call, but that didn't seem to be working. After two weeks of silence, he'd contacted her again by leaving her countless messages. It was clear he wasn't going to let go until he persuaded her to take him back. If she didn't put an end to it right now, then he might well ruin the anniversary party.

She punched the answer button but didn't give him the opportunity to speak. "I told you not to call me again," she said with a determination born of anger and pain. "There's nothing left you can say that's going to make me change my mind."

"Annie, please."

"I don't know how many times I have to say it, Lenny, but it is over. So please leave me alone. Understand?" Her resolve was set, and she had no intention of backing down.

"No, I don't understand," he argued. "I don't understand any of this."

"I can answer that in one word: Nichole . . . and Sadie, and whoever else whose names I don't know."

The words hung in the air between them, as if caught on an invisible wire.

53

"How many times do I have to tell you all this is their fault? They seduced me."

Annie struggled with the fact that Lenny couldn't even own up to his own part in his betrayal. "You're right, you were tricked. It was all a mistake, a life-changing mistake, a break-the-engagement, never-want-to-see-you-again kind of mistake." She'd made that clear for the last six months, but apparently he hadn't gotten the message.

"Where are you?" Lenny asked instead of arguing. "I've been sitting outside your condo for over an hour, waiting to talk to you. Can't you see what this is doing to me? I can't sleep, I can't eat. We've got to settle this once and for all before I go mad."

Frustrated, Annie's fingers bunched up the bedspread. Everything Lenny said related to him, revolved around him. It shocked her that she hadn't seen this earlier. Perhaps her mother was right and she'd fallen in love with being in love. After all the time and effort she'd put into this anniversary party for her grandparents, she would have assumed Lenny would guess her whereabouts. If there was anything to be grateful for, it was his short, self-absorbed memory. "I'm not in Seattle."

"I know." Aggravation bled into his words. "Where did you go? Tell me and I'll come join you and we'll reason all this out. I'm miserable without you, Annie. Have a heart and put me out of my pain."

The last thing Annie intended was to see him. "Lenny, it's over. I don't know how many times I need to tell you that, but our relationship is kaput, finished, done with. We are not getting married."

"My family, especially my mom, once she finds out . . ."

"You mean to say after six months you still haven't told your mother and sister?" Unbelievable! Well, she'd take care of that in short order. "Listen," she said, ever so sweetly, "if you want me to tell your mom and family myself, and save you the trouble and the embarrassment, then I will."

"No, don't."

"Then stop pestering me."

"I can't and I won't until we talk this out." Lenny, as he so often did, ignored anything he didn't want to hear, didn't want to believe.

As far as Annie was concerned, there was nothing left to be said. Her eyes had been opened, and she wasn't going back. Lenny was a fun guy, the kind of person people liked being around because he was witty and charming. He was the perfect car salesman and often the top seller of the month. He enjoyed being the center of attention, but as she'd come to realize, it was all surface with him. Life was a game to be played. Talk was cheap, as her dad said. What she should have recognized long before she did was that there was no depth to him.

"Mom thinks the world of you, and . . ."

"I'm sure she'll like Nichole or Sadie, too." In his mother's eyes, her precious son could do no wrong.

"Annie, please, just tell me where you are so we can talk face-to-face."

"Where I am is really none of your concern." Nor was she about to tell him.

"You're intent on avoiding me, aren't you?"

One thing she could say about Lenny: he missed nothing. She hadn't contacted him in months, and she refused to answer his phone calls or the countless text messages he'd sent, pleading with her to reconsider. Talking to him now was probably a mistake, but she wanted this out of the way so she could concentrate on the family party.

She waited until the air between them went still.

"Annie?"

"Lenny. Please. Listen to me." She made every word distinct, with a short pause after each one.

"Of course. I'll do anything to make this up to you. Anything. Just name it and I'll do it."

She could almost believe him, almost trust him, but at the same time she knew better. "What I want, what I need, is for you to listen, because what I'm about to say is serious."

"I'm serious, too, baby."

"I didn't return the engagement ring because I was angry. I was—"

"I know," he said, cutting her off, rushing his words. "You could have clawed my eyes out, but you didn't. You were so calm, so unemotional, which leads me to believe—"

"Lenny, you're talking. You're not listening."

"Okay, okay, go ahead and say what you want and I promise to give you my full attention."

Annie inhaled deeply and held her breath while she sorted out the words in her mind. She needed to reach him and at the same time be abundantly clear. "I returned the engagement ring because you and I will not, under any circumstances, ever be married." Once she'd finished she gave him a moment to absorb her words and then asked, "Do you understand what I'm saying, Lenny?"

After a brief hesitation he murmured, "I think so."

"Good."

"But when can I see you again?" he asked.

Annie resisted the urge to simply hang up. "You weren't really listening, Lenny. We will never see each other again."

This appeared to shock him. "*Never?* You can't be serious."

"As serious as a bounced check to the IRS." This was a problem Lenny had encountered the year before when he learned it wasn't a good idea to tangle with the Internal Revenue Service.

"You mean to say you don't want to even see me? Not ever?"

Apparently, he hadn't paid attention during the last six months. "Not ever," she reconfirmed, keeping her voice cool and unemotional. He was right about one thing, though—she wasn't angry. Instead, she was resolved. It seemed no matter how she said it Lenny couldn't believe she was serious. Annie didn't know what she could say or do to make this decision any more plain. Lenny couldn't seem to grasp that this was her final decision. He'd gotten so good at persuading people when it came to selling cars that he seemed to think he could use the same techniques in his personal life with the same results.

"What reason would I have to see you?" she asked.

"Ah . . ." Lenny hesitated as if he wasn't sure himself.

Annie resisted the urge to laugh. In all this time since their split she noticed that he hadn't once declared his love. His big concern, it seemed, was how he would explain the broken engagement to his mother.

"Please don't phone me again, Lenny."

"Never?" The word seemed to be stuck in his mind, which might not be so bad.

"You got it. Never. Our engagement, our relationship, is over, and before you can claim I don't mean it, let me assure you that I do. If you continue to pester me and my friends, then you leave me no option but to put a restraining order on you."

"You wouldn't," he said with a gasp.

"Don't try me, Lenny. I can, and I will." Not waiting to hear any further arguments, she ended the call. She waited a few minutes to be sure Lenny wouldn't try to connect with her again, and when he didn't, she dropped her cell back into her purse, with the utmost hope that this would be the end of his harassment.

As difficult and painful as this time apart had been, it was necessary. If Lenny had cheated on her, not once but twice, before the wedding, then she knew it was just a small taste of what awaited her if they were to get married. She knew he liked to flirt, but it was easy to dismiss that tendency because he was so outgoing and friendly. Perhaps it was a downfall of hers not to be the jealous type.

Like Jo Marie's first guest, Annie wasn't interested in eating dinner, either. She read for a while and resisted the urge to call a friend and review the conversation with Lenny. It didn't take her long to decide against it. If she talked to Elise or anyone else, she might admit how much she missed him and how difficult breaking off the engagement actually was. It was far more comfortable to focus her attention on her grandparents and forget she'd ever been in love.

Despite the unpleasant conversation with Lenny, Annie slept the entire night through. It was as if the fresh air off the cove had lulled her into a deep, easy sleep. In the morning, she felt worlds better.

As far as Lenny was concerned, Annie had shed her last tears. These few days away were exactly what she needed. Even if she'd be working the entire time, it was worth it to ensure this was the high point of her grandparents' marriage. The fact that her grandparents had been in love for more than fifty years gave Annie hope that love and commitment could and did last a lifetime. All she needed was to find a good man. Although it was painful now, Annie accepted that she'd made the right decision, and she wasn't turning back.

Mary Smith was already at the breakfast table when Annie came down the stairs. The afternoon before, Annie's conversation with the other woman had been brief. Almost as soon as Annie arrived at the inn, Mary had made an excuse and gone up to her room. She let it be known she wasn't looking for company or in the mood for chitchat. Annie wasn't in the mood to socialize, either, so that suited her fine.

"Coffee?" Jo Marie asked as soon as Annie came into the breakfast room. She stood just inside the room for a moment to soak in the light. The sun sparkled off the windows, filling the room with both light and warmth. This wasn't the typical weather for the end of May, and it came as a pleasant and most welcome surprise.

Annie had dared to hope they'd have sunshine this weekend for the party. Now if only it would hold for the next few days.

Annie reached for her coffee cup, and Jo Marie promptly filled it.

"I understand you two have already introduced yourselves," Jo Marie said, glancing from one to the other for confirmation.

"We did," Mary answered for them both.

"Annie's grandparents and a family friend will arrive sometime today," Jo Marie added for Mary's benefit.

"Followed by a whole slew of relatives, most of whom will be spending Saturday night at the inn," Annie explained. "But not to worry; they aren't a rowdy group."

"It'll be a full house," Jo Marie added.

Mary looked up quizzically. "It's a family reunion?"

"My grandparents are celebrating their fiftieth wedding anniversary," Annie said, and then added, "I hope you get a chance to meet; I'm sure you'll like them."

"I'm sure I will, too," Mary said, but not with a lot of enthusiasm.

"What amazes me is that after all these years, my grandparents are still deeply in love." She enjoyed seeing all the sweet things her grandmother did for her grandfather. Every morning she set out his pills for him. And he helped her make the bed and washed the breakfast dishes. In the evenings, they sat side by side in matching chairs, and while her grandmother knit, her grandfather worked crossword puzzles. They supported each other, helped and encouraged each other, too. Annie felt it was an honor to be part of this celebration of two of the most loving people she'd ever met. They gave her hope that someday she might experience a loving relationship like theirs.

"Fifty years, you say? So they were married in the nineteen-sixties, right?"

"Right. They were college sweethearts, but then Grandpa had to drop out because of money."

"They're from Cedar Cove?"

"No, they're from Oregon," Annie explained, "but they were married here. Grandpa knew he was going to get drafted—this was during the Vietnam War—so he enlisted in the navy, and following his training he got word he was going to be shipped out. They didn't know how long it would be until they saw each other again."

"So Julie came to visit him at the naval base?" Jo Marie asked.

"Yes, and they decided not to wait for the big church wedding but to get married right then and there. It was one of the most romantic stories I've ever heard."

"In this day and age of no-fault divorces, it's wonderful to meet people who've managed to make their marriages work," Mary said.

"It wasn't always smooth sailing. Grandpa worked in construction. There were times when the economy was slow and he didn't have a job for several months. But the hard times seemed to bring them together instead of splitting them apart."

"That happens with a lot of families," Jo Marie said. "Financial problems can put a terrible strain on relationships and marriages."

"I agree," Mary added. "I've seen it more than once myself."

"Are you married?" Annie asked. She didn't mean to pry, but curiosity got the better of her.

"No," Mary responded, not adding any additional information.

Annie wondered if Mary was divorced. If so, this must be a painful conversation for her.

"I apologize if I was being insensitive, Mary."

The other woman held up her hand, stopping her. "You weren't. I think it's wonderful your grandparents have shared fifty years together. I never married . . . I was tempted once, but that was years ago."

A look of such intense longing flashed in the other woman's

eyes that Annie had to resist reaching out and laying a comforting hand on her shoulder.

"It sounds as if you have wonderful grandparents."

"I do."

"I'm looking forward to meeting them," Jo Marie said. She left momentarily and returned with a tray filled with breakfast pastries, homemade muffins, and sliced banana bread, along with thick slices of cottage bread and fresh sourdough.

Annie sat down and helped herself to one of the muffins. She was anxious to see her grandparents. They would show everyone what real love was all about.

Chapter 7

Until this point Mary and Annie were my only two guests. Soon I expected to have a full house with Annie's grandparents and an assortment of other relatives.

As I removed the breakfast dishes from the table, I saw Annie and Mary head back up the stairs. Annie had mentioned something about checking in with the florist about the table centerpieces and had gone upstairs to get her sweater and purse.

Mary followed at a much slower pace. She took four or five steps and then paused as though the effort had sapped her strength.

I paused just outside the kitchen, debating whether I should say anything. Mary seemed to feel my presence because she turned and glanced over her shoulder.

"I'm fine," she said, although she sounded out of breath. "It just takes me awhile."

"You don't need help? I'm happy to give you my arm."

She shook her head. "No, thanks. I'll lie down for a bit and be good as new. I don't have a lot of strength just yet, but I'm feeling much better than I did a few weeks ago."

I was glad to hear it, but still I worried the stairs were too much for her.

After finishing up the dishes, I ran the dishwasher and glanced out the window to the yard, hoping to find Mark. He wasn't anywhere in sight. To be fair, he hadn't mentioned returning this morning, but I'd hoped to see him hard at work.

The phone rang, and I went into my office to answer. "Rose Harbor Inn."

"Thought I should tell you I won't be working on the garden today."

"Oh," I said, swallowing my disappointment. "I was just thinking about you."

He didn't seem to know what to say. "I apologize, but I've got other commitments, too, you know."

"I know," I whispered.

"I promise I won't leave the lawn all torn up like that. I'll have it tidied up before your open house."

"Thanks," I said, "but I would appreciate a timetable of when I can expect the project to be finished." The frustration was back, although I struggled to hide it.

"Can't do it."

"The rose garden or the timetable?"

He muttered something I couldn't understand. "The timetable," he said, and didn't sound the least bit amused by my question. "I already told you this project wasn't a priority."

Like I needed to be reminded.

"If you find someone else who can do the work on your time-table, you're welcome to hire him."

"Aren't you Mr. Sunshine this morning?" I said, fighting down the need to reply in kind. "Really, Mark, there's no need to be grouchy."

He ignored the comment. "I'll bring your plate by later."

"Anytime."

"See you."

He disconnected the line, and I shook my head, wondering what burr was under his saddle. The man was certainly out of sorts. Disgruntled now myself, I went back into the kitchen and took the dishrag to the counter, wiping it down with the same force I used to scrub pots and pans. I'd hoped we'd made some headway these last couple of days, but apparently not.

Rover barked, indicating someone had approached the house. The one sharp knock told me it was Mark. He didn't wait for me to answer the door, but opened it and took one step inside and went no farther.

"I brought back your plate."

I noticed he didn't mention a single word regarding the cookies I'd taken him.

"Did you enjoy the cookies?" I asked.

"Are you searching for compliments?"

"A thank-you or how-thoughtful-of-you wouldn't be amiss." I didn't hide the sarcasm, disappointed as I was about his complete lack of urgency when it came to my projects.

"Okay, fine. Thank you. Now I need to go. I'm already late," he said, one hand on the doorknob.

Rover sat on his haunches and looked up at Mark. I bit my tongue to keep from saying it wouldn't hurt him any to scratch Rover's ears. Then, without my saying a word, he bent down and did exactly that.

Rover lifted his chin and reveled in the attention. "He's a no-good, worthless dog . . ."

I was instantly insulted. Rover was anything but worthless. "He's a good boy," I felt obliged to tell him.

"Worthless," he reiterated, but I noticed that Mark continued to pet Rover's ears and was clearly taken with my dog.

"Can you give me any indication of when you'll be available to work on the yard?" It seemed to me nearly all of our conversations these days centered on my rose garden.

"Soon."

"Tomorrow?" I pressed.

"Can't say."

My shoulders sagged with disappointment.

"I'll see what I can do."

"That would be appreciated."

Mark straightened. "Don't get your hopes up. I'll do what I can to pretty it up for you, but it's still going to be obvious."

"Gotcha."

He tipped his head to me and then left. The door clicked softly as it closed.

It would do no good to chide Mark or remind him that his original estimate had been a couple weeks of work. That had been months ago. It was hard not to be discouraged.

When I'm this out of sorts, I find solace by knitting. It wasn't my habit to knit so early in the day, but trying circumstances called for it. I headed to my room and reached for my project. I sat in the chair in front of the fireplace and relaxed my shoulders.

As my fingers worked the yarn and I tugged away at the skein, I continued to think about Mark, detecting a behavior pattern that had emerged between us. Any time we worked through a barrier, like our most recent tiff, Mark would purposely do or say something that was guaranteed to set me off. It was one step forward and two, or sometimes three, steps back.

By all that was right I should fire him and get someone else. That had been my intention when he'd stalked away madder than a hornet because I'd dared to enter the "danger zone" and use a stepladder to wash windows. We'd both slept on it, but I'd been the one to bring him a peace offering. And while he probably would never have said so, Mark had been happy to see me. I noticed how hard he struggled to hide that fact, though.

We'd mended fences, or so I assumed. Everything seemed back to normal, or about as normal as it ever was between us. And then this morning his attitude had made a complete turnaround. He'd been grumpy and argumentative and couldn't seem to get away from me fast enough.

What was up with that? Frankly, I didn't understand him. I jerked on the yarn so hard it tumbled out of the basket and rolled across the rug. Rover was instantly on the alert and picked it up in his mouth and brought it back to me.

"Good boy," I said, and patted his head.

It was a low blow for Mark to suggest Rover was worthless. The only reason he'd said that was to irritate me. Well, he'd succeeded. I wondered what he'd say if he saw Rover now.

It was times like this that I really missed Paul. Every day there was something to remind me of all that I'd lost, something that seemed to land square over my heart: a hit, a bereft feeling, and a sense of confusion. I wasn't one to fall victim to a pity party, but this thing with Mark was getting me down. My fingers continued to work the yarn, although I was hardly aware of the pattern. I should be paying more attention.

It almost seemed that Mark didn't want to get too close. It wasn't only me, but everyone. Whenever I mentioned to others that he was doing some work for me, he got rave reviews. Few, however, had anything to say about the man himself. He was an enigma for sure. A puzzle that both irritated and intrigued me. It seemed he purposely kept people at arm's length. As far as I could tell, he had no close friends but plenty of acquaintances. He rarely talked about himself. I couldn't help suspecting if he had a deep, dark secret. I wondered if he was part of the Witness Protection Program or was in hiding, living on the run. I immediately dismissed those ideas as proof of having a creative imagination.

I refused to waste another minute on Mark. I finished knitting my row, set the project aside, and returned to the kitchen. Seeing that I had excess energy, I decided what I really needed was a brisk walk. It was still cool out, so I grabbed a sweater, thinking I would use this opportunity to return the book I'd recently finished reading to the library. I hoped to run into Grace while I was there.

The instant Rover saw me get my sweater he headed for the laundry room, where I kept his leash. He was more than ready for a bit of exercise. Thankfully, the library was pet friendly.

As I headed down the hill, my mind continued to whirl. I thought about Paul again. Truly, he was never far from my mind, and the conversation with Lieutenant Colonel Milford was front and center.

I wondered how it was with other widows. Did they continue to think of their husbands every day for years following their death? That was a question I would ask Grace. Did she feel as I did some days, that I was living only half a life? I knew I would never stop loving Paul.

When I arrived at the library I learned that Grace wasn't scheduled to work until the afternoon. I left the book and collected another that had been held on reserve. The walk back up the hill to the inn was steep, reminding me that I needed to get into a regular exercise routine, possibly join the local gym or sign up for an aerobic swim class.

As I approached the inn, I saw a car pull up and park in one of the spaces allotted for visitors. The driver's door opened, and out climbed a rather tall, fit young man who I assumed was in his mid-twenties, possibly close to thirty. He stood and looped his dark hair around his ear before opening one of the back doors and help-ing an older woman out. I noticed right away how gentle he was with her, lending her a hand.

The front passenger door opened and an older man climbed out, and with his hands at his waist, he twisted left and then right as if to settle his bones.

This had to be Kent and Julie Shivers, the anniversary couple.

With Rover straining against the leash, I hurried my steps. "Hello," I called out as I approached. "You must be the Shivers."

"That's us," Kent said.

"Jo Marie Rose." I extended my hand to Kent first and then Julie. "And you're Oliver?"

"Oliver Sutton," he confirmed.

"Welcome."

"Thank you," Julie said, and her gaze went to the inn. "What a lovely place you have here."

"Thank you. I like it, and I hope you will, too."

"Are the rooms ready?" Kent asked. "I could use a nap."

"You napped on the way here," Julie complained, frowning at her husband of fifty years.

"I most certainly did not."

"Then you snored all the way here," she returned.

"I don't know how many times I have to tell you I don't snore."

Oliver went around to the back of the vehicle and opened the trunk to get out the suitcases.

"You'd think we planned a six-week vacation for all the lug-gage Julie packed." The comment was directed at me.

"I only brought what was absolutely necessary."

"Were those ten books necessary?" Kent demanded.

"That's why I asked Oliver to drive us. You're always com-plaining about one thing or another. For once in your life could you kindly keep your comments to yourself?"

Kent made a huffing sound and started toward the house with

Julie following behind at a slower pace. I tried to help Oliver with the luggage, but he refused.

"I'll get it, no problem." He closed the trunk and looked toward the inn. "When do you suppose Annie will arrive?"

"Oh, she's here now."

"Already?" His eyes widened with surprise.

"Not here here," I answered, which probably only confused him more. "She arrived last evening and stayed the night."

"Then she's in town."

"Yes, but she is currently out." I checked my watch and was surprised to notice it was already after eleven.

Oliver looked like he couldn't be more pleased. "Any idea when she'll be back?"

"She didn't say, but I don't imagine she'll be long. You're a bit early, aren't you?"

"A bit," he agreed. "Kent and Julie are early risers."

Julie rolled her eyes. "That's because Kent can't seem to stay awake past nine o'clock these days. I miss all my favorite television shows because of him."

"That doesn't mean you have to go to bed when I do," Kent muttered, taking each of the porch steps one at a time. "Ever think I was looking to get away from you?"

"Fine, then you can sleep by yourself for the rest of your life if that's the way you want it."

I hurried ahead to give Kent a helping hand in case he needed it. Rover raced to the top of the steps and waited anxiously for me to join him. I tucked my hand under Kent's elbow. He smiled and whispered, "I can do these stairs just fine, but if you want to hold my hand, I won't object."

Following us, Julie took hold of the railing. "Don't listen to him. Kent needs his knee replaced, but the fool man refuses."

"I'm not letting any doctor cut me open," Kent sputtered.

"Stubborn old fool."

"I heard that," Kent said, and, glancing over his shoulder, added in a lower voice, "Meddling old woman."

"He has selective hearing as well," Julie told me.

I looked to Kent, who seemed not to have heard that last comment.

Once they were both inside the inn, I watched as Oliver unloaded the last of the two large suitcases, a cosmetics bag, and two smaller travel-size quilted bags.

I led the way into the kitchen, after releasing Rover from his leash. He went straight to his bed but kept a close eye on our guests.

"Where do I sign?" Kent asked, looking a bit flustered as he reached inside his rear pocket for his wallet.

"Oh, not to worry, Annie took care of everything."

"I do hope she'll be back soon," Julie said.

"I'm sure she will be," I promised. "Can I offer you some coffee?" I asked.

All three refused, so I gave them their room keys. Kent and Julie ambled toward their room. Oliver followed with their luggage. I could hear the anniversary couple snapping at each other as they headed down the hallway outside the kitchen.

So this was the loving couple Annie had bragged about? Oh, dear.

Oliver stepped out of their room and closed the door.

"Everything all right?" I asked.

"I think so. I just hope they don't end up killing each other before the party."

Chapter 8

Following breakfast, Mary lay down on the bed and rested. After thirty minutes, she felt refreshed enough to take a short walk. The oncologist had urged her to get back into life as much as possible. A walk in the fresh air would do her good.

She was encouraged. While she still moved slowly, she could feel her energy returning. She wasn't ready to leap tall buildings in a single bound, Superwoman-style, as she once had, but that was fine. This was progress. At least she wasn't hanging over a toilet and clinging to the sides with both hands while losing the contents of her stomach. Despite all the advances in anti-nausea medication, Mary found they just weren't effective for her.

Coming down the stairs, she half expected Jo Marie to race out of the kitchen to check on her. Pausing on the bottom step, she waited for the innkeeper to seek her out. When Jo Marie didn't immediately show, Mary rounded the corner and peeked into the kitchen. The dog was nowhere in sight, either. Apparently, Jo Marie was busy elsewhere, which was just as well.

Her steps were measured and slow as Mary left the inn and started down the steep hill toward the waterfront. She felt drawn to the grassy area by the gazebo. The sun was out, and the day was still young. A big sign posted on a community board advertised the entertainment that was scheduled to start the following month: Concerts on the Cove.

One of the acts scheduled to play was a singer who was advertised as comparable to Tony Bennett, as if that was even possible. George had taken her to see Tony Bennett years ago. Tony had come to Seattle, and knowing how she enjoyed the singer, George had finagled tickets to a sold-out event. He'd held her hand during the entire concert. Oh, how romantic he'd been. Thoughtful and caring.

With the other men in her life, the lovemaking had been frantic, done in a fever, ripping off each other's clothes as they hurried toward the bed. It was never like that with George. With him, the lovemaking was slow, attentive, tender . . . and, oh, so very loving.

George again.

Seeing she was in close proximity to Seattle, it wasn't surprising that George wasn't far from her thoughts. In fact, he seemed to be front and center from the moment the plane's wheels had bounced against the tarmac.

Sitting on one of the picnic tables close to the gazebo, Mary looked out over the waters of the cove and focused her gaze there. Just around the point of land was Seattle.

And George.

Men had come in and out of her life, but there had been only one George. She loved him then, and she loved him now. Biting into her lower lip, she struggled with emotion. Her throat thickened and her chest burned. Again, she blamed the cancer. This blasted disease had taken control of her well-ordered life. Having cancer infuriated her. It wasn't fair. It wasn't right. She exercised; her diet was balanced; she got regular medical exams. She didn't deserve to have to deal with this.

When she'd first gotten the news it'd felt like a death sentence, but she'd decided that if she was going to die then by heaven she would go down fighting. And so with characteristic resolve she'd fought. With every ounce of strength she possessed, with every bit of her will, she faced cancer head-on. She refused to lie down and wait to die. It simply wasn't in her personality to be a quitter, and so she tackled the disease the way she had every other stumbling block in her life.

Feeling disjointed, Mary stood and walked to the railing that overlooked the waterfront. A huge white starfish, the largest she'd ever seen, clung to a rock in the water below. That was how she felt, clinging, holding on, fighting in desperation for her life to go back to the way it had once been.

Mary needed structure. Craved it. As a creature of habit, there'd been order to her day; indeed, to her life. That was the way she functioned best. At eight o'clock she would be at her desk with a cup of coffee. At ten, at noon, at three, at five—she knew exactly what she'd be doing or where she'd be headed. Her life was carefully organized.

Cancer changed all that.

Digging out her cell phone, she went online. For all she knew, George might not even be in Seattle any longer and all this angst could be for nothing. It wouldn't do any harm to check the listings for Seattle attorneys, although she had resisted until this very moment. If his name came up, she'd know, and then she would feel some sense of relief.

It didn't take her long to find her answer. His name was there along with a phone number.

George Hudson, Esquire.

Feeling the need for something to drink, Mary found a coffee shop and went inside. The Java Joint coffee menu was impressive, but then she knew how serious people in the Pacific Northwest felt toward the brew.

She found it astonishing how many latte stands a small town like Cedar Cove boasted. On the ride from the freeway to the inn, she counted six. Six. In a town that stated the population was less than seven thousand. And that was just the ones she'd seen. It boggled the mind that there were obviously others.

The young man behind the counter wore a white apron tied at the waist. His name badge identified him as Conner. He looked to be about fifteen, but surely he was older.

"What would you like?" he asked when Mary approached.

"Just coffee."

"Are you sure you wouldn't like to try our drink of the day?"

"Is it coffee?"

"Well, sure, mixed with a combination of flavors. Today it's a cotton-candy latte."

"Cotton candy?" Unbelievable.

"Hey, it's one of our top sellers."

"Right along with peanuts and popcorn?"

"Funny," Conner said, grinning. "We haven't tried that one yet."

"Just coffee," she reiterated.

"You got it." He poured her a mug and handed it to her.

As she paid, Mary noticed his class ring. "Are you graduating on Sunday?" Then, because she felt like she needed to qualify the question, she added, "I met a young lady who works up at the Rose Harbor Inn who told me the graduation ceremony is this weekend."

"You're staying at the inn?"

"Just for a few more nights, yes."

"You must have met Hailey. The inn's a great place, isn't it?" he said, chatting on as he poured the coffee. "Hailey says Jo Marie is the best. I think it's great the way she was willing to show Hailey the ropes. I know the inn isn't big, but it's a start."

"You know Hailey?" Mary had never lived in a small town, and it seemed everyone was connected to everyone else, which she found just short of amazing. Born and raised on the East Coast in Boston, she'd been employed from the time she was sixteen. Her father had drinking problems and couldn't seem to hold down a job, and her mother had worked two jobs to support the family. Nothing had ever come easy to Mary; she'd worked for everything she got. Caring for her younger brother, who unfortunately followed in their father's footsteps, had shown her she wasn't interested in a family of her own. She had too much ambition, too much drive. She loved the east and George . . . Oh, George again . . . He couldn't ever see himself living outside of Seattle. They'd tried to make a go of a long-distance relationship, but it was doomed.

"Everyone knows Hailey," Conner said, interrupting her thoughts. "She stops by here after work most days and we hang."

"Hang?"

"Yeah, you know, talk and stuff."

"Of course." Clearly, Mary wasn't up on the current teenage vernacular.

"I'm a year ahead of Hailey. I'm working here to help with college expenses."

"Good for you." Mary had worked her way through school, too, and it hadn't been easy. Thankfully, she'd gotten a number of scholarships.

"I'm grateful to get summer work. It isn't like jobs are growing on trees these days."

"I know what you mean." Mary left him a generous tip.

His eyes widened when he saw the five-dollar bill. "You need a refill, just say the word and I'll bring it over to you."

"Thanks." Mary chose a table by the window that overlooked Harbor Street. A woman came by and watered the plants potted in the urns next to the streetlights. Flowers had never been Mary's forte, and she wasn't sure exactly what variety they were, but the colors were a vibrant red and yellow.

"Are you here for the seagull-calling contest?" Conner asked.

"I beg your pardon?"

"Cedar Cove has this contest every year. It's big around here. One year the winner appeared on Jay Leno."

Mary smiled. She wasn't sure how she'd missed that. "Sorry to say I haven't heard about it."

"It's next Saturday morning on the waterfront. The person who attracts the most seagulls with their call wins. If you're in town you might want to stop by. It's a lot of fun, and the farmers' market is up and running, too."

"I'll make a point of doing that."

"Hailey's down there most Saturdays with her mom. They sell homemade jelly. My favorite flavor is chocolate cherry."

"Jelly?" Apparently, there was an entire world of flavors Mary had somehow missed.

"Sounds weird, doesn't it? But trust me, it's the best ever."

Such enthusiasm. Mary sipped her coffee. Her cup was still half full when Conner rounded the counter with a fresh pot and refilled her cup. A new customer, a man in greasy coveralls, stopped into the coffee shop. He glanced in her direction and then quickly looked away. Mary was accustomed to that. Not accustomed exactly, but seeing others' uneasiness at her lack of hair, her obvious battle with cancer, no longer took her by surprise. Nor was she offended.

He was in and gone within a couple of minutes, with carryout.

Mary took her time with the coffee, savoring it until it had cooled to the point that it no longer appealed to her. She really didn't have any place she needed to be or any place special she wanted to go. That bothered her more than just about anything else.

Perhaps coming to the Seattle area hadn't been such a bright idea after all. She wasn't an impulsive woman, and this entire trip had been decided on a whim. What had she been thinking? This was insane. Yet here she was. And just across the water was George.

Glancing at the steep climb back to the inn filled her with dread. It was too much. She should have realized that when she'd started toward the waterfront. She'd need to find a ride, a taxi or something.

Her phone beeped, indicating she had a message. Someone had reached out to her. A friend? A colleague? In her eagerness to free her cell from inside her purse, she nearly dropped it. To her disappointment, the email message was an advertisement from her favorite New York steakhouse.

Her hand tightened around her cell. With a click of one button the phone number to George's office showed on the screen. If he knew she was in the area or even close, he'd want to know. Wouldn't he?

"He's married," she muttered.

"Did you say something?" Conner asked.

Her head shot up; his question had alarmed her and taken her by surprise. "Just talking to myself," she said, while her eyes remained focused on George's office number.

"My grandma does that."

Did she look the same age as his grandmother? This young man was starting to depress her.

"You okay?" Conner asked.

Mary glanced up. "What makes you ask?"

"It's the way you're looking at your phone like . . . I don't know, like it's about to tell you something you need to know."

"I was thinking about calling an old friend." Mary couldn't

believe she was discussing this decision with a teenage boy she'd just met.

"What's stopping you?" Conner braced his elbows against the counter and leaned forward. "Wouldn't you like to hear from an old friend?"

"That depends."

He shrugged one shoulder. "On what?"

"This friend and I didn't exactly part on the best of terms."

"Then make it right."

The teenager seemed to have a quick answer to everything. He made it sound so easy.

Mary continued to stare at the phone.

"Do it," Conner urged. "You won't be sorry."

Wanna bet? Mary looped the long purse strap over her shoulder and started toward the door. "Thanks for the coffee and the conversation."

"Make that call," Conner said, stretching out his arm and pointing at her.

Mary stepped outside and headed back to the waterfront. Maybe she should phone George. Really, she had nothing to lose and certainly nothing to gain. If she was being honest with herself she'd admit he was the reason she'd boarded the flight to Seattle.

But not the only one.

Before she could change her mind, she pushed the button that would connect her with George's office.

On the second ring a woman answered. "George Hudson's office. How may I direct your call?"

"Hello," Mary said, struggling to find her voice. It didn't take her long to get ahold of herself. She straightened and squared her shoulders, and when she spoke again her voice betrayed no hesitation. "This is Mary Smith, an old friend of Mr. Hudson's. Is he available?"

"I'm sorry, Ms. Smith, but Mr. Hudson is in court all day today. May I take a message?"

"No, no, that's fine."

"Can I tell him you phoned?"

"No, don't bother, I'll try again later." Without pausing to say good-bye, she disconnected the call. Her hand trembled as she replaced her phone. The fact that George wasn't available was answer enough. She wouldn't try again. This was fate. They weren't meant to reconnect.

Because the climb up the hill to return to the inn would have sapped her of all her strength, Mary returned to the Java Joint and asked Conner to call for a taxi.

Within five minutes a car pulled up in front of the coffee shop. Conner walked her outside and held the car door open for her.

Mary leaned in and gave the driver the address.

"Lady, it's not that far," the cabbie complained.

"I'll pay you triple what your normal fee is," she assured him, expecting that he would complain.

"If that's what you want, but I'm telling you the inn is only about four blocks."

She didn't wait for him to finish, but climbed into the backseat and closed the door. Taking a twenty-dollar bill out of her wallet, she waved it at him, and he took off without bothering to argue further. When he pulled in at the inn, Mary saw another car had parked outside. More guests, she had to assume.

The excursion had worn her out. She was ready to claim the same chair she'd occupied the day before and sit in the sunshine and rest.

After paying the cabbie, she headed toward the house.

Her cell phone rang, and she automatically reached for it. "Hello."

"Mary? Is that really you?"

It was George.

Chapter 9

Rover greeted Annie when she returned from chatting with the florist, wagging his tail in welcome. As Annie shut the front door behind her, Jo Marie came out of the kitchen.

"Your grandparents arrived with their friend," the innkeeper told her. "Oliver asked that I give them the room off the living room area."

Their friend, but definitely not hers.

"Oh, good." It was thoughtful of him to make sure her grandparents didn't have to climb the stairs. Annie wished she had thought of that. Rather than dwell on her dislike of her grandparents' next-door neighbor, she refocused her attention on Jo Marie. "Aren't my grandparents amazing?" she asked, although she didn't really expect a response. Her grandparents were such a loving, generous couple, she thought Jo Marie couldn't help being impressed once she'd met them.

The innkeeper's response was a decidedly weak smile. A timer dinged from inside the kitchen. "I need to get cookies out of the oven," she said, and excused herself. Rover followed Jo Marie.

Eager to connect with her family, Annie went down the long hallway to their room. Her one wish was that Oliver had chauffeured her grandparents from Portland but had no intentions of lingering for the anniversary party. Casting her eyes toward the ceiling, she prayed Oliver would leave in short order. *Please, God,* she begged, as she knocked against the hard wooden door.

Her grandmother's voice rang out: "Get that, would you, Kent?"

"Get what?"

"Someone's at the door," Annie's grandmother said, louder this time. "Can't you see I'm busy?"

"Hold your horses," Kent shouted.

A couple of moments later the door was thrust open. Annie's grandfather squinted at her. "Annie?" he asked.

"For the love of heaven, put your glasses on," Julie cried, coming out of the bathroom. "Oh, Annie, it is you." She rushed forward and enveloped Annie in a tight hug.

"Grandma," Annie whispered, hugging her back. Next she hugged her grandfather.

"Do I get one of those?"

Annie whirled around. Sure enough, just as she'd feared— Oliver Sutton. He was the last person she wanted to see this weekend. Their history was long and troubled. At one time she'd had the biggest crush on him, but he'd killed that. He was her older brother's age and had teased her mercilessly the entire time they were growing up. Because of his close proximity to their grandparents, Oliver had somehow become part of every holiday function held at their Portland home.

From the time Annie was five until age thirteen she couldn't remember a Christmas or Easter without Oliver teasing her about her red hair . . . and that was only the beginning of their unpleasant history. He'd been unrelenting. If she'd ever come close to hating anyone, it would be Oliver Sutton.

"No hugs for you," she told him, doing her best to let him know she'd rather grab hold of a porcupine than be in his vicinity.

"Oliver was kind enough to drive us up from Portland," her grandmother explained.

"I could have driven without a problem," Kent complained. "But if Oliver wanted to escort us, I didn't mind."

"If you wore your glasses the way the doctor ordered you to—"

"I mislaid them," Kent muttered, looking to Annie. "Which is something your grandmother is far too willing to forget. I can't see worth a darn without them."

"Grandma could carry a spare pair with her—"

"I refuse to baby your grandfather," Julie insisted, cutting Annie off. "He's a grown man. It's not my responsibility to make sure he has his glasses."

"I was available, so I agreed to drive," Oliver said, diverting the conversation from her grandparents.

Annie looked away, uncomfortable under his scrutiny. He couldn't seem to take his eyes off her, which unsettled her far more than it should have. He made her feel like she was thirteen all over again.

"I have to say Oliver has been just wonderful," her grandmother continued, seemingly unaware of Annie's tension. She never knew what her grandparents found so wonderful about their pesky neighbor, and she wasn't about to ask. From her earliest memory, Oliver had been nothing but an irritation. Since she had a brother and another male cousin, she was the only girl, which made her fair game for their nastiness. Oliver had been their ringleader.

"You're looking good," he said.

A natural response would be to thank him, but she refused to do it. As it was, she did her best not to squirm. He couldn't seem to take his eyes off her. It was all she could manage not to glare right back. He had to know how much she disliked him.

"Aren't you going to thank Oliver for the compliment?" her grandfather asked.

She managed to mutter an unintelligible reply. She'd fallen prey to Oliver's so-called compliments before, and she wouldn't again.

"I was just about to suggest we all go to lunch," Oliver said.

"What a lovely idea." Her grandmother seemed far too willing to fall into Oliver's schemes.

"What is?" her grandfather asked.

"Kent, please put in your hearing aids."

"I hate those things. They make my ears itch."

"You know how it irritates me to have to repeat everything I say."

"What's that?"

Her grandmother exhaled a sharp breath. "Never mind."

"Anyone hungry yet?" Kent asked. "It's got to be around lunchtime." It was all too apparent, her grandfather was truly in need of those hearing aids.

"Give me ten minutes," Julie said. "I have a few things to unpack yet, and I'd like to freshen up a bit."

"Of course," Annie agreed.

Annie and Oliver left the room together. She refused to look at him and started down the hall, wanting to escape him and willing to make up an excuse if necessary.

It felt as if his eyes bore into her. It'd always been like this between them. Oliver Sutton was the most unpleasant man she'd ever known.

"When was the last time I saw you, Annie?" he asked, in an attempt to make casual conversation.

"Whenever it was, it wasn't nearly long ago enough," Annie remembered, but she wasn't saying. Actually, she remembered everything about Oliver Sutton, although she'd rather not. It didn't help that he was so good-looking. His features were classic—tall, dark, and handsome as sin. The problem was he knew it. According to her grandfather, who often mentioned Oliver, he was quite the ladies' man. Well, all those other women were welcome to him. And if he left a string of broken hearts wherever he went the way her grandfather insinuated, good for him, but Annie was determined not to be one of them. Early on, Annie had learned her lesson, and she wasn't looking for a repeat performance.

He laughed as if she'd made a joke. "Oh, come on, now, you can't still be mad over me pulling your pigtails. You were eight years old."

She glared at him. "If that was all you did . . ." She stopped abruptly, mid-sentence. It did no good to rehash past offenses. Oliver would only be amused by her litany of wrongs, and she wasn't about to give him that kind of power over her.

"It's a wonderful thing you've done for your grandparents," he said, switching the subject. "This anniversary celebration is all Julie could talk about for weeks."

"I am a party planner. It was the least I could do." She didn't mention how throwing herself into this family gathering, keeping herself focused, had seen her through the bleak period after breaking up with Lenny.

"You're looking good, Annie—I mean that. I've never seen you look more beautiful."

Another compliment from Oliver?

Annie folded her arms around her middle and confronted him. "Why are you here?" she demanded.

He blinked as if the question surprised him. "Your grandmother . . ."

"You know how I feel about you."

"Yes, unfortunately, I do. Julie asked me to drive her and Kent, and seeing that I had the time, how could I refuse?" He grinned and crossed his own arms. "I can see you still have that red-headed temperament."

"The color of my hair has nothing to do with my disposition." Dropping her arms, she tightened her hands into fists.

Oliver's hands flew up in a defensive stance. "Don't tell me you're going to slug me again."

She'd been thirteen, and he'd deserved it. "Don't tempt me."

"Ah, but you do," he whispered. "You always have."

That was an unlikely story. Oliver had been a tease, but Annie wasn't putting up with it any longer. "Don't get in my way, understand? I have a lot to think about, and I don't have time to play silly games with you."

His lower lip jutted out. "That's a shame."

Annie glanced at her wrist. It seemed to be taking her grandparents an inordinate amount of time. Although she had everything for the party under control, she could always use it as an excuse to escape this lunch, especially with Oliver there. All it would take was a word or two, but she'd wait until . . .

"How's Lenny?" Oliver asked.

The question came out of left field. "Who . . . who told you about Lenny?" To this point she hadn't even had time to tell her own grandparents that the engagement was off.

"Your grandmother, naturally. She mentioned him when the two of you got engaged."

"As you very well know, the engagement is off . . ."

His brows arched as though he was surprised. "Since when?"

"For quite a while now, not that it's any of your concern," she snapped, unwilling to fill in the blanks. The less Oliver knew about her personal affairs, the better.

"Is he the reason you're so prickly?"

"You're the reason, and I'm not prickly!" she insisted. "I wish you'd take the hint and just leave."

"No way. This is getting more interesting by the minute. So what happened between you and Mr. Love of Your Life? That's how your grandmother described him."

Annie would stake her life savings on her grandmother saying no such thing. Although she'd talked to her grandparents any number of times while planning this anniversary celebration, Annie hadn't mentioned Lenny. He was a subject she'd looked to avoid, assuming her parents had told them of the broken engagement.

"Lenny drinks too much?"

She ignored the question.

"He's irresponsible with money?"

Rather than listen to his litany of questions, she walked away.

"I know. He has a roving eye."

"Would you stop?" she demanded.

"Ah, so that's it."

No way was she letting Oliver know he'd hit the bull's-eye.

At that precise moment, as if Lenny was aware he was the main topic of conversation, her cell rang. Glancing at the caller ID, she hit the respond button.

"Don't call me again," she all but shouted, and then immediately ended the call.

The door to her grandparents' room opened, and Julie stepped out. "Who was that, dear?"

"No one important," Annie said, forcing a smile.

"Did I mention Betty and Vern are already in town?" Kent called from their room.

Annie knew the couple were good friends of her grandparents'. Vern had been in the navy at the same time as Annie's grandfather, and the couple had stood up as best man and maid of honor for Kent and Julie.

"Unfortunately, they aren't staying at the inn. Betty has a sister in town, and they decided to spend time with Gerty," her grandmother explained. "I do wish they'd booked the inn. It's in such a lovely location. Kent and I are going out to dinner with them this evening. You two won't mind, will you?"

Oliver answered before Annie had a chance: "Not at all. It would be my pleasure to take Annie to dinner."

"Ah . . . that's not necessary," she scrambled to assure her grandmother. "I've got a hundred things to do."

"I'll help," Oliver offered.

Annie fought down the desire to stomp on his foot. "Thank you, but I have everything under control."

"Annie, sweetheart, don't ever turn down a helping hand," her grandmother advised, giving Annie's waist a gentle squeeze. "Now, where's your grandfather? I swear that man is always lagging behind everyone else."

"I'm coming, I'm coming," Kent said, as he stepped into the hallway. He closed the door to their room and then twisted the knob several times to be sure it was locked. "Now, what is everyone in the mood to eat? I say we go out for Mexican."

"Kent," Julie said with a groan. "You know how Mexican food gives me heartburn; besides, all that cheese isn't good for your heart."

A frown darkened her grandfather's face. "I haven't had cheese in weeks. If I want to splurge and have cheese, then I will. You're not in charge of my diet, I am, and I want Mexican."

"We can order a chicken salad, Grandma," Annie suggested.

"Oh, all right. I don't know why it is everyone feels they have to tiptoe around your grandfather."

Her grandparents walked ahead of them, arguing over something new as they all made their way outside to where Oliver had parked the car.

"Were they like this all the way from Portland?" Annie asked Oliver, shaken by their bickering.

"I'm afraid so. They've been snapping at each other from the moment we left."

"Oh, dear."

"How about a truce, Annie?" Oliver asked. "Between you and me. If we can be civil to each other, maybe they'll follow our example."

Annie knew better than to trust him. But then he looked down at her with those deep brown eyes and she almost gave in. "We'll see."

He shrugged. "Okay, have it your way."

While Annie joined her grandparents, Oliver went back to get a recommendation for a Mexican restaurant from Jo Marie. He returned in quick order and slid into the driver's seat next to Annie's grandfather. Annie and her grandmother sat in the backseat.

"Jo Marie said there's a great place not far from here called the Taco Shack," Oliver said as he started the car engine.

Annie's grandmother muttered something under her breath and grimaced.

Annie patted Julie's hand. "I'm sure it will be all right."

Julie looked out the side window and whispered, "I think it's wrong the way everyone caters to your grandfather. It's wrong, I tell you."

"I heard that," Kent growled. "No one is catering to me, especially you."

"Don't you remember . . ."

"Julie has the memory of an elephant," Kent said, leaning toward Oliver. "She brings up stuff from forty years ago as if it happened yesterday."

"I think we're going to have lovely weather for the vow renewal," Annie piped in before the two broke out into a full-blown argument.

"Who said anything about renewing our vows?" her grandfather asked, twisting around to look at Annie. "At the rate your grandmother and I are going, this marriage won't last another week."

"You've been threatening to leave me for fifty years. One would think you'd have done it before now."

"Children, children," Oliver said, chuckling softly.

"Oh, look at that cute restaurant," Julie said, pointing to a pink Victorian-style building as they drove past.

"That's the tearoom I mentioned when I first started looking for someplace to hold the reception," Annie said. "Unfortunately, the restaurant isn't set up for receptions."

"It looks just perfect," her grandmother mused aloud. "I bet they serve incredible lunches."

"You couldn't get me within ten feet of that place," Kent muttered. "You won't see me in a tearoom with my pinkie in the air, sipping tea."

"I wouldn't want to go there with you anyway."

"Ah, here we are," Oliver said, cutting off their argument. He made a right-hand turn into the restaurant parking lot. "This looks to be every bit as good as Jo Marie promised." He parked directly in front of the Taco Shack.

After listening to her grandparents bicker for the entire ride, Annie's stomach was tied into one giant knot. All her memories of her beloved grandma and grandpa had been those of a loving couple. Not once could she recall a cross word between them. Here they were about to celebrate fifty years of marriage and it was almost as if they couldn't stand the sight of each other.

When did this happen? Annie didn't have a clue how she was

going to pull off this event with them constantly picking at each other. Hopefully it was nerves and everything would go back to normal in short order.

As if he was a true gentleman, Oliver opened the back passenger door and helped her grandmother out. Kent didn't wait and was already halfway across the parking lot. Julie hurried to catch up with him.

"Everything will work itself out," Oliver assured her.

"How can you say that?" Annie whispered, ready to weep. "This is a disaster."

"It's not so bad," he said, discounting her fears. "They're just a little stressed out with all this fuss over their anniversary."

"Are you saying I shouldn't have gone to the trouble to plan this party?" she flared. "Is that what you're telling me?"

"I'm saying don't worry; it's going to turn out just fine."

Annie sighed, hoping he was right. She wiped a hand across her face. "Sorry, I guess I'm a little stressed out myself."

"I could help you relax," Oliver offered, and pressed his hand to the small of her back.

"Yeah, right."

"I could always kiss you . . . again."

"You don't want to go there, Oliver Sutton," Annie murmured, and slapped his hand aside.

"Ah, but I enjoyed it so much the first time."

Chapter 10

At the sound of George's voice coming over her cell phone, Mary's knees shook so badly that she needed to find a place to sit down. Thankfully, the Adirondack chair on the veranda was close by. She sank into the wooden seat while pressing the cell phone hard against her ear.

"Where are you?" George asked with a sense of urgency as though she were in desperate need of help.

"Washington."

"State?"

"Yes." Her own voice sounded breathless, as if she'd raced up several flights of stairs.

"Are you all right?" His voice became less frantic. "Do you need anything?"

To her horror, tears flooded her eyes and she found it impossible to speak.

"Mary? Talk to me."

"I . . . I have can . . . cer." She hiccupped the words.

Her announcement was followed by a long pause, as though he was as shocked by the diagnosis as she'd been when she first heard the word. He recovered quickly, though. "When can I see you?"

By the sheer force of her will, Mary managed to gain control of her emotions. She grabbed a tissue from inside her purse and held it to her nose. When next she spoke her voice was steady and strong. "Seeing me isn't such a good idea."

"I beg to differ."

George, sweet George, always so polite and caring. How he ever convinced himself he was in love with her was beyond Mary's comprehension.

"I need to see you," he said.

Clearly the fact that she had cancer had hit him hard. Blurting it out like that had been a mistake. As big a mistake as contacting his office had been.

Mary struggled within herself.

"Tell me where you are," he insisted, "and I'll come right away."

Mary refused to let him even consider leaving. "You're supposed to be in court," she reminded him.

"Screw that."

"George, no."

"Then promise me you'll let me see you."

Squeezing her eyes shut, Mary battled down the nearly overwhelming desire to agree, but she couldn't. Even now she didn't understand what craziness had taken hold of her to seek him out. In any other circumstances she would never have given in to this weakness.

The threat of her own mortality made her weak in areas where she'd always been strong. Nineteen years ago she'd walked away from George. She'd never intended to see or talk to him again and here she was craving his touch, craving his gentleness and caring. It would make everything worthwhile if she could see him again. One last time.

"Mary, did you hear me?"

"Yes," she whispered.

He hesitated, and then softly, ever so softly, he added, "Please."

A sob rose in her throat and escaped, sounding like the cry of a small injured animal.

"Mary, are you crying?"

Even at the very end of their affair, she hadn't shed a tear, and now here she was blubbering like a newborn, swallowing back tears.

George spoke again. "I can take anything but the sound of your tears."

"I'm okay, I'm okay," she insisted. Dealing with weakness in any form was foreign to her. Drawing in deep breaths, she struggled for composure for several seconds. Straightening, she squared her shoulders. "I'm fairly certain your wife wouldn't take kindly to the two of us meeting, and—"

"I'm divorced." George said, cutting her off.

The news rocked Mary. Divorced? "When?"

"Years ago now. What about you?"

For the first time since she'd answered her cell, Mary relaxed. "I never married."

"Never?"

If she had been interested in sharing her life with anyone, it would have been George.

"I never loved Kathleen completely," he elaborated. "She knew my heart belonged to you going into the marriage."

Mary didn't want to hear this, and at the same time she hungered for every word.

"For a while it didn't matter," George went on to say. "We were content with each other, but then, after a few years, we weren't. I wasn't surprised when she asked for a divorce."

"Children?" The word nearly stuck in her throat.

"No."

"If anyone deserved to be a father, it was you."

The line went quiet as he digested her words.

"I'm so sorry," she whispered. She'd robbed him of that opportunity along with everything else.

It went without saying that he knew what she was telling him.

"I know," he whispered back.

They both took a moment to reflect on the past. Mary wasn't willing to break the silence. From the first there'd been a strong connection between them. In the beginning it had manifested itself physically, but this cord, this tie, this link between them, was also spiritual and by far stronger than anything she'd experienced with any other person, even family. Just hearing his voice, it was as if nearly twenty years had evaporated into thin air. Whoosh, and the years disappeared. It felt as if they had never been apart.

"How long have you had cancer?" he asked, his words low, concerned, and fearful.

"I was diagnosed several months ago."

"Where?" was his next question.

She hesitated and then decided he might as well know the worst of it. "My breasts. I had a double mastectomy."

He didn't comment about her breasts being gone.

Mary had anguished over the decision when really there had been only one sensible choice: her life. In retrospect it should have been an easy decision. It hadn't been. It felt as if she'd been stripped of her femininity.

"What stage?" This was asked with a hitch in his breath, as if he was afraid to ask but yet had to know.

"Four."

"The prognosis?"

"Undecided." The one word explained everything, she supposed.

"So that's why you're here. You've come because you want to make your peace with me?"

Had she? Earlier, standing at the waterfront, watching the water lap against the shore, Mary had admitted she'd flown across the country because of George. If she were about to meet her Maker, then she intended to stand before God with the sure knowledge that she had done everything within her power to right her wrongs. She'd lied and misled George and had lived with that guilt all these years. At the time it had seemed the best thing to do under the circumstances. She couldn't be the woman he wanted, the wife or mother he needed her to be. Their bicoastal relationship was doomed from the beginning; if he hadn't recognized it, she did. Because she was the stronger of the two, she'd ended it, and in the process, among everything else, she'd badly hurt George.

"Yes, I suppose I did come to make peace," she admitted softly.

"Then you'll agree to see me." He wasn't about to let up on the subject, she realized.

"Oh, George, is that really necessary?" She wanted to be with him again so badly, but she didn't want him to see her like this.

Her hand automatically went to her head.

Her bald head.

All that remained of her once-thick, dark hair was stubble. She did what she could to disguise it with a silk scarf, but she wasn't fooling anyone. Wigs were a disaster on her. She'd given up on them after the first week.

"I want to see you," George insisted. "You owe me that much."

The truth was, she owed him far more, but still she hesitated. Closing her eyes, her heart heavy with reluctance, she whispered, "I'll see you."

"Thank you."

"But before we meet, there are a few things you should know."

He hesitated. "All right."

"First off, I don't look anything like I did twenty years ago." Those days were long gone.

He laughed. "And you think I do?"

In her mind, he'd never changed. She continued to hold a mental picture of him from the first time they'd met. He'd been young and dashing—in her eyes, anyway. While the years had taken their toll on her, she couldn't picture George any differently than he had been the last time they were together.

"You probably won't recognize me."

He laughed ever so softly and contradicted her: "I'll recognize you, Mary,"

"Okay, whatever you say. It's time for you to go. I shouldn't need to remind you that you have court today."

"I'm coming to see you this afternoon; just tell me where and when." He was so eager, so ready to do whatever was necessary.

"I'll come to you," she offered, and really that was the most practical solution.

"No. You've been sick. Tell me the name of your hotel. You're in a hotel, aren't you?"

This was getting complicated. "No, I'm not."

He waited for her to elaborate, and when she didn't, he asked, "Where are you staying?"

"Ever heard of Cedar Cove?" All Mary could do was hope that she wasn't making a big mistake giving him this much information regarding her whereabouts.

"Of course I know Cedar Cove; it's across Puget Sound from Seattle. For the love of heaven, what made you decide to stay there?"

"I don't know if you'd believe me if I told you."

"Try me."

"Oh, George, I was afraid. I flew all the way across the country on a wild-goose chase. It was a crazy idea."

"To see me." He sounded both pleased by and proud of the gesture.

"Yes, I'm willing to admit I came because of you." But there were other reasons as well, reasons he knew nothing about.

"But you were afraid of being too close." He supplied her reason for staying on the other side of Puget Sound.

"Yes . . . I suppose. As far as I knew, you were still married to Kathleen. I didn't want to disrupt your life."

"I'll be done in court by two-thirty, three at the latest; if not, I'll have my associate take first chair."

Mary glanced at her watch. It was just after noon. He must have collected his messages and phoned on his lunch break.

"I'll check the ferry schedule, but if it's inconvenient, then I'll drive around through Tacoma."

"Okay." Mary could only pray that she'd made the right decision in agreeing to this meeting.

"I'll come directly to your hotel."

"No." Her response was quick and immediate. Letting him know she was in Cedar Cove was a stretch, and one she already regretted.

"Then you tell me where you want me to go."

The problem was Mary didn't really know any place other than the Java Joint. That location would be less than ideal for a variety of reasons. Then she remembered the lovely Victorian-style building she'd seen on her ride into town. The building had been pink and feminine-looking, with dainty lace curtains in the windows and flower beds in bloom. A blossoming cherry tree, filled with small pink flowers, made for a postcard-perfect picture.

Mary had been automatically drawn to it. As little as two years ago, nothing about this tearoom would have attracted her notice.

But two years ago she'd had her breasts. Two years ago her femininity hadn't been in question, at least in her own mind. She'd worn pencil-thin skirts and stiletto heels. These days she battled lymphedema and other adverse side affects as a result of several bouts of chemotherapy.

"There's a tearoom in town."

"A tearoom?"

She smiled at the surprise in his voice. "That doesn't sound like me, does it?"

"Not at all."

"You'll know it right away—it's pink."

"A pink tearoom," he echoed, and it sounded like he was holding back a laugh. The woman he knew twenty years ago would have shunned such a place for fear of being stereotyped.

"I'm not the woman you remember, George. Keep that in mind; otherwise, you're about to be bitterly disappointed."

"Then I'll look forward to meeting the woman you've become."

His gentle understanding made this all the more difficult.

"I'll be at the pink tearoom as close to four as I can make it," he told her.

"Okay," she agreed.

"Good-bye."

"Good-bye." But she didn't disconnect the line, wanting to hold on to him for as long as possible. After a couple of moments she realized George hadn't hung up on his end, either.

After several more moments, he whispered, "I never stopped loving you."

A lone tear rolled down her cheek. "Don't love me, George."

"It's too late to stop now. Did you really think time would change the way I feel about you?"

She had no answer for him.

"Hang up," she insisted, although her voice trembled with emotion. "You'll be late for court."

"You hang up first," he whispered back.

"I'm not the one due in court."

"Hang up, Mary."

Because he gave her no choice, she ended the call, but she clenched her phone in her hand, her grip on it as strong as she could make it.

Oh, my, what had she done? How could she have been so foolish and weak as to contact George? What did she think would come of this?

Nothing. Nothing could.

It was too late for her, and far too late for the two of them.

Chapter 11

Mary was busy on the phone. My other guests had all left for lunch at the Taco Shack, which left me pretty much free, so I grabbed my garden scissors and headed outside to gather some flowers.

Rhododendrons are the Washington state flower and come in a variety of amazing colors. Several bushes dotted the property. The pink blossoms on the one growing along the side of the inn were huge, so I was able to cut enough for several arrangements. I've always loved flowers, and I enjoy having them around the house.

Peggy Beldon warned me that I would need to be sensitive to any guests who might have allergies, so I limited the amount I brought inside. But the rhodies were so beautiful and I was afraid I might have gone just a bit overboard.

I arranged the blossoms and set a few of them about the breakfast area and placed a second equally large vase in the living room, too. A smaller bouquet went in the hallway on a credenza I had on the second floor, and then I took yet another up to the third level. The flowers added color and left a sweet fragrance.

I was coming down the stairs when Mary entered the house. She looked a bit shaken. Although concerned, I hesitated to say anything. Mary seemed to want her privacy, and I honored that, but nevertheless I was worried about her. I noticed how quickly she tired and how hard she tried to hide any weakness. I hoped to make her as comfortable as possible without being overbearing or intrusive.

"Would you like some fresh flowers in your room?" I asked. I'd cut enough rhododendrons to easily fill two or three more vases.

Mary looked away as if this was a momentous decision. "Yes, that would be very nice, thank you."

"I'll see to it right away. Can I get you anything else?"

"I don't think so," she said, and placed her hand on the railing, starting up the stairs.

"If you'd like, I could bring a pot of tea to your room."

"No, but thanks."

She passed me on the stairwell, and kept her head lowered. For a moment it looked as if she'd been crying, but I didn't see Mary as the type of woman who easily gave in to tears.

After I delivered the flowers to Mary's room, I ate a peanut-butter-and-jelly sandwich for lunch. Rover was antsy, I noticed. He couldn't seem to make up his mind about what he wanted. He went into the laundry room a couple of times and then came out and looked intently at me. Then he went to his bed, circled it two or three times, but didn't lie down. Instead he went and stood at the back door as if he needed to go out. Yet when I opened it for him, he stayed where he was and just looked up at me as if I was supposed to be able to read his mind.

"What's with you?" I asked my canine friend.

After a few moments, he returned to the laundry room where I kept his leash.

"You want to go for walk?"

Standing up on his hind legs, he pressed his paws against my thigh with that same intense look. Not knowing what else to do, I went into the laundry room and got out his leash. As soon as he saw it, he did a small happy dance, which told me a walk was exactly what was on his mind.

We'd fallen into a routine and generally took our walks after breakfast. His demand, and that was what it was, came as a surprise, especially since we'd already been out once that morning.

"Okay, okay, but let me finish my lunch first." I grabbed a cookie on my way out the door.

As soon as I connected the leash, Rover started straining down the back porch steps and half dragging me with him. This, too, wasn't normal behavior. "What's going on, Rover?" I asked. Seeing how agitated he was, I decided to let him lead me wherever he wanted to go.

It soon became apparent that Rover was headed to Mark's house. Not once did he stop to mark his territory.

"Rover," I insisted. "Mark isn't home. He's working elsewhere today, remember?" Mark had made a point of letting me know he would be unavailable because he had another project he was working on. A project other than my rose garden!

Rover refused to listen and had me trotting to keep pace with him. He pulled me around the back of Mark's residence, where he'd set up his workshop.

"Rover," I chastised him. "Mark isn't here."

"Who's there?" Mark called from inside his shop. He sounded faint and breathy.

"Mark?" I rushed forward to open the door, twisting the knob hard only to find it locked. I knocked as hard as I could. "Is there anyone there? Mark? Mark, are you all right?"

"Yes." Again it was Mark with that same low, weak voice. "Come in."

"I can't. The door is locked."

"Key," he said, and it sounded as if he were in a lot of pain. "Kitchen drawer by the sink."

"You can't open it?" I asked.

"No."

"Okay. I'll get it." I raced into the house, using the back entrance. Rover remained outside by the workshop and let loose with a howl when I left.

"I'm coming back," I reassured him.

I found it interesting that Mark had locked his shop but not the house. Apparently, everything he valued was in his place of business and not his home. I'd never been inside his house before, and while curious as to what it was like, I didn't dare take time to look around.

To add to my frustration, the key wasn't where he said it was. I slammed open one drawer after another until I located a key chain with a number of odd-shaped keys. Rushing back to the shop, it took two or three tries to find the key to open the door. When I pushed it open, Rover raced into the shop ahead of me, barking erratically.

Mark was nowhere to be seen.

"Down here," he said between gritted teeth.

He sat on the floor with his legs pinned beneath a heavy collapsed table. So this was the all-important project that required his attention.

I got down next to him on my knees and could see he was in a great deal of pain. His face was white with it.

"I'll call nine-one-one," I said.

"No." His voice was hard and insistent.

"Mark . . ."

"I'll be okay, just get this damned table off of me."

Who did he think I was, Superwoman? "I can't lift that thing."
Nor was I willing to sit there and argue with him. He needed more
help than I would be able to give him. Thankfully, I'd brought my
cell with me. I took it out of my pocket and dialed for help.

"Jo Marie," he said, wincing as he spoke, "do you always have
to do the exact opposite of what I ask?"

I ignored him, speaking to the 911 dispatcher and explaining
the situation. After answering a few simple questions, I was assured help was on the way.

"Is anything broken?" I asked Mark.

"How would I know?" he growled back. "Do I look like I'm a
doctor?"

"No need to snap at me," I shot back, and then instantly regretted my outburst. He must be in horrific pain. "Does anything feel
broken?"

"I hate to think I was in all this pain for a scraped knee." He
closed his eyes and turned his face away from me.

"Why was the door locked?"

"I didn't want to be interrupted."

I couldn't imagine what was so important that he literally had
to hide away behind a locked door, but then Mark was nothing if
not odd.

He grabbed hold of his thigh with both hands as though he
wanted to ease the pain.

"Is it your leg?" I asked.

"Yes." The word came on a growl, as if my question irritated
him more than the pain.

I felt so helpless, at a complete loss as to what more I could do
to help him.

"Can I do anything?"

"Leave," he muttered.

"I'm not going to do that."

He snorted. "I figured as much."

We were both silent for a couple of moments before he asked, "Why are you here?"

"Rover. He wouldn't leave me alone until I got the leash, and the minute we got outside, he all but dragged me here."

Mark frowned. "How could he have known?"

I couldn't help but wonder that myself. He really was the most amazing dog. I bet Mark didn't find him so worthless now.

"Do you have an answer?" Mark asked, gruffly.

"No."

"Just leave, would you? The aid car will be here soon enough. You've done your duty."

"I'm not leaving you," I insisted.

"Go," he shouted.

Mark Taylor was the most unfriendly, unappreciative man I'd ever known. Because he seemed so intent on having me out of his hair, I got up from my knees. Seeing he was in no mood to have me around, I figured I'd walk to the front of the house to check if I could see the aid car.

Mark looked up at me as if shocked that I was actually doing as he asked.

"I told the aid car to come in the back, but I thought I'd show them the way."

Leaning back on his hands, he closed his eyes and nodded.

I gave his shoulder a gentle squeeze. "It won't be long now."

A car door slammed in the distance, and I raced out of the shop and called, "This way."

Mark wasn't happy I'd phoned for help, but at the same time I knew he was relieved. He was angry and short-tempered, but I accepted that was the pain and didn't take it personally.

The men from the local fire station did quick work lifting the heavy table off Mark's legs. Right away I could see that his leg and ankle were twisted at an odd angle. Clearly it was broken. The pain must be severe; nevertheless, Mark attempted to stand up on his own.

The firemen put a stop to that, and with Mark protesting loudly, a gurney was rolled into the shop.

"I'm fine now that this blasted table is off me."

"Your leg is broken," I pointed out. Anyone looking at it could see that.

Mark fussed some more, but he was basically ignored.

"Are you his wife?" one of the men asked me. His name badge identified him as Mack McAfee.

Mark must have heard the question, because he snickered loudly as if the very idea was cause for humor.

"Just a friend," I supplied. Frankly, after this morning I wondered if Mark would even consider me that.

"We'll transport him to the Bremerton hospital. Can you meet us there?"

"I don't want Jo Marie anywhere close to that hospital," Mark insisted, as two men rolled him out the door.

I pretended not to hear. "I'm on foot, and my dog is with me. I'll go back to the house, get my car, and head over to the hospital."

"It's a good thing you happened along when you did," Chief Holiday mentioned.

I wanted to tell him Rover was responsible for me finding Mark, but I wasn't sure he would believe me. Really, who would? This was the stuff movies were made of, stories with Lassie or Rin Tin Tin. Rover was a pound dog who appeared to possess magical powers.

Together Rover and I hurriedly walked back to the inn. As far as I could tell, Mary remained in her room, and the others hadn't returned from lunch yet. I had guests due to arrive in a couple of hours and would need to be back.

Now that his work was done, Rover curled up in his bed and promptly went to sleep as if the short walk had completely worn him out. I left a note for Annie and her grandparents, and then headed out the door.

My heart pounded fast and erratically as I inserted my key in the car ignition, and I realized how badly shaken I was by all this.

When I arrived at the hospital, I learned that Mark had been sent down for X-rays. With nothing else to do, I went to the emergency room waiting area and took a seat.

I'd read through one entire magazine and had just started a second when I heard Mark's voice, protesting something. I didn't need a crystal ball to tell me he was not going to be a compliant patient. A broken leg was going to severely hamper his ability to work. Oh, dear, I might as well give up the hope of having the rose garden in before autumn. Right away, I felt guilty for being so thoughtless.

A nurse's aide rolled Mark out in a wheelchair. His left leg was in a cast up to his knee. "Your friend is here," the nurse told him.

He looked up at me and then looked away.

So that was the way it was to be. Fine. One would think the least he could do was show a little gratitude. The ingrate.

"I'll bring the car around," I told the woman, ignoring Mark. Two could play that game.

It took me a few minutes to drive around to the emergency room entrance. By the time I was under the portico, Mark and the nurse's aide were waiting outside for me.

I put the car in park and then hurried around to the passenger side and held open the door. The aide helped him into my vehicle.

"Thank you," I told the young woman. If Mark wouldn't thank her, then I would.

He held himself stiff in the seat beside me.

"It wouldn't hurt you to show a bit of appreciation," I muttered. In his current mood, I didn't expect him to respond.

Debbie Macomber

"The nurse ruined a perfectly good pair of jeans," he complained.

"Would you rather have had her unzip your pants and pull them off over your broken leg?" I could only imagine how painful that would be.

He didn't answer right away, and when he did speak I wasn't able to make out what he said.

"Do you need me to stop by the pharmacy?" I asked.

He shook his head. "They will deliver."

"What about crutches?"

"I have a pair at the house."

So this wasn't the first time around for him. "Did you break your leg before?"

"No." He didn't elaborate, and I wasn't going to pry when he so clearly wasn't in the mood to chat.

It seemed to take forever to drive around the waterfront to Cedar Cove. The silence between us was as heavy as that table must have been. When I pulled up to the front of the house, he didn't even wait for me to stop the car before he had his hand on the doorknob.

"You'll need those crutches," I said. Even Mark had to recognize he wouldn't be able to get from my car to the house without them.

He exhaled and nodded. "Back bedroom closet."

I turned off the engine and started toward the house, doing my best to hide a smile. So I was going to be able to see the inside of his house after all.

108

Chapter 12

Annie didn't know how she'd make it through lunch with Oliver and her grandparents. It was awkward enough being with Oliver, but her grandparents couldn't seem to agree on anything. Annie found it amazing that they had managed to stay married all these years. She couldn't remember them ever being anything but loving toward each other and wondered what had changed. It used to be that she saw them at least three or four times a year, but college had changed that, and then she'd taken a job. The last two Christmases her grandparents had spent with friends in Hawaii.

"I don't understand why you insist on eating Mexican food," Julie said once they were seated and handed menus. Right away a bowl of salsa and chips were delivered to their table.

"I happen to like enchiladas."

Annie's grandmother muttered under her breath. Annie didn't catch what she said, which was probably for the best.

Kent reached for a chip and dipped it in the salsa. "You complain that cheese isn't good for me. Well, I happen to enjoy it, and if I choose to eat cheese, you shouldn't stop me."

"Someone should," her grandmother insisted, grumbling louder this time.

Annie hid behind the menu, embarrassed by the attention her bickering grandparents generated. Her grandfather spoke loud enough for the entire restaurant to hear. Their squabble had attracted the notice of everyone in the room.

"If the enchiladas kill me," her grandfather insisted, "then I'll die a happy man."

"Then go right ahead. You're absolutely right, if you want to clog up your heart valves and die, then that's your prerogative. I'll have the time of my life spending the insurance money."

"Have fun. And like I said, I'll die happy." And with that, Kent ordered three-cheese enchiladas with rice and beans.

Her grandmother had a chicken salad with no sour cream but with extra avocado. Oliver asked for chicken fajitas, and Annie went with an appetizer sampler plate, although she barely touched her lunch.

How could she?

If she wasn't refereeing her grandparents, she was forced to deal with Oliver's stares. With restraint she managed not to kick him under the table and tell him to stop eyeing her like she was a piece of tenderloin. Naturally, he did it on purpose, trying to unnerve her. That had been his game plan from the time they were kids. He found it highly amusing to tease and irritate her. It was easy to see that nothing had changed.

Once they'd paid their tab and were outside the restaurant, Annie whispered, "Would you stop?"

"What?" he asked, playing innocent.

"You know exactly what I mean. I'm telling you right now I'm not putting up with it."

Oliver looked genuinely confused. "Putting up with what?" he asked.

Annie narrowed her gaze and bellowed, "Stop staring at me." Then, to her absolute horror, she turned to find both her grandparents looking at her with their mouths hanging open in shock. Annie had no choice but to explain. "Oliver was watching me," she told them in a low voice. She felt like a schoolgirl tattling on him, hoping to get him in trouble.

"Well, of course he was," her grandmother said, looping her arm around Annie's elbow. "You're lovely, Annie, and Oliver is a young man who appreciates a beautiful woman."

Annie wanted to contradict her grandmother but quickly realized it would do no good.

They headed toward their car, Annie walking with her grandmother and Oliver with her grandfather. The ride back to the inn was tense and silent. It seemed they were all at odds with one another. For her part, Annie couldn't wait to get away from Oliver, and it appeared that her grandparents were no longer speaking to each other.

As soon as they reached the inn, Kent and Julie returned to their room. Annie followed them to make sure they didn't need anything.

"Your grandfather takes an afternoon snooze every day now," Julie whispered to Annie. "Otherwise, he gets cranky."

"I heard that," her grandfather complained. "You make me sound like a two-year-old."

"Well, dear, it's the truth. You're a bear to live with if you don't take your nap."

"Not a word of that is true," Kent said and, shaking his head, closed the door.

That left Annie and Oliver standing in the hallway outside the room. Without a word to Oliver, Annie headed upstairs to her own room. The less said to him, the better.

Sitting on the edge of the bed, she reached for her cell phone and noticed there were six text messages from Lenny. Annie didn't bother to open and read them, determined to cut him out of her life completely. With a few presses of the phone, she deleted each one in turn.

Just as she finished, her phone rang in her hand and startled her to the point she nearly dropped it. Thankfully, it was her mother.

"Mom, I'm so glad you called." Annie couldn't get the words out fast enough. She needed help if she was going to survive this celebration.

"Mom and Dad arrived okay?" her mother asked.

"Oh, yes, and you won't believe it when I tell you how they got here." The mere thought of the insufferable Oliver doing everything he could to get her goat was enough to make her voice tremble.

"Oliver drove them," her mother said, as if this had been planned from the beginning.

Annie gasped. "You knew?"

"Well, yes. Mom phoned last night and told me she'd asked Oliver to drive them to Cedar Cove. Dad refuses to wear his glasses, and she was worried."

"And you didn't tell me?" It seemed the entire family had turned on her.

"I didn't think it was important." How innocent her mother sounded.

"Mom," she cried, "you know how I feel about Oliver. He terrorized me as a kid." To be fair, her mother didn't know the half of it.

"Oh honey, that was years ago. You're adults now, and really it wasn't that long ago since you last saw him. Last summer, wasn't it? By the way, how is Oliver? He's a fine-looking young man."

Annie started to say, *"No, he hasn't changed,"* but swallowed the words in the nick of time. Oliver was exactly as she remembered. As for his being so "fine-looking," she was willing to admit that was true, and her parents and brother certainly thought highly of him—her grandparents, too. Oliver and her brother, Peter, had gone on a hiking trip together, stopping to see her before they took off for two days in the Olympic rain forest. Half the fun for Peter while visiting their grandparents was spending time with Oliver. Naturally, the fun included making her as miserable as possible.

"Tell Oliver I look forward to seeing him, will you?"

Annie struggled to assure her that she would.

"Mom and Dad made the drive okay, then?" her mother asked next.

Annie hesitated, hardly knowing what to say. "They seem fine, I guess."

"It isn't Dad's heart, is it?" Her mother was instantly concerned.

"Not exactly."

"Then what is it?"

Annie exhaled slowly. "They seem to disagree a lot."

"On what?"

"Everything."

"Oh, dear. Is Dad in a bad mood?"

Actually, both her grandparents seemed to be out of sorts. "I don't know . . . It's hard to tell."

"It's just nerves, honey. Don't let it worry you."

Annie couldn't help being worried. She couldn't imagine this was the way good relationships worked. She'd always viewed her grandparents' marriage as the ideal. From what she'd seen to this point, they didn't even seem to like each other.

"More important, Annie, how are you?" her mother asked, cutting into her thoughts.

"I'm good, Mom."

"Lenny called the house looking for you. I told him nothing; you're well rid of him." She hesitated and then asked, "When I realized your grandparents didn't know about your breakup with Lenny, I told them. I hope you don't mind."

"No, that's fine . . . but they must have said something to Oliver, because he was full of questions."

"Oh, dear. Are you upset that he knows?"

"I guess not." Although she'd rather have let him assume she was still engaged. Annie sighed. "Do you mind if we talk about this later, Mom? Talking about Lenny depresses me. I'm just grateful you and Dad and Grandma and Grandpa support my decision."

"Of course we do, sweetheart."

"Frankly, now that the engagement is off, and everyone knows, I feel better than I have in months," Annie continued. And that was the truth. All that she needed was for Lenny to accept that it was over. It surprised her the way he held on, but then he'd recently let it be known he had yet to tell his family, believing that she would eventually change her mind.

To be fair to Lenny, he had a number of fine qualities. He was charming, friendly, and funny, but he lacked the ability to be faithful.

"We'll talk more after this weekend," her mother said gently. "You've been so busy planning events that we haven't had a good chat in far too long."

Her mother was right. Burying herself in her work had been an easy escape for Annie. Once this party was over she planned to get back in the dating scene. If anything would convince Lenny they were finished, it would be her dating another man. She suspected her lack of a social life had spurred him on to believe she continued to love him. He was wrong, though. Her heart had been badly bruised, and she'd needed time to heal.

Wanting to change the subject, Annie asked, "When will you and Dad arrive?"

"We should be in Cedar Cove sometime tomorrow, probably late afternoon. Your father wants to leave around three or four," her mother said. "Do you need me to do anything before then?"

"Not a thing, Mom. Everything is under control."

Annie could hear her mother's relief through the phone.

"You are the perfect person to organize this," her mother went on to say. "We're all so grateful. I want you to know how deeply I appreciate all the hard work you've put into the party for Mom and Dad."

"I've enjoyed it." Now all that was necessary was to keep her grandparents from killing each other until after the big party.

"Call if you need anything."

"I will," Annie promised.

They chatted a bit longer before ending the call. Despite her misgivings regarding Oliver, Annie did feel better about his arrival after talking to her mother. Still, she'd like to clear the air with him, set some boundaries so that she could get through this weekend without the need to strangle him.

Not knowing which room was his, she decided to find Jo Marie. When she opened the door, Oliver was stepping out of the room directly across the hall from hers.

Annie sucked in her breath. Having him in the same inn was bad enough, but learning his room was only a few feet from her own unnerved her.

"Hello, Annie," he said. He had his guitar with him.

She found his smile insufferable, but she refused to let him know. Otherwise, he'd use every opportunity to do whatever he could to make her uncomfortable.

"I thought we should talk, just the two of us," she said, without greeting him back.

"Sure. When?"

In her opinion, the sooner she could lay down the ground rules, the better. "How about now?" Within a short while the inn would be filled with family and friends. By then it would be too late.

"All right. Do you want to come into my room?"

"Hardly."

He grinned and murmured, "Probably wise on your part."

"What does that mean?" she challenged, not afraid to call him out.

"Nothing."

Rather than press the issue, she let it drop. She hoped she could make this conversation as amicable as possible.

"I saw a couple of chairs on the porch," she suggested.

"Sounds good," he said, and led the way down the two flights of stairs.

Annie followed with her mind whirling, going over what she intended to say and how best to start the conversation. Her natural inclination was to confront him with the sins of the past and demand that there not be a repeat. That, however, would start their talk on a negative note. Although there seemed a few scant positives, she would begin with those, Annie decided.

Oliver held open the front door for her to precede him. They settled into the two wooden chairs on the veranda. Although the sun was out, the afternoon was cool. The guitar rested in Oliver's lap.

"What would you like to talk about?" he asked, seeming innocent.

Annie wasn't fooled. He knew. Folding her hands in her lap, she leaned slightly forward. "It's good to see you again."

Oliver grinned. "You're not a very good liar, Annie."

He had her there. Why, oh, why, had she said that? Because he was right, it was a big lie. "Okay, it was a surprise to see you. Why aren't you working?" She'd heard he had a wonderful job working for a high-tech company outside of Portland, designing computer software.

"I decided to quit."

That sounded like something Oliver would do. While others were seeking employment in a down economy, Oliver felt the need to walk away from a high-paying job.

"Why would you do that?" she asked, at a loss to understand anything about this man.

He shrugged as if it were of little consequence. "I've always wanted to travel. I'm young and unattached, and if I'm going to see the world, then there's no time like the present."

"Backpacking through Europe?" How original of him to think of that.

"Australia."

"Oh." She'd always wanted to go there herself, but didn't mention it.

"I have plans to visit New Zealand and the Cook Islands while I'm down under, too."

"That should be interesting," she said, hoping to keep the conversation light and friendly.

He positioned the guitar under his arm and took out a pick before glancing up at her. "I'm sorry I kept staring at you over lunch."

His apology caught her off guard. That was the last thing she had expected from him.

He plucked a few strings. "You've grown into a beautiful woman, Annie."

The urge to assure him flattery wouldn't work tempted her, but she clamped her mouth closed. "Having you watch every move I make unsettles me, so I'd prefer that you don't do it again."

He nodded, strummed a few chords, and started to hum.

"I'd rather you didn't fiddle with the guitar just now, either," she said, feeling it was important that she have his full attention.

Her request took him by surprise, because he quickly glanced up. "Why not?"

"I was hoping we could talk, adult to adult."

"I think best with a guitar in my hands."

She remembered that he had enjoyed making up songs when he was younger. Most of the ones she remembered had verses in which he poked fun at her and her freckles or her braces. Her brother had explained that these days, Oliver used his guitar to attract women. Apparently, females found the fact that he played a real turn-on. Annie wasn't that easily impressed.

He set the guitar down and focused his attention on her, and

Annie realized her mistake. It was much easier to talk to him when she didn't have to meet his gaze.

"This anniversary party is important to me."

"From what your grandmother told me, you've worked exceptionally hard putting it together."

"I have," she agreed, "so you can appreciate how much it means to my family to have everything come off smoothly."

"Of course. If there's anything I can do . . . ."

"There is," she said, leaping on his offer.

"Anything. All you need to do is ask."

"Okay, I will," she said, and stiffened her spine. "Please don't use this opportunity to tease me, to make me the brunt of your silly jokes, or to . . ."

"Kiss you," he offered in a low voice.

The memory of that kiss brought instant color to her cheeks. Oliver had given Annie her very first kiss. Foolish girl that she was, she believed herself in love with him and that he'd come to like her, too. It'd happened late one summer night when her family had visited her grandparents. She remembered that the stars were out in a moonlit sky. Having a romantic heart, she'd lain down on a blanket and gazed up at the heavens. Her brother was in their grandparents' house fast asleep and her parents and grandparents were playing pinochle, unaware that Annie had snuck outside.

That's where Oliver had found her. He'd lain down on the blanket next to her and they'd talked for a long time. The way he'd talked to her was unlike any other time they'd been together. He'd pointed out several of the constellations, and she'd been impressed that he knew so much about the night sky.

He'd told her how he'd always looked forward to her summer visits and that he liked it when she was there. She was thirteen, and he was a year older. He'd held her hand that night, clasping her fingers in his own. Even now she remembered how her heart had leapt with excitement at his touch. It'd seemed wildly romantic. Silly girl that she was, her head had instantly filled with notions of love.

"You still haven't forgiven me for that, have you?" Oliver said, cutting into her thoughts.

"Don't be ridiculous."

"I should kiss you again."

"Don't even think about it, Sutton. I'm not some foolish young girl with my head in the clouds."

"No, you were a sweet girl with stars in your eyes."

"You led me on," she countered, embarrassed even now all these years later by what had happened.

"I'm willing to make it up to you."

"Thanks, but no thanks."

It was easy to see that this conversation wasn't going anywhere. Annie stood, eager to return to the house.

Oliver stood, too, and before she knew it, he planted his hands on her shoulders and turned her to face him.

She could have protested. She should have backed away out of his reach. Instinct told her if she'd protested, he would have instantly freed her. Why she didn't, Annie might never understand.

Then right there on the porch with the sunshine bathing the early afternoon, Oliver leaned forward and kissed her for the second time in her life. His mouth, moist and warm, settled gently over hers, and before she could stop herself she yielded to him, opening her mouth to his, taking in the feel and the taste of him. He wrapped her in his embrace, and she put her arms around him as the kiss went on and on.

It didn't take long for her to come to her senses and break away. This was even worse than the first time. Even better.

"That wasn't so bad, now, was it?" he whispered.

Annie didn't answer; she dared not. Instead, she fled back into the house, letting the door slam behind her.

Chapter 13

Mary arrived at the Victorian Tea Room nearly fifteen minutes early. The friendly hostess with a name badge that read DIANNA placed her at a table by the window. The sun beamed into the room and warmed the chill that had settled over her.

She hated to admit how nervous she was to be seeing George again. Although she had the menu in her hand, her thoughts weren't on food, however tempting. One of her fears was that George would no longer recognize her. As she'd repeatedly told him, she wasn't the woman she had been nearly twenty years ago. Nor was she the woman he remembered. Other than the fact that she'd lost both her breasts, she was much thinner than before, no thanks to the side effects of chemotherapy. She'd wrapped a silk scarf over her head for fear the shock of seeing her bald would be too much for him.

Already she'd regretted agreeing to this rendezvous. No good would come of it. George would be shocked by her appearance, and she wouldn't blame him. She hated to think that in addition to everything else cancer had weakened her ability to make wise decisions. To complicate matters, George would want to discuss the past, the pregnancy, and that was definitely a subject she hoped to avoid.

She was half tempted to get up and leave before he showed, yet curiosity and need kept her right where she was. Mary swallowed tightly as the door opened and George walked into the restaurant.

Her lungs froze, making it impossible to draw in a breath. She recognized him immediately. He hadn't changed in the least. His hair, what he had, was silver now, giving him a dignified, distinguished look. She could see what an impressive figure he would make in the courtroom. He wasn't especially handsome. His face, with his slightly too-large nose and his deep, dark eyes, revealed intelligence and character.

He paused and glanced around the room. The restaurant wasn't busy. Four or five other tables were occupied. A party of six women, dressed in red hats and purple boas, sat in the middle of the room, chatting animatedly. They appeared to be having a wonderful time. Their laughter echoed through the restaurant. A couple sat at another nearby table and talked with their heads close together.

Mary squared her shoulders and nervously clenched the linen napkin with both hands. Even if she found the courage to leave, that was no longer an option.

George paused and waited for the hostess. Like her, he was several minutes early. "I'm meeting a friend," Mary heard him tell the young hostess. "Could I have a table in the sunshine?"

"Of course."

He'd looked around the room as he followed the hostess. Mary had purposely chosen a seat behind a big plant so she was able to see him but he wouldn't immediately see her. As luck would have it, he was seated at the table next to hers. He sat down, with his back to her, and she could tell that he was as nervous as she was. She gave him a few minutes, gathered her resolve, and then stood and walked over to his table.

He glanced up and then blinked, as though even now he was unaware she was the woman he had once loved. Then his eyes rounded with surprise—perhaps it was shock; Mary couldn't tell.

"Mary," he said, as he slowly rose from the chair. "Mary," he repeated, and reached for both her hands, clasping them in his own. "Oh, my sweet, sweet Mary." He raised her fingers to his lips and kissed her knuckles.

"I'm sorry," she whispered, emotion causing her voice to tremble. "I know I look dreadful. I should never have agreed to let you see me like this."

"No," he said, stopping her. "No, don't say that. I . . ." He seemed too choked up to continue and hurriedly stepped around the table in order to pull out her chair. He waited until she was seated and then leaned forward and whispered, "You're even more beautiful than I remember."

To him and to him alone, she hadn't changed one bit. Mary loved him all the more for seeing her as she had been almost twenty years earlier.

As soon as they were both seated, the waitress came for their drink order.

"Tea," George suggested, looking to Mary.

"Yes, please," she said.

The waitress dutifully listed a number of varieties, and George deferred to Mary. "Earl Grey," she said.

"Anything to eat?" Dianna asked next. "We have a Cobb salad on our luncheon special today."

"No, thanks, I've already eaten," Mary said. The truth was, she'd had very little to eat, nervous as she was about this meeting.

Ever since she'd started the cancer treatments, food held little appeal. Her appetite was almost nonexistent, which accounted for part of the weight loss.

"We're known for our pies, too, if I could tempt you with that," the waitress added. Without waiting to be asked, she listed several mouthwatering suggestions.

"Fruit of the forest," George said automatically, and then gestured toward Mary.

"None for me, thanks," she said, looking up at the waitress.

"She'll have a slice of the chocolate cream," George said, contradicting her.

"Oh, George, honestly."

Dianna didn't stay long enough to listen to her objection.

"You love chocolate cream," George reminded her.

How he remembered that, she would never know. It would do no good to argue, and so she gave in. To please him she would take a bite.

George reached across the table and took hold of her hand. His eyes held hers, and in them she read such tenderness and caring that she couldn't meet his gaze. She looked down at the table for fear she would tear up again and embarrass them both.

"How long?" he asked.

Mary didn't need him to elaborate. He was asking what her prognosis was. How long did she have to live?

"The verdict is still out; it's too soon to tell. A great deal depends on how I respond to the treatments." She paused, wanting to give him the basic details he seemed to need. But she hadn't met him to discuss her cancer. "My life is a constant round of tests these days. None of us have any guarantees, you know. I could get hit by a bus and die tomorrow," she added, and forced a smile.

His hand tightened on hers. "What did the doctors say?"

"George, please. I don't want my cancer to be the focus of our conversation. Let's not talk about me, okay? Tell me about you."

He sighed, his shoulders sagging slightly. "I'd rather talk about you."

"Another time," she whispered. "Bring me up to date on you."

He seemed at a loss as to where he should start. "I'll admit I didn't handle it well when you broke it off."

"It wasn't the best of circumstances," she agreed with some reluctance.

"If it's the cancer that brought you back, then I'm grateful."

"George," she warned. "We aren't going to talk about that, remember?"

It looked as if he was about to argue when their waitress returned with their tea and two slices of pie. She set the pot down on the table and then served the pie. Mary had to admit the slice of chocolate pie, piled high with whipped cream and drizzled with chocolate syrup, did look mighty tempting.

George filled their cups. "You were saying . . ."

"It's nothing." Mary would rather not go back to their former conversation. "You've done well."

"Relatively," he agreed. Reaching for his fork, he cut into the mixed-berry pie and sampled it.

Mary followed suit and was surprised by how tasty the chocolate cream pie was. The flavors were rich and silky on her tongue. She savored them for a moment and then reached for her tea.

George set his fork aside. "I've done a bit of research, and I think I might be able to help you."

"Help me?" Mary asked, frowning. "With what?"

"Your cancer."

"George, please, don't." She hadn't seen him in more than nineteen years and she really didn't want their first conversation to result in a battle of wills.

"Hear me out," he insisted. "There's a revolutionary treatment clinic in Europe that's said to perform miracles. I have a few connections, and I can get us an appointment."

Mary wasn't up to traveling to a foreign country. "I appreciate the fact that you looked this up, but . . ."

"You can't give up, Mary."

"I'm a fighter, George; I always have been. You know me probably better than anyone. I'm not giving up."

"I'll travel with you. I'll be . . ."

She held up her hand, stopping him. "Quit. Please."

Frustration showed on his dear face, and it was all she could do not to stretch her arm across the table and cup his chin and comfort him. "I'm going to be fine. Now, stop with all these drastic measures. I'm not dead yet. I'm going to get well, just wait and see."

"I would think you'd know by now that I am not a patient man."

"I disagree." She'd never known anyone with more staying power than George.

"I gave up hope of ever seeing you again," he said, with such feeling that it nearly brought renewed tears to her eyes. "I waited nearly twenty years for that phone call from you."

To hide her emotion, Mary took a second bite of her pie. Once she felt she could speak without her voice giving her away, she said, "I know."

Silence stretched between them. George sipped his tea, and she did, too. They were both afraid, she realized, to discuss the subject they most needed to talk about. He didn't ask about the abortion, and she didn't tell him. Mary, who was fearless when it came to business transactions, found herself reluctant to discuss it. She could stare down a board of directors, but she couldn't tell the man she loved what he had every right to know, what was only fair he did know.

"How's the pie?" she asked instead.

"Delicious. Yours?"

"Good." How silly it was that they could discuss pie but not each other.

Mary cleared her throat and forged ahead. "I'm sorry to hear about your marriage."

George nodded. "It wasn't either of our faults. Kathleen and I simply weren't suited."

"I'm sorry you didn't have children."

"I am, too." He hesitated and gripped his tea cup with both hands. His eyes briefly hardened. "I'd like to think I would have been a good father."

"The best," she whispered, and when her voice cracked, she bit into her lower lip to keep it from trembling. After taking several moments to compose herself, she took another taste of her tea.

"I know you chose to book a hotel in Cedar Cove to maintain an emotional distance from me, but . . ."

She relaxed. "But . . ." she prompted when he didn't finish his thought.

"It didn't work, though, did it?"

"No," she had to agree, and smiled. "Knowing you were so close made it impossible. I shouldn't have phoned, but I'm grateful I did."

"I am grateful, too." His disappointment was gone, and now his eyes seemed to caress her. He couldn't seem to look away. He made her feel as if he was viewing a work of art, a museum masterpiece, such as a van Gogh or a Rembrandt. To him she remained beautiful despite her gaunt features, her paleness, and her lack of hair. To George, she was a beauty.

"When is your flight back?"

"Monday, a little after noon," she told him.

He tensed. "So soon?"

She nodded.

"You can't stay longer?" He looked devastated, as if it was unfair to have found her only to lose her again so quickly.

"No." As it was, she'd gone against her doctor's advice. She had more tests to undergo, and endless appointments.

"Then we only have a few days."

"George, I didn't come to disrupt your life," she insisted.

"I've already cleared my schedule for all of next week."

"George!" She wished he hadn't done that.

"Have dinner with me tonight?" His eyes pleaded with her.

Refusing him would have been impossible. Mary had assumed that this would be the only time she would see George, the only chance they would have to talk. The thought of spending more time with him filled her with happy expectations, with joy. By all that was right she should turn him down, but she couldn't. "Okay."

"Good. We'll drive to Seattle. My car is here."

Mary could already feel her strength leaving her. She tired so easily these days. "Would you mind if we ate locally?"

"Of course, if that's what you want, but I don't know any of the restaurants in the area. Do you?"

"Not really."

George motioned to the waitress and brought her to their table. "Can you recommend a good restaurant for dinner?" he asked.

Dianna smiled and seemed eager to make a few suggestions. "Oh, yes, there are two especially good ones. DD's on the Cove down on Harbor Street, and also the Lighthouse. Both are excellent. Seafood is the best at DD's, and steaks at the Lighthouse."

George glanced at his wrist. "Will we need a reservation?"

Dianna laughed. "In Cedar Cove? No way."

"Thank you," he said, and the young woman left.

"It would be best if I rested awhile before dinner," Mary said. She hated that it was necessary, but a few minutes with her eyes closed would do her a world of good.

"By all means. I have some emails to answer. I'll drive you to wherever you're staying and then find an Internet café, have coffee, and do a bit of work. What time would you like me to pick you up?"

Mary hesitated. She'd taken a taxi to the tearoom and intended to take one back. "You're sure about this?"

"Positive."

"Perhaps it would be best if we waited until tomorrow."

"No," George objected. "We have limited time as it is. I don't intend to waste a single minute."

Limited time. How true that was. "Six o'clock, then?" she asked.

"Six it is." His smile lit up his entire face, as if her agreeing to have dinner with him was the most wonderful thing to happen to him in a very long while. In many ways George was like a child. He appreciated small pleasures, savored the simple joys in life.

The waitress returned with their check, which George paid. He left a more-than-generous tip.

"Will you let me drive you back to your hotel?" he asked.

"Yes."

He helped her up and then tucked her arm in the crook of his elbow as they left the tearoom. His car was one of only a few in the parking lot, and Mary picked it out immediately. It was a luxury model with a vanity license plate: GGH. Mary didn't need to be reminded that his middle name was Gair, which had been his mother's maiden name. George Gair Hudson.

He opened the passenger door and then waited until she was seated and comfortable before walking around to the driver's side.

Mary looked over at him and smiled. "I'm not an invalid, you know." Despite how weak she was physically, there was plenty of life left in her, plenty of fight, too.

His smile faded. "I want to take care of you, Mary. Let me do what I can, okay?"

His words touched her deeply, and rather than respond verbally and risk showing how profoundly his comment had affected her, Mary nodded. Although her body was weak, she felt inspired and invigorated being with George.

She directed him to the inn, and he parked and came around to help her out.

"Tonight," he said, and then hesitated.

"Yes?"

"Can we talk over dinner about what happened years ago?"

Her spirits plummeted. She owed him that much, but she didn't know if she had the courage to confront their past quite so soon. "Not yet," she whispered.

"But we will talk of it."

"Yes," she promised.

And they would.

Chapter 14

All my guests were out for the evening. I wasn't sure where Annie and her family had gone, as I wasn't at the inn when they returned from lunch. I did remember hearing that the Shivers were meeting friends. That left Annie and Oliver to their own devices. Seeing that the house was empty, I could only assume that the two of them had gone out for dinner themselves.

Mary had left a few minutes earlier with a distinguished-looking man. She hadn't said where she was headed, but I had to believe they, too, were going out to eat.

I was on my own for the evening meal, which happened most nights. Rummaging through the refrigerator, looking for ideas, I saw I had shrimp and some hard-boiled eggs left over from breakfast. I'm terribly fond of blue cheese and thought I'd make myself a seafood Cobb salad. The bacon was already cooked, and I had plenty of lettuce.

Humming, I mixed it all together and then was ready to sit down and eat when Rover came into the kitchen and gazed up at me with his incredible deep brown eyes. He had that imploring look as if to say it was a travesty that I would enjoy such a wonderful meal and not include him.

"You have food in your dish," I reminded him.

My words didn't faze him.

"You don't like lettuce," I felt obliged to tell him.

He trotted into the laundry room, and I assumed he was going to his own food dish, but I was wrong. Instead he sat on his haunches and looked up at his leash. I was getting smarter now, and realized he was telling me he wanted to go for another walk.

"Rover, no," I insisted. "We've already been out twice today, and that's enough."

I did my best to ignore him and sat down at the table with my delicious-looking salad. I spread a bright yellow linen napkin across my lap and was ready to dig in when I saw Rover fix his gaze in the direction of Mark's house.

"You know Mark wasn't in the best of moods when I left him," I reminded Rover. The handyman had practically tossed me out of his house. When we'd returned from the hospital I'd helped him up the steps and into his home. We were barely inside the front door when he'd insisted he was fine and he didn't need any further help from me. In other words, he was asking me to leave and he hadn't been the least bit subtle about it.

I stabbed my first bite and made sure I got one of the small Oregon shrimp I enjoyed so much. Rover gave me a mournful look as if I was taking the food right out of Mark's mouth.

"I don't have that many shrimp left," I told Rover.

He lay down on the kitchen floor with his chin resting on his paws and kept his gaze focused on me.

After a couple more bites I couldn't stand it any longer. "Oh, all right," I muttered, but I wasn't happy about it.

Taking everything out of the refrigerator that I had so recently returned, I quickly made up a second salad. To be on the safe side, I added a container of soup that I'd frozen earlier in the week. It was one of my all-time favorites, squash soup made with just a hint of ginger.

After packing everything up and tucking it inside a bag, I begrudgingly made my way to Mark's. I took Rover with me, seeing that this was his idea in the first place. Perhaps if I arrived bearing gifts, Mark wouldn't look at me like an intruder ready to invade his private domain. My heavens, this man was hard to figure out.

Rover strained against the leash as he led the way to Mark's, urging me forward but not with the same urgency he'd used earlier in the day. I walked up the steps to Mark's front door and rang the doorbell.

Nothing.

"It looks like he's out," I told Rover.

As if to prove me wrong, Rover barked a couple of times and then placed his paw against the door.

I could see Rover wasn't going to give up easily. After what seemed like an inordinate amount of time, I pressed the buzzer a second time.

"Be patient," Mark grumbled from the other side of the door.

A moment later it was thrust open. Mark leaned heavily on his crutches and glared back at me as if I was nothing more than a pest.

His lack of appreciation irritated me. It was all I could do not to look down at Rover and tell him this had been a complete waste of time.

"I brought you dinner," I said, and lifted the bag so he could see I had a reason for interrupting his busy social calendar.

Mark frowned. "Why?"

I couldn't very well tell him it'd been Rover's suggestion. "I don't know—silly of me, I guess, but I thought you might be hungry and fixing your own meal would be a hassle." I didn't bother to hide my sarcasm. I was sorry I'd given in to Rover.

Mark stared back at me as if testing my words. His frown deepened as if he suspected I had an ulterior motive.

"Do you want me to leave it on the porch?" I asked, growing more irritated by the moment.

He hesitated and then shook his head. "You can come in."

Well, well, this was a surprise. He was admitting me into his private domain. I wasn't sure I should be happy about this.

The moment he'd opened the door, Rover had bolted inside as if escaping grave danger. Mark scooted to one side so I could enter his living room. It'd been a considerably rocky week for Mark and me. At this point I wasn't sure we were even on speaking terms. The television was turned to a news channel, and the ottoman was scooted away from the chair. It looked like he'd been elevating his leg.

"Would you like me to put this in the kitchen?" I asked.

"Please." He followed me and seemed quite agile with his crutches.

I didn't make a show of looking around, although I did my best to scout out the place, hoping I wasn't being obvious. My curiosity was on high alert. I couldn't see anything of a personal nature. No photos, no knickknacks. The walls were bare. The house looked more like a hotel room, but then I reconsidered. At the very least a hotel room boasted artwork. Mark had next to nothing.

"How are you feeling?" I asked.

"How do you think I'm feeling?"

"Okay, it was a silly question. I was making conversation." I should have realized by now Mark wasn't in the mood for a social visit.

After placing the package on the kitchen counter I turned to face him, my hands behind my back and Rover at my feet. My dog was sprawled out as though he intended on staying awhile.

"Did you take the pain medication?"

"No. I don't like the way it makes me feel."

Now it was my turn to frown, but that was his choice, not mine. I'm no hero, and if the doctor felt I would be more comfortable with pain meds, I'd swallow them down without a moment's hesitation. Clearly Mark and I had a difference of opinion on the subject.

I started to leave when Mark stopped me. "I feel I might owe you an apology," he said, his hands tightening around the grips on his crutches.

He might?

I clenched my teeth before I could tell him I felt I was due an entire series of apologies. Mark had been brusque, short-tempered, ungrateful, and downright inhospitable. By all that was right I shouldn't give a hoot if he ate dinner or not and probably wouldn't have if it wasn't for Rover.

"I appreciate you finding me in my workroom," he murmured, as if he found it difficult to say the words. They seemed to be glued to his tongue, as though he wasn't accustomed to making amends. "I don't know what I would have done if you hadn't come along."

I clenched my jaw tighter this time. This accident should be a lesson for Mark to keep his business door unlocked. What kind of businessman was he, anyway? "You need to thank Rover for that."

Rover raised his head and looked expectantly up at Mark as though willingly accepting his gratitude. He was a forgiving kind of dog, I noted, whereas I didn't quite meet his level.

"I brought you a salad and some squash soup," I said, seeing that the apology made him so uncomfortable.

Mark frowned. "How'd you know that was my favorite soup?"

"I didn't. I just happened to have some in the freezer. Would you like me to heat it up for you? Or would you rather have the salad?"

"I'll take the soup."

"Okay." I saw that he had a microwave, and opening a cupboard, I found a bowl and heated up the soup.

"You don't need to do this, you know."

I was well aware of that but didn't acknowledge the statement. "I'll put the salad in the refrigerator for later."

"Keep it out if you would," he instructed.

"Okay." Then, feeling that I'd worn out my welcome, I reached for Rover's leash. "I'll leave you to your dinner."

He pulled out the kitchen chair and sat down. "You know this broken leg means it might be some time before I'm able to get back to work on your rose garden."

That went without saying. "I figured as much."

"I'm sorry about that."

"Me, too."

For the second time, Rover and I started for the front door.

"Thank you, Jo Marie," Mark called after me. "For everything."

Appreciation. From Mark?

I had to admit it felt good to have him say it. He wasn't as bad an ogre as I'd thought him earlier. The pain in his leg must have been horrific, and that had caused him to be such a grump.

"Would you like me to check up on you in the morning?" I asked. It would be late morning, as I was bound to be busy with providing breakfast and checking in guests before then.

"No," he said flatly.

I couldn't keep from smiling. Everything was back to normal.

When I returned to the inn, I found Kent and Julie Shivers had returned.

"We're waiting for our friends to pick us up," Julie explained.

"Oh, I thought you'd already left for dinner."

"No, Oliver and Annie took us for a ride around the cove, and I pointed out where Kent asked me to be his wife." Her voice went soft, with romance gleaming from her eyes.

"How many times do I have to tell you I didn't propose down by the waterfront," Kent insisted. "We were at the movie theater—"

"We most certainly were not," Julie said, cutting him off. "A woman remembers these things, and we were standing where the gazebo is now. Why else would Annie have the renewal of our vows take place there?"

Kent crossed his arms. "I distinctly remember getting up my nerve to propose while watching Steve McQueen."

Julie rolled her eyes. "We never even went to the movies in Cedar Cove."

"Fine. If that's what you want to believe, then it must have been with some other girl."

Julie's gaze narrowed. "I always expected you met someone else . . . some girl . . ."

"Oh, for the love of Pete," Kent said and exhaled sharply. "There's no talking to you, woman."

With that, he left the kitchen and marched down the hallway to their room, slamming the door.

Julie flinched. "I apologize on behalf of my husband," she said, clearly disgruntled.

I found it interesting that these two people who had managed to maintain a healthy marriage for fifty years could be at almost constant odds. When Annie had told me about her grandparents, there'd been a gleam in her eyes as she spoke of their love and affection for each other. Annie said she hoped that when she married she could have the same kind of loving relationship with her own husband that her grandparents shared.

"I believe I'll wait for our friends in the living room," Julie said, as if nothing had happened and Kent was simply resting awhile before dinner.

"Would you care for some tea?" I asked, playing along. Although Julie did her best to hide it, I could see she was upset.

"Yes, that would be very nice," she said, and with a dignified walk made her way into the other room.

I brought her tea. "Where are Annie and Oliver?" I set the cup down on the end table.

"They went out themselves. Oliver is such a dear, dear boy. I'd always hoped . . ." She let the rest fade.

"You hoped?" I prodded, wondering if she was thinking the same thing I was regarding those two.

"I'd hoped that Annie might be romantically interested in Oliver," Julie admitted shyly. "I'd never say anything, seeing how much she seems to dislike him. I have no idea why she feels the way she does. And now that she's broken her engagement to that car salesman, I guess there's hope."

Based on Annie's reaction to Oliver, I tended to think there really wasn't much of a chance of anything romantic happening.

"I met him once, you know," Julie continued. "His name escapes me at the moment. He was handsome enough, I suppose, but there was something about him that put me off. Something about his eyes."

From what Annie had told me, Julie had hit the nail on the proverbial head. Annie's fiancé—er, former fiancé—did seem to have a wandering eye. Although it'd been difficult, I felt she'd made a wise choice, and from what I was hearing I wasn't the only one.

"He was so sure of himself, cocky-like. Kent said I was imagining things, but I knew all along that salesman didn't have a clue how to make my granddaughter happy."

"Have you said anything to Annie about your feelings?" I asked her.

"No. Kent didn't think it was a good idea. He said I'd look like an interfering old woman, and I suppose he's right."

It was nice to know Julie thought Kent was right about something, I mused, holding back a smile.

"We've interrupted your dinner," Julie said. "Please don't feel you need to keep me company. Our friends will be here any minute." She held up the china cup and motioned toward the kitchen. "Now, go. Enjoy your meal."

The truth was I'd completely forgotten about my salad. I'd been preoccupied by Mark and then by Kent and Julie. I suspected that Julie wasn't in the mood to chat, and so I returned to the kitchen. Rover was curled up in his bed there asleep, exhausted from the events of the day. Good dog that he was, he would remain there until bedtime and then dutifully follow me into my bedroom.

Dinner had lost its appeal, and after a single bite, I decided to save the salad for my lunch the following afternoon. After covering it with plastic wrap, I set it inside the refrigerator.

The Shivers's friends arrived, and Kent came out of the bedroom; within minutes the two couples were out the door. It appeared their squabble was forgotten.

The house was quiet once again. I went to my room and sat down in front of the television with my knitting. As my fingers worked the yarn of the afghan my mind whirled with memories of Paul and the phone call with Lieutenant Colonel Milford.

It was during quiet moments like this that I missed Paul the most. I hadn't felt his presence for several weeks now, and I longed to feel once again that he was with me. I hungered for those special times when it seemed I could close my eyes and pretend that he was sitting close by and the two of us were content just to be together. Words weren't necessary. Several times now I'd felt Paul's presence with me. This sense was so real I was convinced I could reach out and touch him. When I'd first taken over the inn, Paul had come to tell me I would heal here. It was his reassurance and love that gave me the courage to move forward in life. I'd never told anyone about these visits, if, indeed, that was what they were, for fear of what everyone would think. Frankly, I didn't care if this feeling, this sense of closeness, was strictly in my imagination. It comforted me. It soothed my aching heart. Paul might be dead to the world, but he remained very much alive to me.

Chapter 15

Annie didn't like this one bit. She'd been trapped into having dinner with Oliver. Her grandparents were going out with friends for the evening, and naturally Oliver had immediately suggested that the two of them do the same. Although she'd tried to get out of it, first Oliver and then her grandparents had insisted she dine with him.

"Thanks, but I've got plenty to do before the family get-together." That was a small white lie, but three against one wasn't the least bit fair. She'd seen to just about everything and was satisfied that the day would go as smoothly as possible.

"Oh, Annie, you've worked far too hard as it is," her grandmother had gone on to say. "Let Oliver treat you to dinner."

"Yes, let me," Oliver had chimed in. He'd flashed her a cocky grin. He knew exactly what he was doing and that she would do almost anything in order to avoid spending time with him. It seemed like he went out of his way to make her as uncomfortable as possible. Oliver Sutton hadn't changed at all.

"I . . . I . . ." She'd fumbled for an excuse, but neither her grandparents nor Oliver would hear of it. So now she was trapped.

Oliver suggested they dine at DD's on the Cove, and she readily agreed, eager to get this evening over with as quickly as possible. They were led to a table on the deck overlooking the cove, and despite her reluctance, the sun bouncing off the water helped put her mind at rest. It was rare to have such a lovely evening this early in the year.

Sailboats moored at the marina bobbed gently in the water, and multicolored flower baskets hanging from streetlights dotted the water's edge. The scene was worthy of a postcard.

"What looks good to you?" Oliver asked, scanning the menu.

Annie had been absorbed with the scenery and hadn't bothered to look. "I'm not sure yet." She was far too tense to be hungry. "I'll probably just order an appetizer." The minute the words were out she froze, certain Oliver would make some derogatory comment about her weight or something else that would fluster or embarrass her.

"What's wrong?" he asked, after studying her expression.

"I was waiting for you to say something sarcastic," she returned, stiffening as she did so.

"Why would I do that?" He seemed completely relaxed. Leaning back in the chair, he crossed his legs. When they'd first arrived he'd ordered a glass of sauvignon blanc. All Annie wanted was water.

"You look for ways to put me on edge," she insisted.

"Do I?"

"You're doing it right now, turning everything I say back at me in the form of another question."

"Really?"

She glared at him. This was all one big game to him. "You just did it again." Oh, how she'd enjoy wiping that silly grin off his face.

The waitress returned to take their dinner order. Oliver ordered the special, Copper River salmon, which Annie had recently learned was available only a few weeks each year and considered a delicacy. For her part she asked for a bowl of the clam chowder and a side salad.

Once the waitress wrote down their order, she left. Annie gripped hold of the water glass and averted her gaze, waiting for Oliver to comment on the kiss they'd shared earlier. Even now she couldn't imagine how she'd let that happen. It embarrassed her to think about it. It humiliated her even more to admit how much she'd enjoyed it.

"Your grandparents are a hoot," he commented instead, sipping his wine.

Looking up, Annie held his gaze. She couldn't disagree with him more. "They fight like cats and dogs."

"Of course they do."

"Of course?" Annie couldn't believe her ears. She'd been shocked at the way they quibbled over every little thing. If one closed the window, the other opened it. Their behavior was contrary to everything she remembered about them. If this was how they felt about each other, Annie marveled that they'd managed to stay married.

"Don't you see?" Oliver asked.

"See what?" Annie demanded.

"Your grandparents are so comfortable with each other that they can say exactly what they feel. I find that amazing and wonderful."

"Wonderful?" Annie echoed. She'd found it utterly disconcerting. Her childhood memories were full of the loving ways they'd looked after each other, and her grandmother laughing at her grandfather's jokes. They used to hold hands in church and share a hymnal. Now all they seemed to do was squabble.

"Annie, my dear, dear Annie," he said gently, as if speaking to a child, "your grandparents love each other deeply."

"How can you say that after what just happened?" she asked.

"What do you mean?"

"The tour we took them on of Cedar Cove." Oliver had been in the same car as she; surely he'd heard the same thing she had. "My grandparents couldn't find one thing they agreed on. Grandma insists Grandpa proposed on the waterfront, and he claims it was while they were at the movies."

"Does it matter?"

"To them it does. You should have heard them when we got back to the inn. Grandpa went to the room and Grandma pouted in the living room. Honestly, Oliver, I'm afraid of what might happen at the renewal of vows. I'm afraid Grandma might say 'I won't' instead of 'I do.'"

Oliver appeared to have no such qualms and laughed softly.

"This isn't funny." Everything was one big joke to him. On the other hand, Annie was genuinely concerned.

"Everything will work out, Annie, so stop worrying."

She wished it was that easy. "Do you mind if we change the subject?"

Oliver lowered his wineglass to the table. "Sure, no problem. Tell me about you and Lenny."

Naturally he would suggest the topic she least wanted to discuss. "Lenny is off-limits."

"O-k-a-y," he said, dragging out the word. "Tell me about you."

"I'd rather we talked about you," Annie said, feeling good about turning the subject away from herself.

Oliver sat up straighter. "I thought you'd never ask."

Annie didn't know why she hadn't thought of this sooner. Of course Oliver would want to talk about himself. And that suited her just fine. The less attention focused on her and her life, the better.

"What would you like to know?" he asked.

Annie's mind whirled with possible ideas. "You mentioned earlier that you intend to travel to the South Pacific. How long do you plan to be away?"

"A year."

Well, some people might be able to do that, but then there were others, far more responsible, who needed to work. Oliver always had been something of a free spirit.

"And what do you plan to do for a whole year?" She didn't bother to hide her sarcasm.

"Travel."

He made it sound as if that was understood.

"I suppose you're planning to hitchhike." How bohemian of him. How predictable.

"Actually, I've reserved a van."

Australia and New Zealand. Even as a kid she'd been fascinated by the two countries. While engaged to Lenny she'd suggested they honeymoon in New Zealand, but Lenny had quickly put the squash on that. He wanted a Caribbean cruise, and the difference in costs was dramatic enough for her to agree. But, oh, how she would have loved to see the South Pacific.

"You're smiling," Oliver said, cutting into her musings.

"I've always been curious about Australia and New Zealand," she murmured, paying far more attention to him now. "What made you decide to travel there?"

"Same as you, I guess. Curiosity. I've been fascinated with that part of the world from the time I was a teenager."

"Why now?"

"Why not?"

Fair question.

"I could put it off," he elaborated, "but I'm young and single, and I thought if I don't make this happen now it never will."

"Are you traveling alone?"

"A couple of friends were going with me, but Alex can only afford to take three months and Steve has to go back after six, so we're flying into New Zealand first and then heading over to the Cook Islands."

Annie remembered reading about the islands. It was the natives from the Cook Islands who had settled New Zealand. She'd written a report on this island nation while in the eighth grade. Funny that she would remember that now. "From what I understand, the Cook Islands are fascinating," she said, and was surprised to realize she'd spoken aloud. Amazingly beautiful black pearls were said to be found there.

"Come with us."

Despite herself, Annie laughed. "Me and three guys. That would be awkward."

"No, it wouldn't," Oliver countered. "You'd be with me and you'd love it."

No doubt she would enjoy the traveling, but if she was headed down under, it wouldn't be with Oliver. Annie was saved from having to answer by the waitress, who delivered their meal.

They were both quiet for several moments while they ate, although Annie's head continued to spin. When they did pick up the conversation, Oliver did the majority of the talking. He talked more about the trip and how he'd planned and saved for years in order to make it a reality instead of a dream. Annie couldn't help being impressed with the thoughtful care and planning he'd put into this venture. She'd been wrong to think this was a spur-of-the-moment decision and he was taking off on a whim.

Somehow they got sidetracked on politics. It was no surprise to learn they were diametrically opposed. She argued with him for several minutes until it became apparent that he was enjoying egging her on.

"You're doing this on purpose, aren't you?" she said, setting her spoon aside. Although she hadn't been hungry when she'd ordered, she'd eaten everything. "Aren't you?" she repeated. In all her life there'd never been a man she disagreed with more than Oliver Sutton.

In response, all he did was smile.

"You make me so mad, and you do it on purpose." She couldn't forgive that; nor was she willing to drop the subject. "Admit it!"

"Okay, you're right. Guilty as charged."

"Why?" It was probably a mistake to ask, but she couldn't help herself.

"You won't like the answer."

"No doubt," she muttered.

"The truth is, I love watching your eyes light up and sparkle," he said. "You can't hide how you feel, no matter how hard you try."

Annie wasn't amused.

"I enjoy sparring with you," Oliver admitted. "You keep my wits sharpened."

"I'm pleased you find me so entertaining."

"I find you a lot more than entertaining, Annie," he said, his voice soft and low.

She wanted to ask what he meant by that but didn't because she was afraid of the answer. At some point during the evening she'd lowered her defenses and discovered she was enjoying spending time with him. The dinner she'd hoped would be over as quickly as possible went on for more than two hours. They walked back to the inn and detoured along the waterfront.

"You know who this reminds me of, don't you?" he asked.

The night was chilly, and Annie wrapped her sweater more securely around her shoulders. In what she supposed was an effort to warm her, Oliver wrapped his arm around her, bringing her next to his side. The action unsettled her, and she meant to move away but he was warm and she found a certain comfort in being close to him. Even when warning bells rang in her ears, she ignored the voices shouting *Caution!* and stayed as she was.

"Who does this remind you of?" she asked, echoing his question.

"Your grandparents."

That had to be a poor attempt at a joke. "Oh, hardly."

"They argue, too, don't they?"

"Okay, I concede that point."

"They're about as different as two people can get."

"Right again."

"But they balance each other out."

"Okay, okay, we are like my grandparents in certain ways. However," she added, raising her index finger to punctuate her point, "and this is major, I'm not even close to falling in love with you, and I think I know how you feel about me and it isn't anything near affection."

"Don't be so sure of yourself," he countered.

Because she was highly amused, Annie laughed.

Her cell phone chirped, and Annie pulled it out of her purse. Sure enough, it was Lenny. Again. She didn't answer him. Instead, she hit the ignore button and slid the phone back into place.

"Lenny?" Oliver asked, as they slowly walked in the direction of the inn.

"Yeah."

"You're still in love with him, aren't you?"

Annie didn't need to think about her answer. "No." Her emphatic, one-word answer said it all.

"Then why haven't you blocked his phone number?"

Again, his logic left her tongue-tied and unable to understand herself or how to explain it to anyone else.

"Are you hoping he will change your mind? Do you secretly want to marry him?"

"No way." As far as she was concerned, their relationship was dead, with no chance of resurrecting it. She'd told Lenny, and she meant it, that the engagement was off. Forever. They were finished.

"If you're sincere, then block his number."

Oliver was right. She should have done this immediately after she broke the engagement. Reaching for her phone a second time in as many minutes, she clicked a handful of buttons and blocked Lenny's calls to her from a variety of numbers.

"I don't want him to change my mind, and I don't love him," she said when she'd finished. "It was my ego, I think. I wanted to know that he wouldn't give me up easily. I guess I wanted to hear that he was miserable. He hurt me, and I wanted him to be hurt, too. That's a weak excuse, and I find it fairly embarrassing to admit, but it's the truth." Why she felt the need to confess this in front of Oliver was another of life's mysteries. Especially when at some future date he would very likely use this information against her.

"We're all human," Oliver assured her.

She glanced up at him. Once more there was a subtle shift in their relationship. Since the time she was a young teen until just that morning, she'd thought of him as someone to be avoided at all costs. She'd lowered her guard with him once before, and he'd used that blind trust she'd placed in him to humiliate her.

"What's wrong?" he asked.

"What makes you think anything is wrong?" she countered. Two could play the game of answering one question with another.

"Your shoulders just stiffened."

"Did they?" She hoped this irritated him as much as it had her.

"Yes," he said, and then surprised her by gripping both her shoulders and turning her so that she had no choice but to face him. "What are you thinking?"

"What makes you think I've got anything on my mind?"

"It's that stupid kiss again, isn't it?" he asked, frowning darkly.

She tried to back away, but he wouldn't let her, his hands tightening slightly, keeping her in place.

"It might have been stupid to you," she flared, "but it was my first kiss. At the time I thought myself madly in love with you, only to discover it was all one big joke to you."

"It wasn't a joke to me," he said, calmly, smoothly.

"Oh, sure; you say that now, but you sang a different tune back then. If that's the case, then why did you have everyone laughing at me? My brother taunted me for weeks afterward. It was one of the most humiliating moments of my life." She'd been mortified.

Her brother and several of her cousins had caught them kissing. Instead of quieting the others, Oliver had pointed a finger at her and laughed, too. Not knowing what else to do, Annie had run into the house, covered her face with both hands, and broken down in tears.

"I'm sorry, Annie," he said with such gentleness and contriteness that she forced her gaze to meet his. "It was my first kiss, too," Oliver confessed.

"No, it wasn't. You said . . ."

"I lied."

"Why?" she asked with wide eyes.

"Because I was fourteen and sadly not very bright. I was embarrassed and afraid of being teased by my friends, but I was crazy about you."

"And so you threw me under the bus."

"Yes, and I've regretted it ever since. If nothing else comes of this weekend, I hope you can find it in your heart to forgive me for being young and stupid and a complete jerk."

Annie felt herself drowning in his eyes, which seemed to go deep and dark with sincerity. Slowly, she nodded.

"Thank you," he said, and then right there on Harbor Street

under a streetlamp, Oliver kissed her for a second time that day. And for a second time she welcomed him into her arms.

Their first kiss as young teens had been all teeth and lips, but they'd both learned a great deal since then. Oliver's kiss went through her like an electric charge. She felt it in every part of her body. Every cell seemed to hum with anticipation, seeking more, wanting more.

When they broke apart, Annie noticed that Oliver was breathing as hard as she was, as if they'd been involved in a heated race. He held her for several moments and then kissed the top of her head.

Together they returned to the inn, but neither spoke again. They climbed the stairs and went to their separate rooms with little more than a murmured, "Good night."

Not until she was getting ready for bed sometime later did she remember something he'd said: *If nothing else comes of this weekend . . .*

Just exactly what did Oliver intend to happen this weekend?

Chapter 16

I knew Saturday would be a big day for Kent and Julie Shivers, as their family and friends gathered for the celebration of their fiftieth wedding anniversary. I wondered if the couple could pull it off, as they seemed to be constantly at odds.

By eight o'clock I had breakfast ready. The scent of freshly baked scones drifting through the house must have roused my guests. Annie appeared first, slowly making her way down the stairs as if she'd had trouble sleeping. Seeing how she'd been primarily responsible for all the arrangements, I imagined she had spent the night mentally going over every detail one last time. I was about to comment and then decided against it. In addition to the celebration, she must be worried about her grandparents.

"Good morning," I greeted her, and automatically lifted the

coffeepot. From the tired look in Annie's eyes, I figured she would need a caffeine boost.

"Morning." She reached for a mug, and I poured her coffee.

No sooner had I finished when Oliver trotted down the stairs. In contrast, he looked chipper and bright, smiling as if he didn't have a care in the world. He reached for a mug, and I filled his as well. I couldn't help but notice how Annie avoided eye contact with him. In fact, she seemed to go out of her way not to look in his direction at all.

"Morning, sunshine," he said to Annie, and kissed her cheek.

I watched as color automatically flooded Annie's face. She glared at him, and seeing how much the kiss had flustered her, Oliver laughed.

"It's a beautiful day," Oliver said, and after setting his mug down on the dining room table, he stretched his arms high above his head. "A very special day."

The two were soon joined by Kent and Julie. I suspected my other guests who were part of this family gathering would be arriving at the inn soon. The inn was booked solid for Saturday night. Most everyone was involved in one way or another with helping the Shivers celebrate their anniversary—and then, of course, there was Mary Smith.

I'd seen her only briefly and worried about her, as she spent the majority of her time in her room. Although, as I recalled, she'd mentioned earlier that she would be going into Seattle to spend the day with a friend. I hoped the outing wouldn't be too much for her physically.

"I have scones hot from the oven."

"Scones," Kent echoed, and rubbed his palms together. "I love warm scones."

"Since when?" Julie insisted.

Kent scowled back at her. "Since forever."

"You might have told me."

"Why? So you can talk about my dangerous cholesterol levels?"

"Someone needs to watch what you eat, because you seem incapable of doing it yourself. If it wasn't for me, you'd be on twenty medications a day."

Kent looked over at Annie and shook his head. "Your grandmother is impossible."

"Well, so are you," Julie flared, and then immediately let loose with three sneezes in rapid succession. Grabbing a tissue, she held it to her nose. "Your grandfather insisted on sleeping with the window open. I was cold the entire night. I might come down with pneumonia and die, but that's probably what he wants."

"Oh, fiddlesticks."

"I about froze to death."

"I don't know how, when you closed that window every chance you got."

"That's because you kept opening it," Julie complained.

Kent ignored her, and as if to defy her, he reached for a warm scone and slathered it with both butter and strawberry jam and then made a display of taking a huge bite.

"You're acting like a two-year-old," Julie said, and then, looking to Annie and Oliver, she added, "I hope you'll overlook your grandfather's little temper tantrum."

Fearing that their exchange might escalate into a full-blown argument as it had the day before, I hurriedly asked, "Anyone for orange juice?"

Both Annie and Oliver quickly responded. It seemed they shared my fears.

The heated exchange between Kent and Julie the night before had been enough for me. Playing the role of referee didn't suit me in the least.

Julie looked to her granddaughter. "Do you need my help with anything today?" she asked.

Before Annie could respond, Oliver answered, "That's why I'm here. Annie can count on me to be her go-to person."

At first Annie looked a bit startled, but after a short pause, she agreed. "This is a day for you and Grandpa to enjoy," their granddaughter assured them. "Everything is ready, and I know how much family and friends are looking forward to seeing you."

"Your grandmother bought a new outfit for this shindig," Kent said, frowning at his wife. "Cost more than her wedding dress."

"My wedding dress, if you recall, was one I purchased that morning at the J. C. Penney store in downtown Bremerton. I didn't even have a real wedding dress, because you were in such an all-fired hurry to get married."

"As I recall, there was a reason for the big rush. I was being shipped out, and you thought you could be pregnant."

Clearly mortified, Julie gasped.

Seeing that the morning was rapidly deteriorating, I returned to the kitchen, grabbed the pitcher of orange juice, and quickly carried it into the dining room.

"Grandpa," Annie said, "you're not going to mention that at the party, are you?"

"He'll do it just to embarrass me in front of our entire family."

Kent narrowed his eyes. "What'd you say?"

"I'll talk to him later, Grandma," Annie promised. "Don't you worry; he won't say anything to embarrass you."

"If he does, I swear I will just die."

"Don't worry," Annie said again, and patted Julie's hand.

"Would you two stop mumbling?" Kent asked.

I returned to the kitchen and reached for the sausage patties, the bacon, and the cheesy egg dish that my guests seemed to comment on every time I served it. I brought the platter in from the kitchen and set it in the middle of the table, but unfortunately no one seemed to be the least bit interested in enjoying the meal I had so carefully prepared. Oh, dear, I did hope this day didn't turn out to be a disaster for Annie and her family.

With several guests arriving and checking in, my morning was sure to be busy.

Annie and Oliver were the first ones to leave the table. Annie announced she had some last-minute details to see to, and Oliver followed her up the stairs, volunteering to help.

"You can help me set up the hall for the reception," I heard Annie tell him.

"Happy to do it."

I saw Julie's gaze follow them. She caught me watching her. "I would so love it if those two became an item."

"Julie, stay out of it," Kent insisted. "What happens between them is none of your affair."

"I'll do what I darn well please," Annie's grandmother returned, glaring at her husband of fifty years.

Kent snorted and shook his head. "You will, anyway. You're a willful, stubborn woman."

"Willful and stubborn? Well, it takes one to know one."

The two sounded like children on a playground, tossing out insults at each other.

"Forget it. I can't even talk to you anymore," Julie muttered. "I don't even know why I try."

"What'd you say?" Kent demanded.

Sighing with frustration, Julie walked away. A moment later, Kent followed her back to their room.

By nine, the breakfast room was nearly deserted when Mary came down, taking the steps slowly. Her color was good, and she smiled when I wished her a good morning.

"Thank you. You, too."

She automatically went into the dining room and pulled out a chair. After she took her place at the table, I brought her a cup of tea, knowing she preferred that over coffee.

"Thank you," Mary said simply.

"Can I tempt you with a freshly baked scone? They're still warm from the oven."

"Yes, that would be great."

"Eggs, bacon, sausage?"

Mary shook her head. "Thanks, but I don't have much of an appetite these days. A scone and orange juice will do me nicely." Knowing that she preferred her own company, I headed back into the kitchen and started in on the dishes and putting away the leftovers. Rover remained curled up in his bed while he watched my every move. Thinking about the leftovers, I was tempted to contact Mark. Then again, maybe that wasn't such a good idea. He could be such a grouch, I wasn't sure the effort would be appreciated.

The phone rang, and grabbing a dish towel, I wiped my hands dry as I headed into the office.

"Rose Harbor Inn," I answered.

"Jo Marie, it's Dennis Milford."

My knees nearly went out from under me. I'd been waiting to hear from the lieutenant colonel ever since our last conversation. A huge lump instantly formed in my throat.

"I promised to get back to you as soon as I had any information."

"Yes." I could barely squeeze out a reply.

"The remains have been extracted from the helicopter crash site."

My grip on the phone was so tight that I lost feeling in my fingers. Instantly, my head filled with a dozen questions. Try as I might, I couldn't force a single one past the constriction in my throat. I squeezed my eyes shut, tensing. Any hope I had that my husband had managed to survive the crash was about to be dashed against the sharp, rock-hard edges of reality. I braced myself for what was to come next.

"And?" I prodded.

The lieutenant colonel hesitated. "I want to assure you that the crash site hasn't been disturbed by enemy combatants."

"Oh." I was grateful for the chair close by, and I sank into the seat, as my knees would no longer support me.

"All the remains are being retrieved."

That had been his promise to me. Somehow, some way, I would have the opportunity to bury my husband. No man would be left behind. That had been Dennis Milford's promise to me and the army's promise to Paul when he became a Ranger.

"Thank you," I whispered.

He hesitated.

I'd been right. There was more, something he wasn't telling me. I could sense it. Feel it in every pore of my being. "What else?" I managed the question with some difficulty.

"I hesitate to tell you this, Jo Marie."

"Please, whatever it is, I need to know." My ear hurt from the pressure of the phone against it.

"The copter went down with six men."

"Yes," I whispered.

"Only the remains of five bodies were retrieved."

My eyes flared open. "You mean . . ."

"It doesn't mean anything. There's every possibility that the last victim was thrown from the helicopter or carried away by animals. I don't want you to pin your hopes on Paul being alive. He isn't. Accept that."

"Do you know whose body is missing?"

"Not yet. I shouldn't have told you."

"No, no, I'm glad you did." My pulse was going wild. All along I'd had a feeling, call it intuition, call it whatever you want, but this sensation had been with me ever since I'd received word of the helicopter crash. I'd felt that somehow, some way, Paul would have found a means to survive and had been sending me mental notes telling me to go on with my life until he returned.

Perhaps it was because our love was so new and we'd found each other when we least expected to fall in love . . . I'd always felt I would have sensed it if Paul died. Part of me was convinced that in the moment of his death Paul would have managed to come to me and I would know for certain that he was truly gone. In some ways he had come, had surrounded me with his love. This was all so confusing. The problem, I realized, was that I didn't want to believe it, couldn't accept that my husband was actually dead. To be hit with news like this changed everything.

In the weeks that followed the first shocking report of the helicopter crash, I'd been overwhelmed with such horrific grief that I didn't sleep; I didn't eat. At night I laid awake, waiting for Paul to come to me, to appear in my dreams. He didn't . . . not right away.

Not until I'd moved to Cedar Cove did I feel his presence. It was the first night I'd slept at the inn. I remembered that life-altering moment as clearly as I did the night it first happened. I'd been sitting by the alcove, half asleep, with the fire in the stone fireplace flickering gently. It'd been a starlit night early in January and all of a sudden Paul was there, as real as anything I've ever known. I was awake enough to know what was taking place. I sensed his presence as strongly as if he'd claimed the seat next to mine.

I remembered I'd been afraid to open my eyes for fear he would vanish, and I couldn't bear that. I yearned to hold on to this moment for as long as possible. That was the night he'd told me I would heal at this inn and that all who came to stay there would heal, too.

"Jo Marie."

I swallowed hard. "Yes," I whispered.

"Paul is gone."

"Yes," I whispered again, but I felt my heart resist. I didn't want to believe it, nor did I want to accept it as truth.

Chapter 17

After Mary finished breakfast, she returned to her room to get ready to meet George in Seattle. He'd wanted her to spend the day with him, and she'd agreed, although even now, she wasn't sure it was the right thing to do. He'd wanted to return to Cedar Cove and get her himself, but she'd refused. Instead, she would take a cab to the ferry terminal in Bremerton and ride over to Seattle on the Washington State ferry. For the entire time Mary had lived in Seattle she'd never ridden the ferry, and that was a downright shame. The state was said to have the largest ferry system in the world, and considering island nations, such as the Philippines, that was impressive.

Until recently, until she'd been diagnosed with cancer, Mary had been too busy, too involved in her career for such frivolous activities. She was far too impatient to sit in a line and wait for her chance to drive onto a ferry. Far too impatient for many things, including motherhood. This might very well be the only opportunity she would ever have to ride a ferry to Seattle, and she wasn't about to be cheated out of it because George, bless his dear heart, feared that the ride might possibly tire her out or that she'd catch a chill.

The taxi arrived at ten-fifteen, which would give her ample time to walk onto the eleven-ten ferry from Bremerton to Seattle. The sailing time was said to be sixty minutes, which would be ideal. Although the morning was overcast, the weather report claimed the sun would burn off the morning clouds. Mary hoped that would be the case, as she'd enjoy viewing the Olympic Mountains from the ferry.

The cabbie proved to be a friendly fellow who chatted easily during the thirty-minute drive between Cedar Cove and the ferry terminal in Bremerton. Mary couldn't help being amused by his ongoing dialogue. As little as eighteen months ago, she would have found him an irritation, but a great deal had changed in that time period. She took pleasure in studying him and listening to his stories.

When they arrived at the ferry terminal, she paid the fare and added a healthy tip. The walk up the platform tired her, but she took it slow and easy, letting the other walk-on passengers speed ahead of her. There'd been a time when she had felt the need to keep up with everyone else and would often lead the way. That was no longer the case. The sounds of the cars driving onto the ferry echoed in the morning as she paced herself, reserving her energy as best she could on the steep climb up the ramp.

As soon as she was on board, Mary found a seat and gratefully sat down. She looked out over the dark green water and viewed the scene with appreciation and wonder. Seagulls swooped overhead; the sound of their loud caws made her smile, remembering the young man's comment from the day before about the annual seagull-calling contest in Cedar Cove. She was about to get up and wait in line at the small galley for a cup of tea when George slipped into the seat across from her.

"George," she said, unable to hide her surprise. "What are you doing here?"

"I wasn't about to let you travel to Seattle without me," he stated calmly, as if he made a trip on the ferry a routine part of his weekend. "I want to spend every minute I possibly can with you."

George had always been wildly romantic. It was one reason she'd fallen so hard for him. "How did you get here?" she asked, thinking he must have driven around.

"How else?" he asked. "I rode the ferry across from Seattle, walked off, and then walked on again."

Mary smothered a laugh. "Are you nuts?"

"For you, I'm more than willing to be a fool." He moved to the seat next to her on the padded bench, slipped his arm around her shoulders, and gave her a gentle squeeze.

Despite what she said, Mary was pleased to see him. Sharing this ride with George would make it all the more meaningful.

"Can I get you anything?" he asked.

She nodded. "I'd love a cup of tea."

"I'll be right back." He stood eagerly, and seemed more than willing to get her anything she might possibly want or need. After taking a step or two, he abruptly turned around.

Mary raised her head expectantly, and with a smile George bent down and briefly pressed his lips to hers.

Funny how such a small display of affection could profoundly affect her. Emotion tightened her chest. Really, she mused, furious with herself, she had to get over this ridiculous desire to weep at the drop of a hat. She found it embarrassing in the extreme.

Within minutes George returned with two steaming cups of tea. He'd doctored his own and kept hers just the way she liked it best, hot and strong. That he remembered shouldn't have surprised her. He'd always been detail-oriented.

"What are our plans for the day?" she asked, seeing that he'd been the one who'd asked to spend this time with her. "Although after our wonderful dinner last night, I doubt I'll be hungry again for another month." George had insisted she try the clam chowder before the entrée, and later dessert, a delicious bread pudding, which he shared with her. He made no effort to hide the fact that he wanted to get some meat on her bones. They hadn't dealt with the past yet. She'd been tired and anxious, so George hadn't pressed the issue, and Mary had been grateful.

"I have a number of plans for our day," he said, and reached for her hand, folding both of his over hers. "First I wanted to take you to my office."

"Good idea." In the past, his office would have been the first thing she would have wanted to tour. Work had been her life, the focus of her attention, and where she felt most at home, most in her element and comfortable. Her corner office with the incredible view of the New York City skyline, a view she rarely noticed, had once been her kingdom from where she ruled. Cancer, like it had so much else, had put an end to her reign.

"Then I thought I would take you to my condo."

"Perfect." How thoughtful he was to make sure he didn't tire her out by filling their day with tourist activities. Mary squeezed his fingers, letting him know she approved.

"I've arranged for us to have lunch there."

"Wonderful."

"My view is great, and there's probably nothing in Seattle that you haven't already seen."

"True."

"If you have your heart set on . . ."

"I haven't," she assured him. His plans suited her. She didn't have the energy for a lot of physical activity. It shocked her how quickly she tired, and being reminded of her limitations only served to depress her. Cancer had threatened nearly every aspect of her life, and she refused to allow it to rob her of this day with George.

"I'd like to go outside for a while," she said, as the ferry reached the middle point of its journey. Seeing the view of the Seattle skyline from the front of the ferry was an opportunity not to be missed.

George hesitated, and Mary could see he was worried.

"I'll be fine," she was quick to assure him. She'd worn a jacket with an extra scarf over her shoulders. Plus, her near-bald head was well protected from the wind.

Still holding her hand, George led the way outside and onto the area in the front of the ferry. As promised, the view was spectacular. The Space Needle jutted up, reminding her that this was where they'd first met. Wind whistled around her, and the bite of it brought an instant chill to her. Nevertheless, Mary refused to leave. She wanted to hold on to this moment. George was with her, making it all the more precious.

Ever thoughtful, George moved behind her and wrapped his arms around her torso, offering her his warmth and protection. Closing her eyes, she placed her hands on his arms and savored his warmth and his love.

The ride seemed to pass in seconds instead of the sixty minutes. When they docked in Seattle, the cars drove off the ferry, making the same clanking sound they had while boarding. George and Mary walked off, following the crowd on the passenger ramp and through the terminal.

Once on the street they took a short, leisurely stroll down to the waterfront. George kept her close, with her hand around his arm. Mary immediately noticed that a great deal had changed in the years since she'd been away. New businesses had sprung up, and yet much was the same. The original Starbucks was close by, and the Seattle Aquarium was just down the street. The climb up the hill to Pike Place Market would be too much of a challenge now.

The market held a special place in her heart. She recalled that George would present her with a fresh floral bouquet from Pike Place Market each week. With care, they would often last a full seven days, and the arrangements were usually colorful arrays of exotic flowers, whose names she would never hope to pronounce. She kept them on her desk at work and was reminded of his love every time she glanced in their direction.

"Are you thinking about what I think you are?" he asked. He'd placed his hand over hers in the crook of his elbow and walked at a slow pace so as not to overly tire her.

"And what am I thinking?" she asked, glancing at him.

"Pike Place Market."

"The flowers."

George laughed. "Remember the time the fishmonger tossed a salmon right over your head?"

It wasn't something she was likely to forget. It'd been a magical moment. The entire day had been. If she were to guess, it was that very night that she'd conceived his child.

Sadness, mingled with regret, settled over her, and she swallowed hard. Always sensitive to her moods, George noticed right away.

"You okay?" he asked.

"I'm fine. Now, what was it you said about showing me your office?"

George led her to the line of taxis outside the ferry terminal and held open the rear passenger door for her. Once inside, he gave the driver the business address, and almost immediately the cabbie sped off in such a rush that the car bounced as they flew toward Fourth Avenue.

The tour of his office told Mary a great deal. George had done well for himself. His corner office, with its cherrywood desk and credenza and original artwork, couldn't help but impress. Pride in him, this man she had loved, stirred in her, and she smiled.

"This room is so you," she commented.

"How so?"

"Look at your desktop."

"What about it?"

"It's clean and polished and . . ."

"I have a janitorial service that takes care of that sort of thing."

Mary was undeterred. "You're focused and brilliant, and any client should consider themselves fortunate to have you as their counsel."

Clearly embarrassed by her praise, George looked away. "I can see it's time for us to leave." He wrapped his arm around her waist and gently guided her toward the elevator.

Although his condo was only a few blocks away, George insisted on getting a cab. Mary could have easily walked the short distance, but she was grateful for this thoughtfulness. His home was on the twenty-fourth floor of a modern high-rise. His living room offered a stunning view of Puget Sound and the Olympic Mountains. Mary felt drawn to the windows the moment they entered the condo.

"Oh, George."

"You like it?"

"How could I not? This view is incredible."

He helped her off with her jacket and hung it up in a hallway closet. Mary saw that the kitchen table had been set and that lunch was ready to be served.

"Shall we have a glass of wine first?" George asked.

Mary looked away. "I can't . . . the medication."

"Tea?"

"Perfect."

"Coming right up." He walked into the kitchen, which was separated from the living area by a long counter.

"Let me help."

Although she offered, Mary knew George wouldn't allow it, and she was right.

"Stay put and relax. I don't want to wear you out."

From where she sat, Mary had a good view of George as he set about brewing the tea. He fidgeted about the kitchen, opening and closing drawers. At one point he went completely still and held on to the counter. Mary didn't need anyone to tell her the cause of his restless uneasiness. He'd brought her to his home because he wanted to delve into the regrets of nineteen years ago.

This was exactly what she'd feared would happen, and yet he had a right to know the truth, as painful as it would be to tell him.

"George," she said softly.

He whirled around, his look expectant.

"Come, sit with me." Her hand bounced against the cushion beside her.

"Your tea . . ."

"I'll drink it later."

He returned to where she sat, but he didn't take a seat. Instead, he paced the area, rubbing his palms together. "Tell me, Mary, why wouldn't you marry me? We could have made it work. I wanted nothing more than to raise our child and love you."

Mary lowered her gaze and struggled for the words. "We tried, we both did, but I could see, even if you didn't, that it was impossible." She didn't mention the pregnancy . . . She would, but not now. Later she would be stronger; later she would be better able to deal with his anger and disappointment.

He ignored her response. "How could you have taken that transfer without discussing it with me first?"

This was an old argument. "You know the answer to that better than I do, George. Please, can we put that decision behind us for now . . ." This awkward discussion was what she'd feared would happen, and she didn't have the emotional fortitude to deal with it now. "I could never have been the kind of wife you deserved or the mother a child needs—you know that, George. I had my own goals, and you knew, you always knew, that I never had any desire to be a mother. And then I couldn't even imagine dragging a child from one side of the country to the other. That's no life for anyone. I did what I had to do. I know you wanted to marry me, especially after I told you I was pregnant, but this is my body, and a pregnancy was never part of my plans."

Her words hung in the air between them. As if he couldn't face her, George walked away and seemed to mull over her words.

"Answer me this: Have the years brought you happiness?" His look was intent.

What a question. Had she been happy? "I don't know," she said, being as honest as she could. "But I felt a deep sense of accomplishment."

"Did reaching the top of your profession give you what you needed?"

This question was even more difficult to answer. "In a way, I suppose it did."

He shook his head. "I don't believe it. I can't believe it." He clenched his fists at his sides. "Was it worth it, Mary? Was killing our baby worth it?" The words were calm, but his pain was much louder than any outburst. "I wanted that baby," he said, his voice trembling with barely restrained anger and gut-wrenching pain.

Mary's eyes filled with tears, knowing how badly she'd hurt him. "I'm sorry."

"You should be."

She opened her purse for a tissue and clenched it in her hands as she looked down. "I went to the abortion clinic—"

"I don't want to hear this." He started to walk away. He stood with his back to her, his shoulders stiff, looking out the picture window.

Mary squeezed her eyes closed. She needed to tell him. "George, listen to me . . . I should have told you this long ago. I went to the clinic, met with the doctor—"

"I don't want to hear it," he repeated, louder this time.

"I couldn't do it, George. I couldn't do it."

George froze, and then slowly, ever so slowly, he turned around, his face revealing his shock. "What did you just say?"

"I was on birth-control pills . . . The chances of getting pregnant were a hundred thousand to one. I didn't forget my pills. I took them religiously every morning, and still I got pregnant. As I sat in the clinic, it came to me that this baby was no accident. This child was meant to be born."

All George seemed capable of doing was staring at her, his mouth open in shock and disbelief.

"We had a daughter," she whispered.

George was silent for a long time, and then the words burst out as if he couldn't say them fast enough: "Why didn't·you tell me?"

"I . . . I couldn't. I'd left, severed the ties. I didn't want to hurt you anymore."

"Hurt me? You didn't want to hurt me?" he repeated and glared at her, his eyes wide and accusing. "Is this your idea of a joke? You gave birth to my daughter and then didn't tell me . . . All these years you've deprived me of my own flesh and blood, and the reason is you didn't want to hurt me?"

"George . . ."

He held up his hand, stopping her. "I didn't want to keep loving you. God knows I tried not to. I married someone else, hoping, praying that would purge you from my mind. It didn't. Kathleen knew I was simply going through the motions. She always knew that despite all my claims I'd never stopped loving you."

Mary covered her mouth and sobbed. "Oh, George . . ."

He sank into a chair and covered his face with both his hands. "And now to find out you gave life to my child and then kept her from me all these years . . ."

"I didn't keep her from you." Mary stood, walked over to him, and placed her hand on his hunched shoulder.

He jerked away from her as if her touch had scalded him. He looked up, his eyes rimmed with tears.

In her heart she believed she'd done the right thing, the only thing she could have done for her and for their daughter. "I gave our baby girl up for adoption."

George tore his gaze away from her, covered his face with his palms again, and released bitter sobs that wrenched at her heart.

Unable to bear his grief, Mary bent over him and set her hands on his shoulders. Tears rained down her cheeks as she whispered softly, "I'm so sorry, so sorry."

George reached for her then; gripping her around the waist, he buried his face in her stomach.

Chapter 18

Annie walked a complete circle around one of the tables that had been set up in the reception hall where family and friends would be gathering later that afternoon. The hall was beautifully decorated with flower centerpieces and balloons waiting to be attached to the chair backs. Her fear was that this anniversary party was destined to be an unmitigated disaster. It would be a miracle if her grandparents didn't end up killing each other before the end of the day. What had happened? What had changed? Where was the loving couple she remembered from her childhood?

"Where would you like these chairs?" Oliver called out from the other side of the hall. Folding chairs lined the walls, ready to be placed around the tables.

Annie couldn't do anything but stare back.

"Annie?"

She scooted out a chair and slumped into it. "This isn't going to work," she whispered.

With his hands braced against his lean hips, Oliver surveyed the room. "I think the setup is perfect."

"I'm not talking about the room. I'm talking about my grandparents." It was hard to believe that just a few days earlier Annie had told friends she wanted a marriage just like theirs. They had built their lives around each other. They'd raised their family; they'd supported and encouraged each other through the years. They were living proof that love lasts a lifetime.

Oh, my.

"Annie?" Oliver asked, cutting into her thoughts. "What's the problem?"

"You need to ask?" she cried. Her stomach was tied up in one huge knot and she could easily picture the entire anniversary party going down in flames. If her grandfather mentioned one word that they'd rushed into the wedding because of the fear of pregnancy it would mortify her grandmother and shock their friends.

Oliver joined her, sitting down across from her. He leaned forward and reached for her hands, gripping them both with his own.

"Are they always like this?" Annie asked, pleading with him to tell her this behavior wasn't the norm.

"No," he assured her.

"Thank God." But his words didn't help ease her worries. "They've done nothing but argue from the moment they arrived. Grandpa won't wear his hearing aids, and then Grandma shouts at him. Then he gets irritated with her for yelling."

"I know."

Oliver chuckled, although what he found amusing Annie couldn't guess.

"Kent gets dressed, and Julie says what he's wearing isn't appropriate and insists he change," he said, adding to her list.

"Exactly." Annie didn't know what to do. She felt sick to her stomach. "I thought I wanted a marriage just like theirs," she said, and was surprised the words had been audible.

"Annie," Oliver said gently, reassuringly, "people show love in different ways."

"By fighting? I don't think so."

"Your grandparents are nervous about this party. This celebration wasn't your grandfather's idea. He'd much rather be back in Portland, playing poker with his buddies. Saturday afternoon he plays cards. He's going ahead with this whole setup because he thinks this is what your grandmother wants, but he'd prefer to not be part of any of this. It's not his thing."

Frustrated and a little hurt, Annie tilted her chin up. "He might have said something to me about how he felt. I could have toned down the party, made it a small affair."

"He didn't want to disappoint your grandmother," Oliver explained.

Annie wasn't sure what to think. It was far too late to back out of the celebration now, at the very last moment. Within a few hours the band would arrive, the caterers would set up the buffet tables, and her grandparents' closest friends and family would gather at the waterfront for the renewal of the wedding vows.

Oliver rubbed his thumb over the tops of Annie's hands. Concerned as she was, she hadn't realized he was holding her hands. As soon as she did, she tugged them free.

"Do you remember the summer you were fourteen?" he asked.

"Of course," she snapped. Why he would bother her with nonsensical questions irritated her all the more.

"You came to Portland for two weeks with your mother. Do you remember why?"

"What I remember about that summer was doing everything I could not to get anywhere in the same vicinity as you." Annie did her best to hide how annoyed he made her with all these useless questions. After that disastrous kiss she'd been determined never to speak to Oliver again. Annie had done everything she could to avoid him, which made Oliver seek her out with more determination than ever. He'd gone above and beyond the norm to make her as miserable as possible, it had seemed to her.

"You were dreadful to me," she reminded him.

"I know."

"You know? Why would you do that? What did I ever do to you that warranted such meanness?" Other than make a complete idiot of herself and let him kiss her.

Oliver released his breath in a slow sigh. "I wanted to kiss you again."

"Well, you had a funny way of going about it."

"True I didn't show a lot of finesse, but you made sure I paid for it."

She didn't know how that was possible, but she didn't want to get into any of that now. It was a long time ago and not the least bit important. "What does any of this have to do with my grandparents?"

"You don't remember why you came to Portland that summer?"

"We visited every summer."

"Sure, for a few days, but that particular summer you spent two weeks."

"We did?"

"I should know," Oliver insisted. "It was torture for me having you right next door."

Despite herself, Annie smiled. "If I made you miserable that summer, then good. It was what you deserved."

"Your grandfather had surgery, remember," he said, ignoring Annie's comment, "and your grandmother refused to leave his side."

Annie blinked. She vaguely recalled that her grandfather had been sick. What remained prominently in her mind was how much she'd detested Oliver and how miserable he'd made her. It boosted her ego to learn that she'd returned the favor, although she couldn't imagine what she had done that was so awful.

"Your grandmother had recently opened her own gift shop, remember?"

Annie did, because the shop sold dolls. Not play dolls for children but high-end porcelain ones that women cherished and collected. Annie remembered that some of those fancy dolls cost several thousands of dollars. The shop had been successful for a number of years before the doll market crashed.

"Yes," she admitted. "I remember Grandma's shop."

"Your mother came to work in the shop while your grandfather was hospitalized."

Frowning, Annie's mind drifted back to that summer. Although her annoyance with Oliver played heavy in her mind, she did recall that her grandfather had been gravely ill. "Grandpa's appendix burst. Mom was afraid he might die."

"So was your grandmother and just about everyone else. I can remember hearing someone say that it was your grandmother's love that pulled him though. She was with him nearly twenty-four/seven."

Annie couldn't remember ever seeing her grandmother during that trip.

"A love that strong doesn't change, Annie."

She desperately wanted to believe what he said was true. "I find that hard to believe, seeing how they snipe at each other now."

"Your grandfather is overwhelmed, and your grandmother isn't accustomed to being the center of attention. They're nervous, and this irritation with each other is how it's coming out."

"I wish I'd known . . . Oh, Oliver, I think I've done them both a grave disservice." Annie felt dreadful, as if she'd forced them into an awkward situation for which neither of her grandparents was prepared. She'd given this party her best effort. She'd immersed herself in the details because it had helped her deal with the emotional pain of losing Lenny. The knot in her stomach tightened. She'd been the one to bring up the idea of a large anniversary celebration. She'd been the one who'd set the agenda and then refused to listen when they said she didn't need to go to all this trouble; what they'd really been saying was that they wanted something small.

"Oh, Oliver, I've made such a mess of things."

"No, you haven't. Everything you did was out of love for them."

Bolting to her feet, Annie said, "I've got to set matters straight, reassure them. I'll call the whole thing off if that's what they want." She'd find a way to get them out of this, although she didn't have a clue how she would manage it. Grabbing her jacket and purse, Annie headed toward the door.

"What are you going to say to them?"

"I don't know . . . I'll figure it out when I get there."

Oliver started after her. "Do you want me to come with you?"

She shook her head. "You stay here and . . ." Annie looked around the room. "Go ahead and set up the rest of the chairs and attach the balloons. Just assume we're moving forward until I tell you otherwise."

"Okay. Do you want me to kiss you for luck?"

"No." She left no doubt as to her feelings on the matter.

"Sure you do," he called after her. "But I'll collect that kiss later."

Annie waved him off. Oliver had always been a tease. For most of her life she hadn't appreciated it. This day was different. She was grateful that he'd taken the time to explain to her what was happening between her grandparents.

Back at the inn, Annie raced up the porch steps and burst through the front door. Rover barked furiously at her.

"It's me, Rover," she announced.

As soon as the canine recognized her, he gave one more short bark and then returned to his spot in the kitchen. Jo Marie stepped out of the other room, and it might have been Annie's imagination, but the innkeeper looked deeply troubled.

"Is something wrong?" Jo Marie asked.

"Do you know where my grandparents are?"

She shook her head. "I haven't seen them since breakfast."

For one horrifying moment, Annie feared her grandparents had run away or disappeared. Hurrying to their room on the main floor, she pounded on the door as hard as she could, until her hand hurt too much to continue.

Her grandfather opened the door and, taking one look at her, asked, "Annie, good grief, what's wrong?"

"I need to talk to you." She was breathless and panicky.

"Come in." He stepped aside so she could enter the room. Her grandmother was apparently in the bathroom, because she wasn't in the room.

"Where's Grandma?"

"She's pouting."

The bathroom door swung open, and Julie Shivers came out, dressed in her housecoat with her hair in giant rollers. "Annie, dear heart, what are you doing here?"

"I just asked her the same thing," Kent said.

Julie sat down on the bed. "Tell us what's got you so upset," she said in the coolest, calmest voice one could imagine.

Annie felt dreadful, and now that she was with them she didn't have a clue where to start, so she blurted out, "I feel like I railroaded you into this huge party that neither of you want. I am so sorry."

Both her grandmother and grandfather stared back at her wordlessly, as if at a loss for what to say.

"I got carried away with myself because I wanted . . . needed a distraction after Lenny. It never occurred to me that you wouldn't want any of this." To be fair, her mother and her aunt Patty had both thought the party was a wonderful idea, too.

"Who told you that?" Julie demanded.

"A little birdie."

Julie quickly confronted Kent, her eyes flashing fire. "What did you do now?"

"It wasn't Grandpa," Annie jumped in. "It was Oliver."

Her grandmother sucked in a deep breath. "He had no business telling you any such thing."

"But I'm so glad he did," Annie cried. "Listen, we can put a stop to the party right now. I'll make everything go away. You don't need to worry. In fact, if you want, you could leave right this minute. I'll . . . I'll tell everyone you eloped a second time."

Julie glanced toward her husband, seeking his opinion. "What do you think, Kent?"

"Well," her grandfather said slowly, thoughtfully turning his attention back to his wife. "I've sort of gotten used to the idea, but we'll do what you think is best."

"A lot of people have come from out of town," Julie murmured. "Betty and Vern drove all the way from South Dakota. It would be so rude of us to walk out on our guests."

"I agree," Kent said. "I feel we should go through with the party, renewed vows and all."

Although relieved, Annie felt she had to do something more. "What can I do to make you more comfortable?"

"Oh, sweetie, we'll be fine." Julie stretched out her arm toward Kent. "Isn't that right, honey?"

"Of course we will," Kent agreed. He slipped his arm around Julie's waist.

"We've behaved so badly," Julie said. "Oh, Annie, I do apologize."

"Hey, you could apologize to me, too, you know."

Her grandmother pressed her hand against Kent's jaw. "We're a pair of old fools, Kent Shivers."

Annie's grandfather chuckled and gave his wife a little squeeze. "You hit the nail on the head with that one."

Julie smiled and told Annie, "Now, you get back to whatever it was you were doing."

"You're sure?"

"Positive," her grandfather assured her.

"You go, and I'll finish getting dressed."

Annie turned to leave when her grandfather stopped her.

"Hey, Annie, what do you think of your grandmother's new push-up bra?"

"Kent!"

Her grandfather chuckled. "I like it. The girls are upstairs."

"Kent," Julie protested again. "You mean the twins are upstairs," she said, and giggled as if she were twenty years old all over again.

Feeling much better, Annie left the inn and returned to the reception hall.

When she arrived she found that Oliver had the chairs all set up. "How'd it go?" he asked.

"Good, I think," she said, as she shucked off her jacket and set aside her purse. "I gave them the option to elope a second time, but they decided to go through with the party."

"I thought they probably would."

Annie owed him. "Thank you," she whispered. "I think this entire day would have been a disaster if you hadn't said something."

Oliver shrugged off her appreciation.

"No, really."

The space between them seemed charged with electricity. Annie tried to break away, but found herself trapped in the moment. This feeling was gratitude, she tried to tell herself. Appreciation. She couldn't actually be physically attracted to Oliver. Couldn't long for him to kiss her again, couldn't . . .

Even as the thoughts were zipping through her head, Annie felt herself leaning toward him.

Oliver didn't need any more encouragement. He reached for her, and his lips descended toward her when the outside door to the hall opened.

"Annie, what can I do to help?"

Annie and Oliver broke apart, and she quickly turned aside. "Aunt Patty! Hi. Thanks for stopping by . . ."

Chapter 19

When I'm upset or worried, I find the best antidote is for me to do something physical. Lieutenant Colonel Milford was right. Paul wasn't alive. He wasn't coming home. In my heart of hearts, I had to accept the fact that my husband had died in a helicopter crash in Afghanistan. Six men were on board that aircraft when it went down; six men died. I couldn't pin any hope on the fact that the remains of five men had been found and one had survived. And that one could be Paul.

I greeted two sets of guests and saw them to their rooms, but I didn't remember anything I'd said to them. What I needed, I decided, was hard physical labor, and seeing that Mark couldn't work on the rose garden, then I would.

Putting on rubber boots, I grabbed a coat and headed outside with Rover dutifully following behind. Once I retrieved a shovel from the shed, I headed toward the half-completed garden space, unsure exactly where to start. If nothing more, I could put the sod back so the yard didn't look so torn up. While I strained with effort, I might manage to hold back my churning emotions.

Rover seemed to sense that something was wrong, because he whined for several moments until I stopped digging and petted him. Tears clouded my eyes. I did my best to ignore them, sniffling several times until it became necessary to pull a tissue out of my pocket. I dabbed at my eyes and then blew my nose. All too soon I gave up any effort to hold back the tears and was quickly out of tissues. I'd worked myself into a frenzy carting the sod across the yard, sobbing as I worked. My fear was that I'd made an even bigger mess of things.

Mark wouldn't be pleased, but this had to be done. Being the perfectionist, he wouldn't take kindly to me meddling in what he considered his area.

By the time I returned the shovel to the shed my back ached and my legs felt shaky. Although I had a dozen other tasks that required my attention, as a result of my outside exercise, I needed to shower and change clothes. My emotions were all over the board, and I hoped standing under a hot spray of water would help settle me down.

As I headed back into the house, the front door opened and out stepped the Shivers. The morning had definitely gotten off to a shaky start with the anniversary couple. I sincerely hoped that everything would turn out the way Annie had planned. I knew the young party planner had put her heart into organizing this event, wanting to honor her grandparents.

Julie Shivers stood with Kent on the porch. She took one look at me and immediately knew something had upset me. "Jo Marie, my dear, whatever is wrong?"

It wasn't like I could hide my red runny nose or the fact that I'd been weeping. "I apologize," I said, but my voice was barely above a whisper. "I got some distressing news this morning." I hadn't realized the couple was still at the inn. I assumed they'd already left for the festivities with their younger daughter and her husband.

"Is there anything we can do?" Kent asked.

I shook my head. Wanting to change the subject, I smiled as best I could. "You both look amazing." And they did. Julie wore a pink double-breasted suit with a pencil skirt that had a pleated hem. Kent's dark brown suit complemented Julie's outfit perfectly. They made for a handsome couple.

"In other words, we clean up well," Kent joked.

"Indeed, you do," I said, and was pleased to know my voice had found itself again.

"You really think so?" Julie asked, brushing her gloved hand down her front. "Kent and I waited to dress until the very last moment. Oliver is due to pick us up in a few minutes. Kent was too restless to wait inside."

"Too uncomfortable, you mean." Kent ran his index finger along the inside of his shirt collar. "Never did enjoy wearing a suit and tie. I can only put up with this for a few hours."

"All this will be over with before we know it," Julie assured her husband, gently patting his forearm.

"That's what I keep telling myself," Kent grumbled.

"Why don't you sit with us a bit?" Julie invited, gesturing toward the porch swing.

"I'm a mess," I protested. My boots were covered with mud, and I was more than ready for a shower.

"Sit," Kent ordered. "Help us take our minds off all the fuss and bother of this anniversary."

I could see the invitation was more for them than for me, and so I sat down on the top porch step while Kent and Julie chose to sit on the swing. Rover came and lay down beside me, and I ran my hand down his back, finding a gentle comfort in this special friend.

"So what's going on?" Kent asked, in that no-nonsense way of his.

More as a distraction for them than a need to talk, I said, "I got a phone call this morning from my husband's commanding officer. He's back from Afghanistan. When the helicopter my husband was in went down, the crash site wasn't accessible," I explained. Then I went on to tell them what I'd learned that morning.

"Do you think the one body not retrieved might be Paul and that he survived?" Julie asked, her eyes growing round and hopeful.

"I keep telling myself to accept the fact that he's dead."

"But you can't help believing he might have survived the crash," Kent filled in for me.

I nodded. No one needed to tell me it was a fool's game. "Every wife, every mother, is thinking the same thing I am. Each one of us clings to the hope that the missing body is their loved one and that by some miracle their son or husband is alive. We all want to believe that he's living in the mountains, working his way slowly but surely back to civilization."

"How could you not cling to that hope?" Julie asked.

Kent agreed. "Frankly, I don't think you'd be human if you didn't. It's never easy to let go of a loved one."

That these two would be so sympathetic helped chase the chill of the morning away. "Paul and I had such a short time together," I said, staring off toward the calm waters of the cove. "I'd like to think if he had survived the war that we might have had the chance to celebrate our fiftieth wedding anniversary one day."

"I worried myself sick when Kent was in Vietnam," Julie said. "I was so afraid I would lose my husband. Every night the newscaster would report how many more young men had died. My greatest fear was that one day I would get word that Kent wouldn't be coming home. I couldn't bear the thought."

Kent reached for his wife's hand, and the two exchanged a long look.

"Julie wrote me every day," Kent remembered. "Her letters are what got me through the war. I think I would have gone stir-crazy if it hadn't been for her letters."

"And when I didn't hear from him, every imaginable scenario went through my mind," Julie added. "A week would often go by without a letter from Kent, and I was certain I'd lost my husband."

It hadn't been nearly as bad for Paul and me. "Thankfully, we were able to keep in touch," I recalled. My entire day centered on when the two of us could talk. I'd moved my computer into the bedroom and even in my sleep I was able to recognize the pinging sound that indicated an email. More nights than I cared to remember, I would wake and then the two of us would spend an hour or more with instant messaging. Afterward, I would fall back into bed and sleep, feeling my husband's love wrapped all around me despite the fact he was half a world away.

"It's much easier to stay in touch these days with email and Skype and cell phones," Julie agreed.

I would be forever grateful for those late-night sessions. I had reread his emails often, especially those first few months after I got word of the helicopter crash. Some I had even put to memory. I printed them out and placed them in a binder. These days I took them out only when I felt especially lonely. I would sit with Rover cuddled up next to me and read through them again and again. Perhaps I would do that this evening. I hesitated, unsure if that would be wise. Sometimes the emails comforted me, and other times they had the opposite affect and I would be hit with wave upon wave of grief. I'd wait until this evening and decide.

"It looks like Oliver is here now," Kent said, and pointed toward the street. He stood, and so did Julie.

"He's been with Annie, getting everything set up at the reception hall," Julie told me. "I'm sure he was a big help."

"You know, you just might be right," Kent said, looking down on Julie.

"About what?"

"About Oliver being the one for our Annie."

Julie couldn't have looked more pleased. "I've said that for years. I would love to make Oliver an official part of our family."

"He might as well be family," Kent muttered. "He spent as much time with us as he did with his own parents."

"Kent, that's not true. Oliver only came to visit when the grandkids did."

"And if they weren't around, he found an excuse to stop by," Kent added, but he didn't seem to have minded.

"Oliver has been a big help to us over the years, so quit your complaining."

"I'm not complaining," Kent insisted. "I'm making a comment is all."

"Oliver shoveled the snow from our sidewalks, and if there was something Kent could no longer do, then he took on the task. We're really going to miss him while he's traveling in the South Pacific."

"True enough," Kent agreed.

"I just wish . . ." Julie let the thought fade.

"What do you wish, sweetie?" her husband asked.

"You know . . . that Oliver and Annie."

"I'll admit it would be nice, but they need to discover this without help from us. Now, Julie, I know how much you enjoy matchmaking, but we can't be meddling in young people's lives."

"I know, I know." But Julie didn't look happy about it.

Oliver hurried up the sidewalk. "Your chariot awaits you," he said, all smiles.

"Are you ready?" Kent asked Julie.

She sighed and then nodded. "I think so. What about you?"

He nodded solemnly. Then, reaching for her hand, the two walked down the porch steps.

I knew that everything would be fine. Kent and Julie would be surrounded by family and friends. This day would long be remembered as they celebrated their marriage and their lives together.

I continued to sit on the porch after the car pulled away. I'd learned a valuable lesson from watching the Shivers. If Paul had lived, I was convinced we would have probably behaved as they had after so many years of living together.

Only we wouldn't have that opportunity.

But then, I hadn't ever expected to fall in love or marry, either. Would I trade having known and loved Paul Rose for anything else life had to offer? My heart instantly knew the answer.

No.

Even with the pain of loss that I would carry with me the rest of my days, I had no regrets. Despite my hopes, my husband was gone from me physically and yet at the same time he would always remain a part of me.

As I started to walk into the house, I heard a car pull into the yard. Looking over my shoulder, I saw it was Peggy Beldon and Corrie McAfee. Peggy and her husband owned another bed-and-breakfast in town. Corrie was married to a retired Seattle police detective who took on investigations in the private sector. Come to think of it, the young man who'd arrived with the fire department to help Mark had been named McAfee. I wondered if they were any relation.

The two women were good friends, and I knew they made a point of having lunch together at least once a month. I'd been invited to join them, but had only been able to make it one time.

Peggy and her husband, Bob, had helped me with many of the practical applications of running a B&B, too. They'd introduced me to other inn owners operating in the area. I was amazed by their willingness to reach out to someone they might consider com-petition. Instead, their attitude was that of friends. Peggy insisted that all the B&B operators needed to stick together. I knew that part of the Shivers family who had traveled from out of state would be staying at The Thyme and Tide on Cranberry Point this eve-ning. I had been happy to recommend their B&B. Peggy and Bob would make all their guests feel welcome.

I met Peggy and Corrie on the sidewalk leading up to the inn.

"Hello," I said, more than pleased to have company. I could use a few distractions, especially this day. "What are you two up to?"

"We're heading out for lunch and thought we'd stop by to see if we can do anything to help you get ready for the open house," Peggy offered.

"Now, that's a friend."

"A good friend," Corrie teased.

"You're right. It isn't just anyone we'd offer to help clean," Peggy added. She looked around and frowned when she viewed the half-completed rose garden. "I thought you said Mark would have this finished by now."

"That's what he said." No one was more disappointed than I. "But it didn't happen, and now he's got a broken leg."

"How long will he be laid up?"

"Can't say." Mark wasn't exactly a font of information, espe-cially about anything personal.

"I hope you aren't upset with me for recommending him," Peggy said.

"Not at all," I assured her. "He does a great job, and his prices are more than reasonable." For the most part, Mark was a bless-ing. He was a grumpy one, but still a big help to me in a number of areas. "He's completed quite a few projects for me now, and I've always been happy with his work."

"Glad to hear it." Peggy did sound relieved. "Like I said, he's a bit of an odd duck."

When I'd first met Mark, I'd thought the same thing, but gradually as I'd come to know him better, I realized he was a private person.

"Do you know his story?" I asked, looking from one woman to the other.

"No," Peggy said, and just as eagerly asked, "Do you?"

I shook my head. Mark was as much an enigma now as when we'd first met. Perhaps even more so. The more I learned about him, the more I realized I barely knew him at all. We'd played Scrabble and he was good, and he'd recommended a few books that I'd enjoyed.

"All I know is that he does good work."

I had to agree.

"Do you want to come inside for coffee?" I asked. It seemed a little ridiculous for us to be standing in the middle of the sidewalk when we could be inside.

"Thanks, but not today. We were headed out to lunch when we saw your sign and I remembered the open house. I'm happy to help any way I can," Peggy said. "Honestly. Seeing that I was the one who suggested this, it's the least I can do. If you want, I can bring a few appetizers."

Again, I thanked her, but I had already decided on cookies, and had finished the last of my baking. I wanted to keep it simple and have my guests concentrate on the inn rather than the food.

The two left within a few minutes. My mood had lifted. I had loved my husband, and I would miss him.

Slowly but surely I was learning to build a new life for myself.

A life without Paul.

Chapter 20

Mary knew that the news that she'd given their daughter up for adoption had badly shaken George. He appeared stunned, shocked. He continued to stare at her as if he didn't know what to say or how to react.

Leaning forward, he braced his elbows on his knees and hid his face in his hands as if he was still unable to absorb what she'd told him. He looked like a man burdened with more troubles than one person could possibly bear.

If only he would say something. Mary could deal with anything but this silence. He wouldn't look at her. She'd rather he shouted, ranted and raved, or even tossed her out of his home. What she couldn't take was witnessing this pain, this grief, this horrific sense of loss.

Gradually, he looked up. He opened his mouth as if to say something, but closed it again.

"I didn't expect to have any feelings for her," Mary whispered. "I tried to think of her as a mass of cells, and then she started to move. I felt her stretch and grow inside of me. As hard as I tried, I couldn't ignore what was happening to my body, to my heart."

George straightened slightly and leaned toward her as though to hear more.

"I remember the first time I felt this living being, who was our daughter," Mary continued, seeing how eager George was for more details. "The doctor told me that I should expect to feel life at any time. The sensation was so slight, so fragile, I thought at first that I must have imagined it."

He continued to stare at her, again as if he was at a complete loss as to what to say.

Mary moistened her lips and went on. "Over the next several weeks I grew accustomed to her being part of me. I found my hand pressing against my stomach as if to shield her. In some odd way, I think I was reaching out to her . . . to you."

She thought she detected a hint of a smile in him.

"After those first few times when I felt her kick, she moved more often, and I knew right away it had to be the baby. I came to expect it, wait for it. No one even guessed I was pregnant, although several people commented that I . . . had a certain glow about me, as if I'd fallen in love. My colleagues were convinced I had met someone."

"Had you?"

"Yes," Mary admitted.

His face tightened.

"That someone was our baby," she told him.

George wasn't amused by her little joke, and his look told her so. "You said you grew to care for her?"

Her hands, which had been fidgeting, went still. "How could I not, but it didn't change what I knew about myself. I simply wouldn't make a good mother and I knew it. Still she was part of you and me, the very best part. It was because I loved her that I decided to give her a family, a real family."

It took him a few moments to digest her words. "When did you learn it was a girl?"

"I saw her for the first time after the doctor ordered an ultrasound. Because I was a bit older, the obstetrician wanted to be sure the baby was developing as she should. He told me there were no guarantees, but it looked like a girl to him."

George nodded. "Tell me more."

Mary wasn't sure what she should say. "I used to sing to her at night before we went to sleep . . . well," she said and smiled softly, "before I went to sleep. I thought she would turn out to be a soccer player. My goodness, that girl could kick."

He smiled. "I wish . . ." He didn't complete his thought. He didn't need to; Mary understood.

"I know. I wish you could have felt her move, too." So often Mary had wondered if she'd done the right thing by leaving George and not telling him of her decision. A hundred times over the course of the pregnancy, Mary had wanted to contact him, especially toward the end of her third trimester, when she'd been so bloated and so terribly uncomfortable. She'd successfully hidden the fact that she was pregnant from her staff. Some might have guessed, but it was never discussed. The last ten weeks she'd taken a leave of absence, letting the company assume she'd gone home to take care of an ailing parent. Those last few weeks of the pregnancy had been dreadful. Her hands and feet had swollen until they felt like overstuffed sausages.

"You were alone when you had her?"

Mary nodded. Because of her age and fear of other complications, her OB had suggested a cesarean. It was only as a precaution. After weighing her options, Mary had opted for a vaginal birth. This would be her only pregnancy and birth, and she wanted the full experience. And she got it. In spades.

"I would have given anything to have been at your side," he said.

"No, George, be glad you weren't there. I was a horrible patient."

"It was bad?"

Mary shrugged. "For obvious reasons, I didn't take those natural birthing classes. So I watched a couple of movies and read a few books and assumed I was prepared."

"You weren't?"

Mary responded with a short laugh. "Nothing can prepare a woman for what labor is like. After four hours I was thinking this was taking much longer than it should, and I demanded the doctor do something to speed up the process. The labor room nurse went out of her way to assure me it would be hours yet, and I was having none of it."

"How long did the labor last?"

Mary smiled at the memory. Knowing how sensitive George was, she felt it was best not to fill in the gory details. By the time she'd been ready to deliver, she'd used language that would shock a sailor. This birthing business wasn't for sissies. Despite the pain and repeated reassurances, she'd held fast, insisting she wanted a natural birth for fear of what drugs would do to the baby. She'd managed it, too. In retrospect, the entire experience had been nothing short of incredible.

"Labor takes as long as it takes," Mary said, answering his question, "but our daughter seemed bound and determined to stay right where she was. Apparently, it was comfortable and warm and she could suck her thumb."

"She sucked her thumb?"

"Constantly."

"In utero?"

"Oh, yes," Mary said, and then explained, "I felt this rhythmic kicking from her, which kept me up most nights in the last trimester. Then after she was born I watched as she sucked her thumb and I realized that was what was happening when I was trying my best to find a comfortable position in which to sleep."

George now had a full-blown smile. "I sucked my thumb until I was five," he admitted. "I had my favorite blanket that I dragged along with me everywhere I went. It drove my father nuts. Mom was smart, though. She washed it every week and cut a small strip away until the blanket was a little more than a ten-inch square."

"Didn't you suspect what she was doing?"

"I had my suspicions. Mom insisted it shrank, and after a few months she told me the washing machine had eaten it."

"Clever woman."

"I hated that washing machine," George said, chuckling. "For years every time I went near it, I'd kick it, until I realized I hurt my foot far more than I did that machine."

How dear he was, Mary thought, as she smiled over at him. Her heart ached with love for him and for the daughter they would never know.

His smile faded. "What did she look like?"

Mary nodded. "Newborns are notoriously ugly. No one will say it, of course, but the birthing process isn't much easier on the baby than it is on the mother."

"Our daughter was ugly?"

"No, that's just it. Despite everything, she was a beauty, George, simply beautiful. I stood outside the nursery window and stared at her for hours."

"Were you"—he hesitated as if unsure how to say what he meant—"sore?"

"No. In fact, I felt amazing. I wanted to pound my chest like

Tarzan and yell at the world, 'Look what I've done.' I don't believe I've ever felt more empowered than after giving birth."

George chuckled a second time and then grew sober. "Did you . . . hold her, or were you required to give her up right away?"

If only he knew. "I held her every chance I got. It was important that I knew in my heart that I was making the right decision. I was bringing a life into this world. A precious life that was part you and part me. It was up to me to give her the very best future that I could, and I had to accept that that future wasn't with me."

Scooting closer, George reached for her hand.

"This pregnancy, this infant, was bigger than just you and me," Mary said, locking her eyes with his.

"Do you know who adopted her?"

"Yes. I personally chose the family."

His eyes widened. "You chose them?"

It'd taken her weeks of reading applications and going over family studies before Mary felt ready to make her final decision. "I went through a private adoption agency. One I had researched extensively and had a flawless reputation."

"Did you meet the . . . parents?"

"No . . . not face-to-face. The option was mine, but I chose not to have an open adoption. In retrospect, I feel I made the right decision."

"How so?"

Mary broke eye contact and looked down. "If I'd had contact," she said, swallowing against the thickness in her throat, "I think I might have been tempted to change my mind and try to nullify the adoption."

"You missed her."

"I didn't sleep through the night for weeks, agonizing over my decision. Then everything changed."

"What happened?"

Mary found it more difficult to tell him than she'd ever thought it would be. So much of what she told George had been buried deep in her psyche. As she relayed the details of the pregnancy, birth, and adoption, more memories floated to the surface, like flecks of snow blowing off a fast-moving car.

This was what had been happening ever since she'd been diagnosed with cancer. It seemed as if someone had hit a speed button and she was hurled into a time machine, with her life whirling forward at an impossible speed.

After handing their daughter to the agency representative who would take the baby to her new family, Mary had suffered with doubts and indecision. For a while she considered seeing a counselor. As a private person, she'd never been comfortable sharing herself with strangers, especially something this personal. In addition, she feared this information would get back to the investment firm where she was employed. Seeing a mental health specialist might give the appearance of weakness, and she dare not risk that.

"Giving our baby up for adoption was harder than you expected, wasn't it?"

She nodded rather than spoke, afraid her voice would give away exactly how difficult that decision had been. After taking a few seconds to regain her self-control, she said, "Everything changed after the agency forwarded a letter to me from the adoptive mother. The family named her Amanda."

Mary had thought to avoid the details, but the more they talked, the more comfortable she became discussing this painful subject. Besides that, George had a right to know.

"Amanda," George repeated slowly, thoughtfully. "I like the name."

"If . . . If I'd raised her, I would have named her Elizabeth."

"Elizabeth. After your mother?"

Mary grinned. "She died long before Amanda was born . . . I

loved my mother; I'm grateful she never knew about my decision; she would have been disappointed in me."

"Don't be so sure; you gave our daughter life," George reassured her.

Mary squeezed his hand, appreciating his words of comfort. "If I needed confirmation that I'd done the right thing, I got it. The adoptive family named her Amanda Elizabeth."

"Oh, Mary."

"I know. Their letter was filled with gratitude and love. I had every assurance I would need that Amanda would be deeply loved and that the family would provide for her emotional, physical, and spiritual well-being. They're good people, George. I chose well."

"Have you heard from the family since that time?"

Mary heard the hopeful tone in his voice. "No. Not once. It was the way I wanted it, for Amanda's sake as well as my own."

"And everything went along smoothly after that?"

"Pretty much."

"Until the cancer," he added.

"Until the cancer," she confirmed.

George knelt down in front of her. His arms circled Mary's waist and held her close to his heart. For a long time they clung to each other.

Neither of them spoke.

George broke the silence, straightened, and pressed his hand against the side of her face. His eyes were warm and gentle, filled with love.

"Thank you," he whispered.

Mary had anticipated disappointment, even anger. His gratitude took her by surprise. "For what?" she asked. She had rejected his love and marriage proposal, and left him. He had every reason to detest her.

"For giving my baby life."

"Oh, George." Wrapping her arms around his neck, she clung to him.

When they broke apart, she wiped the moisture from his cheeks and then smiled as he did the same for her.

Mary was tempted, so very tempted, to tell him the rest.

But she couldn't. Not yet.

Chapter 21

I enjoyed seeing Peggy and Corrie. I waved them off and then sat for a short while on the step, enjoying the sunshine.

Rover lay down in the grass for a while before chasing after a butterfly. I kept a close eye on him, but he seemed to understand that this was his home and where he belonged. Whenever I let him outside, he never ventured far. I suppose I should count myself lucky that he was this well behaved. It made me wonder if he'd been trained by someone . . . someone who missed him and was concerned about what had happened to him. Perhaps one day I'd have the answer to those questions, but for now, I was happy to have him with me.

The mail was delivered, and I decided to check it when I finished setting a few flower pots about the area where one day my rose garden would be.

Afterward I walked down to the mailbox. The majority of the mail was advertisements, an assortment of bills, and a magazine. Only one envelope was hand addressed, and it looked to be a formal announcement. I tore it open and saw that my guess was right. It was a wedding invitation. As soon as I read the names, I smiled.

It was from Abby Kincaid. Abby was one of my very first guests who'd come to stay shortly after I took over the inn in January. She'd arrived for her brother's wedding and seemed withdrawn, reticent, and decidedly uncomfortable. Soon afterward I learned she had been behind the wheel when her best friend, Angela, had been killed in a car accident the year they were college freshmen. From that moment forward, Abby's entire life had been placed on hold. It was as if she'd lived in limbo, avoiding all contact with friends and classmates.

What made this wedding invitation so wonderful was the fact that it confirmed what Paul had told me soon after I moved into the inn. This bed-and-breakfast would be a place of healing, for me and for those who came to stay.

For Abby, returning to Cedar Cove for her brother's wedding had set everything that had happened to her since into motion. The last place on earth she'd ever wanted to be again was this town, fearing whom she'd see. Perhaps even worse was being forced to confront the memories of that horrible winter's night when Angela had died.

"Rover, oh, Rover," I said, in my excitement, "look. Abby and Steve Hooks are to be married."

Rover, who rested next to me on the top step, cocked his head to one side and regarded me quizzically.

"This is wonderful news. Don't you remember her?" It was a silly question, because clearly he didn't have a clue who or what I was talking about. The news was too good to keep to myself.

Leaping up, I hurried into the house, set the mail down on my desk, and reached for the phone. I could think of only one person to tell.

Mark answered almost right away.

"How are you doing?" I asked.

"I was just fine until my nap got interrupted. I hate taking these damn pain pills. They put me to sleep."

"I'm sorry. I woke you?" I asked, feeling guilty.

"You didn't, the phone did. What's up?" he asked.

"I heard from Abby Kincaid."

"Who?"

"Abby. She was one of my first two houseguests back in January."

"Oh, yeah, I remember her. Real quiet . . . was in town for her brother's wedding, right?"

"Right. I received a wedding invitation from her in today's mail." I was more than a bit reluctant to share this news with him, seeing what a grump he was.

"Nice," he said, surprising me. "Is it the guy she met at her brother's wedding? Wasn't he her brother's old college roommate?"

How he knew about that I could only speculate. "Yes. How'd you know?"

"How do I know anything? You told me."

"When?" I certainly didn't remember saying anything about Abby and Steve.

"I don't know, but how else would I know?"

Good question. I must have said something, but I certainly didn't remember.

"What about Josh and Michelle? Do you ever hear anything from them?" Josh had been at the inn at the same time as Abby. Abby and Josh had been my very first guests.

I hadn't. "I saw Michelle in the grocery store not long ago, but it was only in passing."

"They'll get married," Mark said matter-of-factly.

"Oh, and what makes you such an expert on matters of the heart?"

He chuckled.

Actual amusement from Mark? Now, that was a switch. The sound took me by surprise, and it was all I could do not to laugh myself.

"The two of them had the look," Mark explained.

"The look?"

"Didn't Josh stay on a couple of extra days from what he'd originally planned?"

"He did." I had no idea Mark would be so detail oriented when it came to people.

"Thought so."

"It was because of his stepfather, remember? Richard died, and Josh felt obligated to settle Richard's affairs."

"That's the excuse he used. He stayed because of Michelle."

"You chatted with him, and he spilled out his heart to you?" If ever there was a joke, this was it. Neither Mark nor Josh was the type to discuss their personal lives.

"In a manner of speaking, you could say so."

"I don't believe it."

"Believe what you want," he said. "Can I get back to my nap now?"

"By all means." I was ready to hang up the phone when he stopped me.

"Jo Marie."

"Yeah?"

"I hope you'll overlook me being cranky. I didn't mean to snap at you like that."

"You're excused," I said, making light of his bad mood. He was worried that I'd taken offense. It surprised me.

"It's these stupid pills."

"Of course it is," I joked. "If it wasn't for the medication, you'd be a regular Marvin Sunshine."

He chuckled. "I take it that's a bit of sarcasm."

"Just a tad," I said with a smile.

"Listen, I'll do my best to get working on your rose garden as soon as I get out of this cast."

"I know." And I appreciated that he remained concerned about the job. "I'll stop by later this evening and bring you dinner."

"No need. I've got peanut butter and jelly."

"I'll bring you a real dinner," I insisted.

"Peanut butter is real food."

"Right," I agreed, knowing it would do no good to argue with him. "I'll be by sometime after six."

He sighed as if he was far too weary to fight me. "Okay, I give in. Do whatever suits you."

Shaking my head, I docked the phone and picked up Abby's wedding invitation, reading it a second time. The wedding was scheduled for August and would take place in Florida. I brewed myself a cup of coffee and sat down at the small kitchen table.

I remembered the day Abby and I had talked and she'd told me about the car accident that had claimed her best friend's life. The car crash had basically robbed Abby of her future. She'd been dating Steve Hooks at the time and had broken it off with him, partially out of guilt and partially out of a sense of unworthiness. It didn't seem right to her that she should be happy, should fall in love and continue on with her own life when Angela was dead.

The doorbell rang, and Rover barked and rushed to the front door. It was the woman who lived next door. A real sweetheart, Mrs. Coryelle had to be close to eighty. I'd chatted with her daughter several times and had gone to check on the older woman now and again.

"Mrs. Coryelle, come in, please." It was rare for her to venture to my house.

"No, no, I need to get back. One of those cable channels is running an all-day marathon of my favorite TV show and I don't want to miss any of that." She grinned, scratching the side of her head. "I've seen them all before, I know, but for the life of me I can't remember how they end. Best part of my failing memory is being able to enjoy things again as if it's the first time."

"What can I do for you?" I asked. Surely she hadn't made the walk to tell me about television reruns.

"Oh, yes, I nearly forgot," she said, laughing softly. "The mailman put this envelope in my box, but it's addressed to you." She removed it from her pocket and handed it to me.

"Thank you," I murmured, and scanned the return address. It wasn't a name I recognized at first glance, so I set it aside, more concerned about my elderly neighbor than opening the letter.

"Let me walk back with you," I said.

"No need."

"I insist, and so does Rover." I stepped onto the porch, and Rover immediately followed me. It didn't take me long to walk the short distance between our houses. Mrs. Coryelle was a talkative one, and she filled me in on the television marathon, mentioning her favorite characters as if they were her personal friends. She was particularly enamored with Mark Harmon, who played the lead, chatting on and on about him and what a fine-looking man he was. "I might be eighty-three, but I recognize a handsome man when I see one."

"So do I," I returned, remembering how attracted I was to Paul the first time we met.

Once I saw her inside her home, Rover and I made our way back to the inn. I hadn't finished everything I'd hoped in preparation for the open house. In retrospect, I wished I'd delayed mailing out the invitations and had waited until the inn was in the shape I envisioned. I probably would have canceled if several Chamber members hadn't already mentioned how they were looking forward to touring Rose Harbor Inn.

By the time I returned to the house, I'd nearly forgotten the letter. It was Rover who reminded me. He parked himself by the entryway table and barked. It took me a moment to realize what he wanted.

"Oops, you're right, the letter." I said. Thankfully, his memory was a bit longer than mine.

I reached for the envelope and carried it into the kitchen with me, setting it on the tabletop. Because Rover seemed so curious, I sat down and opened it. It was a couple of pages long, with a note attached.

Dear Jo Marie,

    Forgive me. Paul asked me to give you this letter if anything were to happen to him while he was in Afghanistan. I've had it all this time and simply forgot about it. I know it's probably hitting you out of the blue, and for that I apologize.

An illegible name was scribbled at the bottom of the page.

Turning aside the first page, I found a single sheet, a letter addressed to me in my husband's handwriting.

The letter was from Paul.

Chapter 22

Sun poured in over the waterfront gazebo as Annie's grandparents stood holding hands and facing each other as they prepared to renew their wedding vows. Father Donovan looked out over the small gathering and opened his prayer book.

One of Annie's biggest concerns about this anniversary celebration had been the weather. Although she'd never gotten the story straight on exactly where her grandfather had proposed, Annie had gone with her grandmother's version. Even if her grandfather insisted he'd popped the question during a Saturday matinee, the waterfront scene was far more picturesque and practical than renewing their vows in the parking lot at the movie theater.

Kent and Julie were surrounded by their closest friends and immediate family. Annie's mother and father, plus her aunt Patty and uncle Norman, stood in a semicircle around the anniversary couple. Annie and her cousins, along with their young families, were the outer edge.

Oliver stood next to her. She tried to ignore him, but that wasn't as easily accomplished as she would have liked.

The elderly priest looked up from his Bible and smiled at the small gathering. His gaze then rested on Annie's grandparents.

"Kent and Julie, the two of you are prime examples of what it means to love and cherish each other."

Julie turned and looked deep into her husband's eyes. Kent looked back, and Annie's breath caught. Even now she wasn't sure what she'd do if her grandfather started grumbling. Instead, she saw love radiating from him to his wife of the last fifty years. All he seemed to be able to see was Julie, and the love they had shared appeared to touch all who had gathered for this special moment.

The pastor's words were lost on Annie. Frozen, she watched as her grandmother's lips moved, repeating the vows with such heartfelt meaning that her eyes clouded with tears.

Tears sprang to Annie's eyes, too. It was then that she felt Oliver reach for her hand, entwining his fingers with hers and giving her a gentle squeeze. She wanted to jerk her hand free but discovered she couldn't make herself do it. He stood close, too close for her to be comfortable. Instead of stepping aside, the way she wanted, Annie remained exactly where she was. The citrus scent of his aftershave reminded her of oranges and lemons, and of the lazy summer night when she'd gazed up at the night sky with him close to her side on the blanket.

He'd held her hand that night, too. She'd been young, thirteen, and even after all these years, as much as she didn't want to, she thought of that night as one of the most memorable, romantic experiences of her life. She'd thought Oliver was the cutest boy in the universe and had pined after him all that summer.

Annie supposed every girl thought back fondly on her first kiss, holding the memory of it against her heart. Oliver had ruined the moment for her, and she hadn't forgiven him until now. How could she not, when his apology had been heartfelt and sincere?

He'd mentioned that it had been his first kiss, too. She felt his eyes on her, and despite the tumultuous memories of their youth, she met his gaze. The attraction was there, as strong and powerful as it'd been that summer night. It had always been there, she was forced to admit, despite her determined effort to ignore it.

As dreadful as Oliver had been to her, she'd longed for him to kiss her again. Twelve years had passed and nothing had changed. She wanted to close her eyes, tilt up her chin, and receive his kiss. Their eyes held as the ceremony continued. Oliver couldn't help but know what she wanted.

Sucking in a deep breath, he bent his head to claim her lips just as her grandfather all but shouted, "I sure do."

A burst of laughter followed, pulling Annie out of the romantic dream that had somehow woven an invisible web around Oliver and her. Coming to her senses, she removed her hand from his, and after Father Donovan's final words, she applauded long and hard.

Oliver did, too, but not with as much enthusiasm as she did. When he finished, he wrapped his arm around her waist and edged her closer to his side. She sent him a disgruntled look, which he chose to ignore. This attraction wasn't real. It couldn't be.

This thing between Oliver and her was a by-product of breaking off her engagement with Lenny. Some part of her ego, the part that embarrassed her, needed to feel attractive and desirable. Oliver was just the one who happened to be handy. She didn't want to believe that, but it was the only thing that made sense.

The wedding party started to break up, and Oliver reluctantly moved from her side. "I'm driving your grandparents to the reception hall," he said. Still, he didn't move. Reaching for her hand, he raised it to his lips and whispered, "We'll talk later."

"No, we won't," she returned, but he'd already left, and if he heard her, then he pretended he hadn't.

Annie didn't have time to analyze what was going on between her and Oliver. Nor did she want her unwelcome feelings for him to distract her from what was important, and that was celebrating her grandparents' marriage.

The reception was being held at the yacht club just down from the gazebo. It would be easier to walk the short distance than to search out another parking space. The walk, however, would probably be too much for her grandparents, and Oliver had volunteered to transport them.

"Hey, sis, what's with you and Oliver?" her brother, Peter, asked as she headed across the waterfront parking lot.

"Nothing," she answered, a little too brightly.

"Okay, if that's what you say. But I'm not blind. I saw the way the two of you looked at each other while Gramps and Grandma said their vows. For a moment there I thought the two of you were going to kiss right in front of everyone."

"It was your imagination," she insisted, walking at a faster clip now. It mortified her to know others had been watching them. She couldn't help but wonder how many other family members had seen her gaze longingly into Oliver's eyes and practically beg him to kiss her.

"Oliver's a good guy," Peter said, keeping pace with her. "If you decide to marry him, that would be fine by me."

"I'm not marrying Oliver."

Peter abruptly stopped. "Frankly, he'd make you a much better husband than Lenny," her brother said, in what could be described only as hopeful happy anticipation.

"Stop it, Peter," she cried.

"Well, it's true. Lenny's a loser."

"I sort of figured that out on my own." It shocked her that no one in her family had mentioned their feelings about Lenny until after she'd broken off the engagement.

"Well, thank goodness you wised up in time. You don't seem that broken up about it," Peter continued, keeping pace with her.

"It's been six months."

Annie had been too busy to think about her feelings toward Lenny and the fact that he would no longer be part of her life. In that moment, she knew without a doubt she was completely over him, otherwise she wouldn't be this attracted to Oliver.

"What about you and Oliver?" Peter asked. "I mean, he's been stuck on you from the time we were kids."

"Oliver?" She didn't even bother to disguise her shock. "You've got to be kidding."

"You mean you didn't know?"

"No."

"Good grief, are you blind? He pined after you like a lovesick dog most every summer, but you wouldn't have anything to do with him. I was thinking you might have wised up and that is why you two were all goo-goo eyes just now."

"Goo-goo eyes?" she repeated and laughed. She hadn't heard that term in years.

"You can't deny that you were. Oh, wait, you already did. So whatever."

"Whatever," she repeated.

"All I ask is that you give the guy a chance."

"Forget it, Peter."

"Yeah, you're probably right," Peter mumbled. "He's more or less given up on you and heading for the South Pacific. It's a shame, too. He'll probably marry some girl there and never come back."

"Good," she said, but even as she flippantly tossed out the word, her stomach tightened at the thought.

Peter opened the door to the reception hall ahead of her, and

Annie stepped into the room. It took a moment for her eyes to adjust to the lack of light, and when she did, the first thing that came into view was Oliver helping her grandparents. He was so gentle with them, so patient and caring. Her grandfather must have told the same story ten times. It was about an incident that happened aboard his ship while he served in Vietnam. Annie could almost recount it word for word, and yet Oliver had listened intently each time as though this was the first he'd ever heard it.

Then, as if he felt her gaze resting on him, Oliver turned and looked her way. When he saw her, he smiled softly. Julie said something, and he immediately turned his attention back to Annie's grandmother.

Annie couldn't believe what her brother had said was true. Had Oliver really cared for her all these years? Every summer he'd made an effort to talk to her but she'd rebuffed him, convinced he would use the opportunity to win her attention simply so he could embarrass or humiliate her later.

The caterers had arrived, and Annie left to make sure everything was going according to schedule. The reception would take place first for those who could stay only a short while. The three-tiered cake resembled a wedding cake. In addition, Annie had ordered two sheet cakes.

One cake displayed a photo of Kent and Julie on their wedding day fifty years ago. They looked young, happy, and so deeply in love. The second sheet cake had a more recent photo of the couple.

Later in the afternoon the buffet dinner would be served. Annie had reviewed the menu countless times, choosing fresh Northwest ingredients, salmon and then chicken for those who couldn't eat seafood. There were salad greens with sliced early strawberries from California, almonds, and goat cheese. And her grandfather's favorite side dishes: potatoes in three different variations, plus two other salads, fresh green beans, and rolls still warm from the bakery oven.

The party would end with dancing. To this point, the event had gone off without a hitch, and Annie was grateful.

After speaking to the caterers, Annie turned to leave the kitchen and nearly ran headlong into Oliver. He steadied her by gripping her shoulders. Otherwise, she would have stumbled backward.

"Sorry," he said.

Annie's mouth went dry as she stared up at him. Her heart beat like a drum in a rock band. Hard, loud, and strong. It surprised her that no one else could hear it.

"I don't believe it," she said, thinking about the conversation with her brother. If Oliver had a crush on her, her brother would have taken delight in razzing him. She hadn't heard a word, and she'd visited her grandparents practically every summer of her childhood and teen years, until college.

Oliver frowned. "Believe what?"

Annie hadn't realized she'd spoken aloud. Shaking her head, she broke contact and stepped away from him. "Never mind."

"No," he insisted. "Tell me."

Straightening her shoulders, she stared back at him. "I have better things to do than stand here and argue with you."

As though dumbfounded by her behavior, Oliver stepped aside. But before she walked past him, he caught her arm. "What's bothering you?" he asked.

"You," she whispered, knowing she was being unreasonable and unfair. From the moment he'd arrived Oliver had been a huge help to her grandparents and to her. Annie wasn't sure how she expected him to respond, but his smile took her completely by surprise.

"I'm under your skin, then?"

"No . . . Don't you realize we have nothing in common?"

"What do you mean?"

"Okay, if you want me to spell it out, then I will. You're opinionated and stubborn and . . . and that doesn't even scratch the surface."

"And it confuses you because you want me to kiss you again."

"Yes," she cried without thinking, and then decided that his knowing how strongly she was attracted to him wasn't a good idea. "I mean no, absolutely not."

He shook his head as though her answer amused him. "If that's what you want to believe, then go ahead."

"I don't trust you." And really that was the crux of the matter.

Once more, he took hold of her shoulders and turned her so they were eye to eye. "If you don't hear anything else I say, Annie, hear this: I'm not Lenny. Understand?"

She bobbed her head and was eternally grateful when the caterer called her away with a question. Annie more than welcomed the distraction. As she met the other woman, she realized how badly shaken the encounter with Oliver had left her. If the caterer noticed, she didn't comment.

Family and friends started drifting into the reception hall, and soon Annie was busy making sure everyone was greeted. Her grandparents had been adamant that there be no gifts, but if someone felt the urge, then they offered the name of their favorite charity, an organization that helped homeless families. Soon cards stacked the table next to the cakes.

Annie's youngest cousin, Catherine, served the cakes, and another cousin, Eva, was in charge of pouring coffee and tea. Her aunt and uncle, along with her parents, circled the room, visiting and making sure everyone was comfortable.

Her mother and aunt Patty had done a great job of assembling photos of her grandparents through the years. The photographs arranged in albums and displayed in frames around the hall were a big hit.

Earlier in the year, her grandmother had given Annie a few items that had been wedding gifts that she still used. It astonished Annie that her grandmother had not only held on to these gifts but also that they were still in use. Annie had them on display as well, along with the names of those who had gifted them. Her favorite was an apple-shaped cookie jar. The lid had a small chip in it that Peter had put there when he was five, trying to steal a cookie.

Annie was too busy talking with the visitors to pay much attention to Oliver. That was a blessing in disguise. When she couldn't stand it any longer and sought him out, she noticed that he was doing what he could to make sure everyone was comfortable. Had he always been this helpful? she wondered.

Soon the food was being set out for the meal, and once again, Annie headed for the kitchen. She was close to the entrance when Oliver waylaid her.

"I have things I need to do," she said, looking to step around him.

"Fine, but I want it understood that before this day is over the two of us will talk."

"Ah . . ."

"Before this day is over, Annie."

She wanted to argue, but she wasn't given the opportunity. Oliver was already gone.

Chapter 23

Mary was tired. She tried to hide how drained she felt both emotionally and physically, but George knew. Neither one of them had
eaten much lunch. They'd barely touched their food, which had
been so beautifully prepared. Mary ate little because her appetite
was gone, and George because her news had shocked him. They
hadn't spoken again of the child as George absorbed the information.

Hardly able to keep her eyes open, Mary said, "It's time I head
back to the ferry."

"No," he said instantly.

"George, I'm sorry . . . my strength . . ."

"I'm not taking you to the ferry," he insisted.

"But . . ."

"I'll drive you back myself."

"Cedar Cove is a good hour's drive, possibly longer. That's a two-to-three-hour commute for you. I can't let you do that." George had always been so thoughtful, so loving, and the years hadn't changed him.

"I don't care how long the drive is, you're not taking the ferry."

"George, please." Surely he understood how difficult this was for her, and she wasn't talking about the cancer. Being with him, loving him the way she did, made this visit painful and difficult.

"I can't let you go," he said. "Not yet. Not when I have so much I need to learn about Amanda."

This was what Mary had feared. He would ask her questions that were better left unasked, and he would do it when she was at her weakest point emotionally. George was the only man who had ever broken through the natural reserve that had always been a part of her.

George Hudson was the only man who had ever made her feel weak, and at the same time he was her strength. Mary couldn't explain this phenomenon. His love made her weak because with him her heart was vulnerable; he made her believe they could be together despite the fact that they lived separate lives. At the same time, his love made her strong. With him, she'd come to understand contentment and joy. She could be herself. He'd been the only man to break through the hard shell of professionalism that had dominated her life. Who could understand how one man was capable of bringing out both weakness and strength in her? Not Mary.

Try as she might, and she did try, Mary couldn't talk him out of personally delivering her back to the Inn at Rose Harbor. He escorted her to his car, helped her inside, and then left the parking garage and drove into the heavy Seattle traffic.

For the first ten minutes, neither spoke.

Then, out of the blue, George asked, "Did the adoptive parents ever mail you her picture?"

Mary tensed. "No."

"Why not?"

So it was to begin. Mary waited to answer for so long he glanced in her direction. She swallowed tightly and then whispered, her voice so low she wondered if he could hear, "I asked them not to."

She watched as George's hands tightened around the steering wheel. "Weren't you curious?"

A rogue tear slid a moist trail down her cheek. "Oh, yes, I was curious."

"Then why . . ."

"I did my best not to think about her," she said, rushing to explain. "I tried to let her go completely."

Another lengthy pause followed as they entered the freeway on-ramp. "Did you . . . forget her?"

"No." Mary looked out the side window and hoped he didn't notice when she wiped more tears away. She couldn't allow herself the luxury of thinking about her daughter. Their daughter.

It was pointless to hide anything from George. He reached for her hand and gently squeezed it. "Oh, Mary, my beautiful, smart Mary, I'm sorry. This is painful for you. It's just that—"

"No, I understand," she said, interrupting him, because she did understand. This was all new to him. It was only natural that he would want to know everything. "I hit you with this and you haven't had a chance to absorb it, while I've been living with this secret for the past eighteen years."

Seeing how his questions had upset her, George fell silent. She had deprived him of so much already that Mary felt obligated to tell him what she remembered.

"When she was born, she had a head full of curly dark hair."

He smiled and patted his bald spot. "Guess she didn't get that from my side of the family."

"They say that it's impossible to tell what color a newborn's eyes will be, but hers were blue."

"Like yours."

"Like mine," she whispered.

Quiet again. "Anything else you can tell me about our . . . daughter?"

Mary remembered everything, every minute detail of the babe she'd held so briefly in her arms. "Both her little fingers were slightly crooked."

"A sign of genius for sure," George said, a smile in his voice.

"No doubt," Mary said, grinning herself. "And, George, she had the cutest, tiniest toes."

"As I recall, you have beautiful feet."

George said the funniest things. "Oh, George, honestly."

"Well, you do."

Mary remembered how he used to place her feet on his lap and would rub her toes after a long day at the office. It had been sensual and romantic all at once.

He glanced at her, and from the smile that teased his lips, she knew he remembered, too.

"I'm grateful she inherited your feet and not mine," he muttered.

"Why's that?" Mary couldn't remember what George's feet looked like.

"I've got stubby toes."

"I never noticed."

"Good. I guess you were too blinded by my stunningly handsome features to pay attention to my feet."

"Clearly, that was it." Even now George could make her smile.

"You find that amusing, do you?"

"Oh, yes."

"Anything else I can tell you that will make you smile?" he asked. "You've done precious little of that this afternoon."

She grinned again. George made her feel comfortable and relaxed. With him there were no pretenses; she could be herself.

"Do you still think about her?" he asked, growing serious once again.

"Of course I do." How could she not? "I might not have raised our daughter, but she'll always be a part of me."

"And me," he added.

"The very best of us both." Mary was certain of that. "On her birthday . . ." She hesitated and swallowed against the hard lump that had formed in her throat.

"Yes?"

"I celebrated her birthday every year. No matter where I was or what I was doing, I had a little ceremony for the two of us . . ." It was time to be honest, really honest. "For the three of us," she corrected.

"You thought of me, too?"

"Oh, George, did you really think I could forget you?"

"Yes," he said, his voice tight with pain. "You cut off all contact with me, remember?"

She didn't need the reminder. Of course she had regrets. But then, who didn't? It would fill a dump truck if she were to dredge up the past and some of the decisions she'd made. But when it came to the choice she'd made for their daughter, Mary had no reservations. She'd done what was right for Amanda Elizabeth.

"What did you do to remember, to celebrate?" he wanted to know.

"You'll think it lame and predictable."

"Mary Smith doing something predictable? I don't think so."

Just to prove him wrong, she stuck out her tongue at him.

George laughed. "Are you going to tell me or not?"

"Oh, all right. I ate cake."

"What kind of cake?"

"German chocolate."

He grinned sheepishly. "My favorite. You tried to bake me a chocolate cake once."

Again, she didn't need the reminder. The entire experience had been a disaster. If any proof was ever needed that she was never meant to darken the inside of a kitchen, that was it. She'd spent a fortune getting everything she needed at a high-end home-goods store, purchased the very best of ingredients, and then painstakingly followed the recipe.

For whatever reason, the cake had fallen flat, but that wasn't the worst of it. After piling four layers of cake and frosting together, the entire monstrosity had unceremoniously slid from the plate onto the floor. George had claimed he loved her all the more for the attempt. The next day, Mary had given everything she'd purchased to charity.

The car was warm, and after a couple of moments she felt herself drifting off to sleep.

"Rest," he whispered, and gently patted her thigh.

Mary fought it. She didn't want to waste a moment of this weekend. Not a single moment. When she flew back to New York, she would hold on to this day, review it again and again in her mind. She would always hold on tight to the memory of the look that came over George when she told him she hadn't aborted their baby and that she'd delivered his daughter. It was a look of pain mingled with profound joy, as if he wasn't sure which emotion would take dominance. Pain for all the years he had lost not knowing his child, and joy, sheer, undiluted joy, that she had given birth to his daughter.

In that moment, Mary made the decision. "George?" She said his name, barely able to speak.

"Yes."

"Is there an exit close by?"

Immediately, he was concerned. "What's wrong? Do I need to get you to a hospital?"

"No."

His stricken face searched hers. "Are you feeling ill?"

"I'm okay." She wasn't, but this had nothing to do with the cancer.

He swerved across two lanes of traffic so abruptly that he cut off another driver, which caused several other cars to blast their horns at him. "What do you need me to do?" he implored.

"George. Don't panic. I just want to talk to you."

"I thought we were talking." His words were rushed, harried, frantic.

Despite the urgency in his voice, Mary remained cool and calm. "We are talking, but there's more."

"More about . . ."

"Amanda Elizabeth."

He took the exit at nearly double the speed posted, and when he pulled to a stop at the red light, the seat belt tightened and held her in place as the car rocked forward. He went to the first available parking area, pulled in, and shut off the engine.

"Okay, tell me," he said. "Whatever it is, I have a right to know."

"I . . ." Her throat closed up on her, and once again she looked out the side window while she composed herself.

"No matter what it is, I need to know."

She swallowed again, lubricating her throat. "When I found out I had cancer . . . I felt the urgency to get my affairs in order."

"Of course." He reached for her hand, holding it tightly within his own.

"A large portion of my estate will go to charity."

George didn't comment, as if it was too painful for him to discuss these details. It hadn't been easy for Mary, either. She was relatively young yet, and she'd felt she had a number of years to think these matters through. Oh, she'd completed the most rudimentary basics of her estate, but not the details. Being hit in the face with cancer had put everything into sharp focus and changed her perspective.

"I wanted to be sure Amanda would always have what she needed."

Again, George said nothing. It seemed like he was holding his breath, waiting for what she would tell him before he was comfortable enough to exhale.

"I came to Seattle."

"I'm so glad you did, so grateful." Both of his hands held one of hers now.

"But, George, my dear, wonderful George, finding that you still lived here was a bonus, a gift."

His gaze delved into hers as it dawned on him what she was telling him, what she was really saying. For a long moment, George went still and quiet as his shock rippled though the interior of the vehicle.

"Are you . . . Are you saying our daughter . . . Are you telling me the couple who adopted our daughter lives in Seattle?"

"No."

George frowned.

"They live in Cedar Cove."

He blinked as if he hadn't heard her. "Cedar Cove," he repeated. "How do you know?"

She looked away. "I hired a private investigator."

"Amanda is happy and healthy?"

"Very much so. She's beautiful, George. Smart and beautiful."

He smiled, and the hold on her hand tightened. "Like I said before, she's like her mother."

"The curly hair is gone, and just as I suspected, her eyes are blue."

He touched Mary's face, cupping her chin. "Then you've seen her?"

"Not yet. What I saw was a photograph."

"Where?"

"There were a couple of photos on the Internet from newspaper articles regarding school functions."

"Will you see her personally?"

"No, I don't suppose I will. I'd like to more than anything, but I won't disrupt her life. I can't."

"Yet you came to Cedar Cove."

"Yes," she whispered. "I came because I thought . . . I hoped that I might be able to hear her speak."

"Speak?" George frowned.

And then, with sadness mingled with pride, Mary added, "Our daughter will graduate from high school Sunday afternoon."

"Cedar Cove High School?"

Mary nodded, and with pride that flooded her eyes with tears, she added, "Like me, Amanda is the valedictorian of her class."

Chapter 24

I clenched Paul's letter in my hands and stared down at the message scrawled across the top in my husband's stark handwriting: TO BE GIVEN TO JO MARIE IN THE EVENT OF MY DEATH.

I remained frozen, unable to move. I didn't breathe, I didn't blink; all I seemed capable of doing was staring down at Paul's words. The last words he would ever say to me.

I should read this letter. I knew that in all probability my husband was dead. But until I received absolute verification that his remains had been found and identified, I refused to read what would be his final words to me. Hurriedly, I folded up the letter and tucked it back inside the envelope. It seemed to throb in my hands, pulsing and pounding.

I hurried to my room with such urgency that Rover barked furiously and charged ahead of me. When I arrived, I was panting and breathless, my shoulders heaving with both emotion and exertion. Opening the drawer to my nightstand, I reached for my journal and slipped the letter inside.

Until someone could assure me that the missing body wasn't that of my husband, I wouldn't give up the possibility that Paul Rose was alive. Hope was a heady commodity, and I clung to it with desperation, letting myself hold on to the dream that the impossible had happened and Paul had managed to live.

Stepping back from my nightstand, I clenched my hands together to help stop the trembling. I drew in a deep breath, closed my eyes, and tried to center myself. I had an inn full of guests, but I would be forever grateful that the house was currently empty.

As if to remind me I couldn't give in to my emotions, the phone rang, jarring me back to reality. I waited until the third ring before I felt composed enough to answer.

"Rose Harbor Inn," I said, as calmly as my pounding heart would allow.

"Jo Marie?"

Mark. "Yes."

"You don't sound right. Is anything wrong?"

"No."

He hesitated, swore under his breath, and then muttered, "I need help."

If anyone didn't sound like himself, it was Mark. His voice was low and gravelly, filled with frustration and dread. "What's wrong?"

Again he paused, as if asking anyone to come to his aid was miles outside his comfort zone. "I tripped with these blasted crutches, and I can't seem to get myself off the floor."

It was time to put aside my own personal struggles and help a friend. "I'll be right over."

"I wouldn't have called you if it wasn't necessary."

"I know."

"You're the one who keeps butting in to my life, and I thought . . ."

"Do you want my help or not?" I snapped, losing patience with him.

"It's either you or call nine-one-one again."

"I'm on my way." Before he could argue further, I replaced the phone. Really, I had never met a more unreasonable human being. At least this time he had his cell phone with him. The doctor, Mark had told me, had suggested he keep his cell close, in case something like this happened. That had proved to be good advice.

"Come on," I said to Rover. "Mr. Personality has fallen and he can't get up."

Rover cocked his head and looked up at me as though my words puzzled him. Nevertheless, he dutifully followed me. When I entered the laundry room, he immediately recognized that we were going out, and he trotted to the door and patiently waited for me to join him and attach his leash.

Once we reached the street and he realized the direction we were headed, Rover strained against the leash. He liked Mark, which confused me, because Mark wasn't all that likable. My dog seemed to have a special affinity for the handyman that I found difficult to understand. Normally, Rover felt it his dog-given duty to mark his territory every few feet, but he seemed to sense the urgency in me and dragged me along.

When we reached Mark's house, I didn't knock. It wasn't like Mark could answer the door. But when I tried to open it, I found it locked. Oh, great, so we were going to go through this again.

I pounded on the door. "Are you there?" I shouted.

"No, I'm outside playing tiddlywinks," Mark shouted back from the other side.

"The door is locked. Do you have a key hidden somewhere outside?" I looked around for the normal hiding places, a flower pot, a fake rock, but the porch was bare.

"No."

If Mark assumed I'd be willing to find an open window and hoist myself inside, then he was sadly mistaken. As much as he'd hate it, I'd contact the fire station that had come to his aid earlier.

"I think the back door might be unlatched," Mark suggested, yelling again.

"Okay, I'll try that."

Rover and I made our way to the back of the property, where his shop was situated. A cement walkway curved slightly between the two buildings. Four steps led to the house. I'd been through the back door only once, and that was when I'd been in a frantic search to find the keys to unlock his door the last time around.

To my relief, the door handle turned, and I stepped into a mudroom, something I hadn't noticed on my first visit.

"Where are you?" I called when I walked from the mudroom into the kitchen.

"Hallway."

The one word was clipped and impatient, as if he was upset it had taken me so long. Sure enough, he was sprawled out in the narrow hallway. His crutches were askew at an awkward angle several feet away. I frowned and then scooted down and sat next to him on the hardwood floor.

"Are you going to tell me how this happened?"

"No."

"Why not?"

"You'll gloat."

"Oh?"

"That's what women do. They take pleasure in telling a man 'I told you so.'"

"Really?" I found his attitude more amusing than irritating, but then, he was on the ground and unable to stand, while I, on the other hand, was free to move any which way I wanted.

"Don't try to deny it." He scowled at me as if I'd been the one responsible for this latest fiasco.

"In your vast experience with women, you know this for a fact?"

"Yes. Now, are you going to help me or not?"

"I'm thinking about it." I was enjoying this, probably far more than I should.

As if to prove how cruel I was being, Rover walked up to Mark and licked his face. I expected the handyman to shoo him away, but he didn't. Instead, Mark tucked his free arm around Rover and brought him close to his side. "At least I can count on us men sticking together."

Without a lot of grace, I got back on my feet and picked up his crutches. It looked to me as if he'd tossed them down the hall in frustration, but seeing how grouchy he was, I decided against asking.

"I can't stand using those as leverage," Mark growled, frowning. "I already tried. Several times."

"So you really have fallen and you can't get up." I couldn't resist.

His scowl darkened. "If you find this so amusing, you can go home right now."

"Testy, testy," I murmured, wagging my finger at him. I stepped behind him and looped my arms under his and tried to hoist him upright. Mark wasn't a big man, but he wasn't easy to lift, either.

"Stop," he all but shouted. "You'll hurt your back doing it that way."

"Do you have a better idea?" I asked.

Exhausted, I slumped down on the floor next to him. I held my hand against my forehead as I tried to figure out the best way to get him back on his feet.

"You okay?" he asked, studying me.

"Yeah. Give me a minute to think this through." His scrutiny was uncomfortable. It seemed as if he was looking straight through me. He was exhausted and short-tempered. One look told me how difficult it was for him to ask for help.

"You didn't sound like yourself when I called," he commented, still watching me closely. "Did I, you know, interrupt anything?"

"Like what?"

He shrugged. "I don't know? A visitor?"

"No." Generally, I was more forthcoming with information, but I didn't feel I could mention Paul's letter.

Mark frowned at me.

"What?" I asked, pretending nothing was amiss.

"Something's wrong. I can sense it," he insisted.

"What are you, psychic now?" I snapped, unable to hide my irritation.

His eyes widened at my heated response. "No."

I realized that I'd given myself away, and tried to cover it with an excuse. "It's probably the open house. I've never done anything like this before, and I'm a bit out of sorts."

"A bit?" he challenged, arching one brow.

I slapped his upper arm. "Listen, buddy, I could walk away right now and leave you here for the next twenty-four hours, so show some appreciation."

He didn't take my threat seriously. "Let's try this again," he said, sitting up straighter. "Instead of you trying to lift me, let me use your arm for leverage."

His idea worked, but it wasn't easy. By the time Mark was back on his feet, we were both so exhausted one would think we'd been scaling the sides of Mount Rainier.

With Mark leaning against the wall, I handed him the crutches. He hobbled into the living room and collapsed onto his recliner. I needed to rest myself, and slumped onto the sofa. Rover leapt up and rested his chin on my thigh. I slowly petted him while I caught my breath.

On a small table alongside his chair was a knife and a pile of wood shavings. I had no idea Mark did whittling. Whatever he was working on seemed intricate.

"What's that going to be?" I asked. Clearly it was a bird sitting on a tree branch.

"An eagle."

We certainly had plenty of those around Cedar Cove. "It's beautiful. Do you sell these pieces?" It would be perfect for a spot on my bookcase in my room.

"It's yours," he said starkly. "I'm making it for you."

I jerked my head up and hardly knew what to say.

"I have to do something or I'll go stark raving mad. You've been great through all this and I've been a jerk. I wanted to thank you."

Again, I was dumbfounded. This thoughtfulness came from a side of Mark I'd never seen. "Thank you."

"Don't go all soft on me now. It's been a while since I did anything like this, so there's no guarantee how it's going to turn out."

"I'll treasure it."

His reply was a gruff, dismissive snort, as if he was embarrassed.

"Can I get you anything before I leave?" I asked after a couple of moments.

He shook his head.

"What about dinner? Do you want me to set it out for you?"

"No, thanks."

I started to leave, but Mark stopped me before I reached the kitchen. "You aren't going to tell me, are you?"

I turned back.

"It's about Paul, isn't it? My guess is that you heard back from that officer friend of his."

I stiffened. "No."

"Then it's because you didn't hear back."

"I really don't want to talk about this, okay? I don't pry into your private life."

He raised both arms as though I'd pointed a gun in his direction. "Sorry."

"It's none of your business," I continued, my voice quivering. "Leave it alone." With Rover at my heels, I marched out through the kitchen.

As if to punctuate my departure, Rover turned back and barked once at Mark, and then trotted after me.

By the time I reached the house I realized how badly shaken Paul's letter had left me. Mark was painstakingly making me a gift and I'd snapped at him and left in a huff.

Rover sensed something was wrong as well, and whined softly as I put on water for tea. I enjoyed both coffee and tea, but when I was upset or out of sorts I chose tea. If ever there was a time I needed comfort, it was now.

Sitting in the kitchen, with a teapot next to my china cup, I closed my eyes. Despite my best efforts, my thoughts refused to leave the letter. The last piece of communication I might ever receive from my husband.

What had Paul said to me?

Did I want to know?

Curiosity was strong, but if I gave in and read the letter I would be as good as admitting hope was lost. I refused to do that.

The lump that formed in my throat made it almost impossible to sip the tea. If anyone were to return to the house now, I wouldn't be able to hide my emotions.

What I'd told Mark about the open house was true. I'd never

done anything like this before, and I was nervous. Frankly, I wasn't sure I'd be able to pull it off.

Seeing that I'd already dispersed the invitations, it was too late to cancel, especially at the last minute like this. Yet here I was, an emotional mess. The more I thought about it, the more upset I got.

Unable to remain still, I scooted out of the chair and started pacing the kitchen while rubbing my palms together. Rover was in his bed, and his head followed my movements.

Not knowing what else to do, I walked into my office and reached for the phone, although I didn't know whom I could call. Not my family. My parents worried about me enough as it was, and I didn't want to add to their concern. While I had friends in Seattle, good friends, I wasn't sure this was something I could talk to them about.

Clenching the phone in my hand, I continued circling the kitchen. My thoughts whirled at an incredible speed while I tried to reason out the best course of action. If there were any.

Then I remembered something I'd heard. Someone I knew right here in Cedar Cove. Someone who would understand. A woman I had met soon after I'd made the move. A woman I liked a great deal, and who had gone through something similar, although completely different. Her husband had disappeared, and it'd taken more than a year for her to discover where he'd gone and what he'd done. Perhaps she could offer me advice. I needed to look up the phone number, so I took care of that in short order.

With a push of the button, the line connected. It was picked up almost right away. "Cedar Cove Library."

"Grace Harding, please."

Chapter 25

Annie remained busy through the dinner buffet, making sure all the food was fresh and hot. Working with the caterers, she carted the food onto the warming trays and worked in the kitchen. As soon as the buffet line dwindled, Annie greeted her grandparents' most recent guests whom she didn't immediately recognize while refilling cups with coffee or tea. Oliver made himself useful as well, she noticed, although she tried to pretend he wasn't in the room.

All the while she couldn't help thinking about the conversation she'd had with her brother. She wondered if what Peter had told her could possibly be true. Of course, all this talk of Oliver having a crush on her could be a figment of his overactive imagination. Peter had always been something of a pest, especially when they were kids. He might have made the whole thing up in order to stir up trouble. Annie immediately dismissed that thought. Peter was nothing like that these days. He was a husband, father, and responsible employee. They got along great.

The band came onto the stage and played a medley of songs from her grandparents' era. Annie recognized several as classics, many of which she enjoyed.

It wasn't long before her grandfather stood and reached for Julie's hand. Her grandmother protested, her hand against her chest, and shook her head, but Kent bent forward and whispered something in her ear. Julie laughed, and then without a word of complaint stood and took her husband's arm.

Annie watched, transfixed, as her grandfather led her grandmother onto the dance floor and brought her into his arms. With more energy than she would have expected, Kent whirled his bride of fifty years around the dance floor. Annie couldn't ever remember seeing the two of them dance. They were fabulous; their steps synchronized perfectly. Annie didn't know if they'd taken classes, but they appeared to be in such harmony with each other that all she could do was stare. She wasn't alone. The entire room watched, mesmerized.

At the end of the song, Annie set down the coffeepot and clapped wildly. She wasn't the only one. The entire roomful of guests spontaneously broke into applause. Her grandfather bowed, and in gentlemanly fashion escorted his wife back to their table.

While other couples stood to dance, Annie started carting the dirty dishes into the kitchen. The next time she looked up, she saw her grandparents on the stage with the band. Both had tambourines and were slapping them across their open palms to the beat of the music. Amazed at their energy, Annie hurried back into the kitchen with another armload.

Oliver stopped her on her return trip to the hall.

"Enough," he said, while his hands cupped her shoulders.

She blinked up at him.

"Let the staff do the work you hired them to do."

"But . . ."

"Come and enjoy the party."

Her mother and aunt Patty had said the same thing to her twice already. Annie knew they were right. She smiled and nodded. "Okay."

"Good." Oliver reached for her hand and led the way, weaving in and around tables in a crooked, meandering path.

"Where are you taking me?"

"To the dance floor."

Annie hadn't danced in years. The last time she could remember had been while she was still in high school. Her skills were nowhere close to what her grandparents could do. She was sure to look foolish.

"I . . ."

"No excuses."

"Oliver," she protested, reluctance causing her to drag her feet.

He ignored her objection and pulled her along until they were on the outskirts of the other dancing couples. Thankfully, the song ended just as he turned to take her in his arms.

"This isn't a great idea," she felt obliged to tell him.

He arched his brows in question. "Why not?"

She bit into her lower lip and looked down. "The truth is, I'm not a very good dancer."

"You don't need to be. Just follow me."

"What are you going to do?"

The music started up again before Oliver had the chance to answer. Annie groaned when she realized it was a slow love song. This was even worse than a fast number.

Oliver reached for her and gently brought her into his arms, wrapping one arm around her waist and gripping her hand. After a couple of moments he whispered in her ear, "Relax. I'm not going to bite you."

While that was true, she wouldn't put it past him to nibble on her earlobe. She made a sincere effort to release the tension that held her in its grip. Not only was this unfamiliar territory, but this was Oliver. Despite that, after a few moments she grew more comfortable.

"See, it's not so bad, is it?" Oliver whispered again.

"Not so bad," she echoed. He made it easy for her to follow, and he stayed with the basic dance steps.

"Ready?" he asked, as the tempo picked up.

"Ready for what?" She was almost afraid to ask.

Tightening his grip on her waist, he started to whirl around the room in sweeping circles, taking her with him.

Annie gasped, strengthening her grip around him. "What are you doing?" she asked in a panic.

"Dancing."

"Well, don't."

He chuckled as though her comment amused him. "We're doing great."

The song continued, and Annie sighed with gratitude when he effortlessly returned to the slow, uncomplicated steps he'd used earlier. Again, it wasn't hard to follow his lead. He made it far too easy to find comfort in his arms.

Because she was curious, she asked, "Where'd you learn that whirling move?"

"You won't believe me if I told you."

"You took dancing lessons?" Oliver didn't seem the type.

"In a manner of speaking, you could say that."

In a manner of speaking? Either he did or he didn't. She looked up at him and found his eyes twinkling with mischief. "Are you going to tell me?"

"If you must know, your grandfather is the one who taught me that little trick."

"You danced with my grandfather?"

"No." Oliver laughed. "According to him, it was the technique he used to sweep your grandmother off her feet."

"I imagine you've used that little dance-floor maneuver before on other unsuspecting partners," she said, enjoying teasing him.

Oliver's finger touched her cheek, turning her face toward him. "No."

"No?"

"Only with you, Annie, only with you."

This was information she didn't want to hear. She looked away and did her best to ignore the soothing warmth she felt in his embrace. As much as she didn't want to feel anything for the boy, now the man, she'd spent the last ten years despising, Annie did. The sexual current between them was strong, arcing with every move and impossible to ignore. At thirteen, she'd been crazy about him, and here she was, as an adult, and that same euphoric high hit her all over again.

The song ended, and Oliver reluctantly released her. Annie used the opportunity to step away from him. He was about to say something when a distant preteen relative raced up to him.

"Dance with me, okay?" Tammy Lee pleaded, and grabbed hold of his hand with both of her own. "Twirl me around the way you did Annie."

Oliver chuckled and said, "Now, that's an invitation I can't refuse."

"My turn next!" another cousin cried.

It was apparent that Oliver would be occupied for the next several minutes. Annie was grateful for the breather, and not because she was winded. Her head whirled with what was happening between her and Oliver, and she had yet to sort it out.

Her grandparents were seated at their table now, and seeing that they were alone, Annie joined them.

"Oh, Annie," her grandmother said, patting the seat of the empty chair next to her. "Sit with us for a few minutes."

Her grandfather scooted closer, and his gaze was warm and sincere when he spoke: "This has been a lovely party."

"It's been just perfect," her grandmother concurred. "More than either Kent or I had imagined . . . above all our expectations."

"I'm honored to do this for you," Annie told them, and she was. A lot of hours and hard work had gone into this special anniversary party. She'd stressed over every detail. But it had been worth it a hundred times over just to see the way her grandparents' eyes had lit up when they walked into the reception. They'd been shocked and amazed to see so many of their family and friends awaiting their arrival.

Julie looked toward Kent. "I don't know why we were so worried."

"We're just a pair of old fools," her grandfather muttered, leaning closer to Annie.

"Speak for yourself," her grandmother teased.

Annie soaked in their praise. "I have to say I had no idea the two of you were such wonderful dancers."

"Oh, it's really Kent who's fast on his feet," her grandmother was quick to tell her. "Back in the day, all the girls wanted to dance with him."

Without meaning to, Annie's gaze found Oliver on the dance floor with her young cousin, who gazed up at him adoringly.

"I see you notice that Kent isn't the only one who's got some fancy footwork," her grandmother commented, her eyes following Annie's.

That reminded Annie of what Oliver had told her. "Oliver said you're the one who taught him how to sweep a woman off her feet," Annie said to her grandfather.

Kent chuckled. "He told you that, did he?"

"He claimed it was that dance move that won you Grandma's heart."

"Kent," her grandmother protested.

"Well, it was."

Julie leaned forward. "I am not that fickle, Annie. Don't you believe your grandfather for one moment. While it is true that Kent could dance circles around any other boy I ever dated, my falling in love with him had nothing to do with his moves on the dance floor."

"You're denying it?" Annie's grandfather asked, his question full of challenge.

"Well, okay, to be fair, I was impressed by what a great dancer he is, but it was his eyes that really won me over."

Kent frowned. "My eyes?"

"I found them absolutely adorable. Still do," her grandmother confessed with a soft sigh.

Instead of being pleased, Annie's grandfather frowned and scratched the side of his head. "Well, that certainly comes as a surprise."

"For heaven's sake, Kent, after fifty years you should have been able to figure that out."

"Guess you're right," he murmured, although he continued to frown.

"That's a compliment, Grandpa," Annie said, surprised by his reaction.

"I know. It's just that I told Oliver . . ." He snapped his mouth closed as if he'd said more than he'd intended to.

"What did you tell Oliver?" her grandmother asked.

Annie was curious herself. "Yes, what did you tell Oliver?"

Kent shook his head as if it was of no concern. "We chatted about women in general. Oliver asked me a few questions, and I answered him as best I could."

"Kent!"

"He wanted my advice when it came to Annie here."

"Kent!" Her grandmother's eyes widened. "You told me whatever happened or didn't happen between Annie and Oliver was none of our affair and I should stay out of it."

Annie's gaze shot between her grandfather and her grandmother. "What are you two talking about?"

They ignored her. "Oliver said he wanted a marriage that would last fifty years, the same as the two of us, and asked my advice."

"It sounds to me like you wandered down the same path you insisted I not take," her grandmother said, and appeared none too pleased.

"He wanted specifics."

"Specifics?" Annie asked, wanting details herself.

"Yes. Like how did I convince Julie to fall in love with me? I thought it was my dancing, but apparently I got it wrong."

"You old fool, it was a lot more than that. You were thoughtful and loving."

"And my sister, God rest her soul, fed you information."

"True," her grandmother admitted, somewhat reluctantly.

"So what does it hurt if I answer Oliver's questions about Annie?"

"Well, seeing that it's Annie . . ."

The two of them spoke as if they'd completely forgotten that Annie was sitting only a couple of feet away.

"Hey, you two. Remember me?"

"Of course," her grandmother said, without looking at her. She stretched out her arm and patted Annie's knee. "Just be patient while your grandfather and I settle this. Kent Shivers, it seems to me you've been something of a hypocrite."

Her grandfather did look slightly guilty. "We both want the same thing—we just have different methods."

While her grandparents became involved in their discussion, Annie didn't notice that the music had stopped. When next she looked up, Oliver was standing at her side.

"I believe this dance is mine," he said, and held out his hand to her.

Without even realizing what she was doing, Annie rose to her feet, her gaze holding his.

Oliver's arms went around her, and she pressed the side of her face against his chest. It felt good to be in his arms. Right.

"It is true, isn't it?" she said, more to herself than to question him.

Oliver kissed the top of her head. Even without knowing what she asked about, he answered, "Every word."

Chapter 26

I was barely able to distract myself until Grace arrived. I'd spoken briefly with the librarian, although I hadn't given her any of the details of why I'd called. She must have heard the anxiety in my voice, because right away she promised to visit as soon as the Saturday movie finished. It would be over in less than an hour.

I felt mildly guilty for bothering her in the middle of the afternoon event, but she'd assured me it wasn't a problem. Rover, my constant and faithful companion, sat with me as I waited.

When I heard a car door close, I walked around to the front of the porch and was grateful to see it was Grace. Her pace quickened when she saw me. Although she was several years older than me, probably close to my mother's age, I considered her a friend. If not for Grace, I wouldn't have Rover. She wore a denim jumper over a long-sleeved red turtleneck shirt.

As she approached, she held out both hands to me. "Jo Marie, is everything all right? You sounded so upset."

I could lie and tell her everything was hunky-dory, but it wasn't, and I was unable to pretend otherwise.

"Do you have time to talk for a few minutes?" I asked, instead of answering her question.

"Of course."

We sat down right where we were on the porch steps. She continued to hold my hands, and Rover, my wonderful Rover, sensed my distress and pressed his chin against my thigh.

"Do you mind if I ask you a couple of questions first?" I asked.

"You can ask me anything," Grace assured me, and then laughed softly. "Well, anything within reason."

"Your first husband died?"

Sadness bled into her eyes, and a faraway look stole over her. "His name was Dan, and we were married nearly thirty years."

"I heard . . ." I sincerely hoped I wasn't bringing up a time so painful that it was difficult to speak of it.

"What did you hear?" Grace pressed.

"Mark told me Dan was missing for several months before you knew he was dead."

The sad look in her eyes deepened. "He was missing for over a year."

"A year . . . and did you hold out hope that he was alive during that time?" I couldn't help asking, wanting so desperately to believe in my own situation.

"Oh, yes, I was convinced of it. Dan had left like this before, a couple of times, actually. He'd disappear for a day or two without a word. The first time I panicked, not knowing what to think. Because I was worried out of my mind, I called the sheriff and reported him missing. When he returned, Dan was furious with me."

Grace's circumstances were completely different than my own, but the feelings she experienced, not knowing one way or the other, were achingly familiar. This was the nightmare I had been living with ever since I'd gotten the phone call from Lieutenant Colonel Milford.

"The next time he disappeared, it was for much longer. In a short period of time, he returned to the house twice. Both times it was while I was at work."

"How'd you know? Were things missing from the house?"

"Not that I noticed, at least not right away."

I could see this was difficult for her, bringing up memories Grace would rather forget, and I was sorry to cause her to relive all this again. "If you'd rather not talk about . . ."

"No, it's fine."

I thanked her with a small smile.

"It's funny," she said. "Not humorous funny, but a weird sort of funny. The minute I walked into the house, I sensed Dan had been there. I even called out his name, thinking he was back. I stood in the middle of the room and waited for him to reply. He'd vanish for a few days, then return and act as if nothing had happened, as if he hadn't been gone for two nights or longer and I should just ignore the fact that he'd disappeared."

"So when he was gone for an extended period of time, longer than a couple of days, did you have any idea where he'd gone or what had happened to him?"

She smiled, but I could see it wasn't one of amusement. "I assumed he'd left me for another woman."

"What made you think that?"

"A couple of things. First off, I found his wedding band. He'd left that behind, as if casting me aside, dismissing our wedding vows. A month or so after he disappeared the last time, I found a charge on our credit card from a jeweler I didn't know. I was so angry. I contacted the jewelry store, but all they could tell me was what he'd purchased: a ring. I assumed the jewelry was for another woman. What hurt was the fact that he'd left me to pay for it."

"Was it for someone else?"

Grace clenched her hands together. "Not until later did I learn he'd bought himself another wedding band. Apparently, he thought he'd lost the one I'd found, and he wanted to have his wedding ring on when he killed himself. In retrospect, I realized this was his twisted way of honoring me, our daughters, and our marriage."

Seeing how painful this was for my friend, I squeezed her hands. "You don't need to tell me any more."

"I'm sure you have a reason for asking, and I think talking about Dan helps. Finding his wedding band and the bill from the jeweler weren't the only reasons I assumed there was someone else."

"Oh?"

"Not long after he disappeared, I was working at the library when someone came running in and said they'd seen Dan in town. He was in his pickup and he wasn't alone. There was another woman with him. To flaunt her like that, to embarrass me in front of the entire town, was more than I could take.

"I was determined to confront him for the agony he'd put me and the girls through. I can still remember how angry and frustrated I was. In my rush to find him, I raced out of the library like a madwoman. I fell and badly scraped my knee and then sat and wept."

"Was it Dan? Was he with someone else?"

"No. It couldn't have been him. By this time several weeks had passed, and when his body was recovered it showed he'd been dead long before that incident."

"You were angry?"

"Angry?" she repeated. "That doesn't even begin to explain how furious I was. Shortly after that, I had some sort of emotional

244

breakdown, I think. The neighbors were so concerned they called my daughters."

I could only imagine the pain and anger Grace must have felt. "What happened?"

She laughed, and the sound was genuine. "I emptied Dan's side of the closet. I carted armload after armload of his clothes outside and hurled them onto the lawn. To my way of thinking, if he wanted to leave me, then he should have taken everything with him."

"It was a hellish time for you, wasn't it?"

Grace looked blankly into the distance. "Dan was a different person when he came back after serving in Vietnam. I'm convinced he was a victim of post-traumatic stress disorder, but neither Dan nor I knew what was wrong.

"I didn't know how to help him. Our marriage wasn't wonderful, but it wasn't bad, either. We were content with each other. To the best of his ability, Dan loved me and our daughters. Unfortunately, he couldn't let go of the past. It tormented him."

From articles I'd read, I understood how tension and anxiety had profoundly affected our soldiers in and out of combat. Thankfully, there were programs in place to help, but there weren't nearly enough, and many of those coping mechanisms had come too late to help men like Dan.

"He suffered for years. He never felt he was worthy of anything good. I remember one time I found the Christmas gifts the girls and I had given him in the garage. He'd destroyed them, cut them into pieces, and then for whatever reason he hid them there."

It was all too apparent Grace's first husband had undergone a great deal of mental anguish.

"Death was a release for him. He carried the burden of guilt and shame from an incident that happened in the war. At the time, he was nineteen years old, and he was never able to forget it."

"He's at peace now," I whispered. Although I desperately longed for Paul to be alive, more important, I wanted him to know serenity and peace.

"Does hearing about Dan help you?" Grace asked me.

It was time to tell Grace my dilemma. "Mrs. Coryelle stopped by the house this afternoon," I said, plunging right in.

"Marion Coryelle?"

"Yes. She lives next door." It wasn't exactly next door, but down the hill from me, which was why I kept an eye out for her, seeing how elderly she was.

"I assumed she was housebound. Her daughter stops by the library and gets the large-print books for her. She loves to read."

"She's a good neighbor . . . a letter to me was placed in her mailbox, and she brought it to me herself."

"The letter is what upset you so much?"

I looked away, for fear I wouldn't be able to continue without my voice cracking. "It was from a friend of Paul's."

Grace scooted a bit closer to me.

"It seems Paul gave him a letter to deliver to me in the case of his death. His friend apologized and said he'd forgotten about it and recently came across it and mailed it off right away."

"Oh, Jo Marie, no wonder you're upset."

That was an understatement.

"Did you read the letter?"

"No."

"Do you want me to be with you when you do?"

"No. I refuse to read it . . ."

"Would you like me to read it first?" Her voice was soft and gentle.

"I won't read it . . . not until I have proof that Paul is dead." I broke into sobs then, and Rover started to whine and lick my face. Wrapping my arm around his small body, I brought him onto my lap.

Grace placed her arm around me. "You may have to accept that his body may never be located."

I realized then she didn't know about Lieutenant Colonel Milford's phone call. Sniffling, I straightened and drew in a deep, calming breath.

"I heard from the army, Lieutenant Colonel Milford, earlier in the week," I continued. "The site where the helicopter went down is now accessible, and the bodies were retrieved. Six men were on the helicopter, and the remains of five men were located. The army is running DNA tests now. However slight the chance, there's a possibility that one man might have managed to survive.

"It could be Paul. He could be alive. I refuse to give up hope . . . If he were dead, I'd feel it. I know I would." I don't know why I argued so hard or adamantly, as if it was necessary to convince Grace that my husband might be alive.

She didn't say anything for a long time, and when she spoke, her voice was so low I had to strain to hear. "All that year Dan was missing, I thought I'd know if he was dead, too. I was convinced I'd feel it."

"Did you?" I asked.

"That was part of the reason I believed he'd found someone else who could make him happy." Leaning forward, Grace looped her arms around her knees. "It made no sense that he would decide to kill himself when he did. None whatsoever. Our first grandchild was about to be born, and Kelly and her father were especially close."

"You didn't feel it?"

"No, and you won't with Paul, either. As much as you love him, as much as I loved Dan, he had his own life path, and Paul had his, too."

I thought about the letter awaiting me in my nightstand.

Grace reached over and touched my arm. "You don't need to

read his letter now. Wait if you wish. You know where it is, and your heart will tell you when the time is right."

Her advice was good, and I recognized the wisdom of her words. I had other questions but felt unsure how best to phrase them. "How . . . How did you go on?"

The same thoughtful look I'd seen earlier was back. "A death of someone so close to us, like a husband or a child, hurts beyond comprehension. The pain is strong enough to kill a person, and unless you've been through it personally, no one could ever understand. I know how badly my friend Olivia wanted to help see me through Dan's disappearance and death. She'd lost a son, so she understood, but there are no words of comfort, nothing anyone can say to ease this kind of pain. There simply are no words."

I swallowed and nodded.

"It's a wound, but unlike a physical cut, there is no medication that will take the pain away, nor is there a prescribed time in which it will heal. You know if you broke a bone in about six weeks it will mend itself. It isn't that way dealing with a death. Do you believe you'll get over losing Paul?"

"Will I?" I needed answers, not more questions. "Did you get over Dan?"

"No," she whispered. "He was my husband, the father of my children. I spent the majority of my adult life with him—I will always love Dan. But at the same time, I can assure you that life goes on. In the beginning, you won't want it to. It feels like everything should stand still; life as you know it should stop while you try to absorb what has happened."

That was how I'd felt when I'd first gotten the news about the helicopter crash. It felt as if life had come to an end for me, too. I dragged myself from one day into the next with no sense of time or distance, stunned, horrified, shocked, and disbelieving.

"You remarried." Grace had a new life now, and this was more statement than question.

"I have," Grace said, and her eyes brightened. "This is another life lesson that attaches itself to the death of a loved one. Because life does go on, no matter how hard we try to cling to the way it once was, we are pulled along, too. In my case, I went kicking and screaming. I'd had a year without Dan. A year to learn to live without him."

"Me, too . . . It was a year April twenty-seventh." I needed her to tell me that this grieving would get easier, that I'd survive the same as she had. The way I felt just then, it seemed impossible. Death would be preferable to this agony.

"I will tell you from personal experience, you will heal, Jo Marie. The scar of losing Paul will mark your heart, but you will heal."

Everyone insisted there was no possibility my husband had survived. My heart told me so, but in my stubbornness I refused to believe it, clinging to hope. And yet everything Grace said rang true. In time, the same as she did, I would heal. Paul had come to me that first night after I took over the inn. Like Grace, he'd assured me this inn would be a place of healing.

"One day you might even fall in love again," Grace went on to say.

I laughed outright, seeing how long I'd remained single. "It took me thirty-six years to find Paul. If it takes that long again, I'll be in my seventies."

"Life just might surprise you."

I never had been much good with surprises, but I had time to wait and see.

Chapter 27

A slow, easy smile came over George as he wrapped his arm around Mary's shoulders and brought her head close to his own. "Our daughter is the class valedictorian?" Pride echoed with each word.

"Yes. Oh, George, I'm so proud of her."

"I know it's crazy, but I feel personally responsible for fathering such a brilliant child," he added, and his voice shook with emotion.

For a long moment, they simply held each other. Mary knew how he felt, because his emotion mirrored her own when she'd first discovered Amanda had been awarded top honors. Like mother, like daughter, even if she had no right to feel anything.

"I've only known about Amanda for a few hours, and I think the buttons could burst off my shirt, I'm so proud."

Mary ran her hand down the side of his face, loving him with such intensity that it felt as if her heart would burst. The only thing she had contributed to their daughter, other than her DNA, was giving her life. Amanda's adoptive family had nurtured and loved her. It was her adoptive mother who'd stayed up nights with a sick baby, who'd kissed her scraped knees, who'd sat with Amanda while she'd learned to read. Her family deserved the right to be proud of their daughter, and no doubt they were.

"Now, what's this about being unable to attend the graduation?" George asked, growing serious.

"It's a huge graduating class."

"And your point is?"

Mary knew his look of sheer determination all too well. "Tickets are handed out to family and friends only. No one is allowed into the auditorium without a ticket."

"So we'll get tickets."

"That's the point, George. There are none to be had. I tried, believe me."

"Are you seriously going to allow that to stop you?" he challenged, and then amended his thought. "Stop us?"

In any other circumstances, Mary would have gone toe to toe with the person who would try to keep her from attending that ceremony, but unfortunately, the cancer had taken the fight out of her.

"We're going to hear our daughter speak," George insisted.

"I don't think I could bear a scene at the front door," she whispered. "And I doubt that I could sneak in unnoticed." Unfortunately, she stood out in a crowd with her bald head.

"Not to worry," George stated calmly. "I have connections. One way or another, I will have two tickets by tomorrow afternoon."

Mary could hardly believe it was possible. She thought just being in the vicinity would be enough. Hailey Tremont, the teenager who worked for Jo Marie, had fed her tidbits of information about Amanda, and so had Connor from the coffeehouse. She'd savored each tiny bit and hoped to hear more.

Mary had learned that the following Monday's newspaper would run a copy of the speech from the valedictorian. Being able to read her daughter's thoughts was as good as Mary assumed it could be. To see and hear Amada herself with George at her side was more than she could have dreamed.

George released her and wiped the moisture from his cheeks. Mary did, too, and then they looked at each other and started to laugh.

"Look at us," George said.

"We're nothing but a pair of softies." Oh, how she loved him. She'd never stopped loving George, but seeing him, being with him intensified her feelings a hundredfold. Yet in less than forty-eight hours she would need to find the courage to leave him again.

Both appeared caught up in their own thoughts as George started the car and headed back to the freeway on-ramp. Mary made an honest effort to stay awake until they arrived back at the inn, but it was a lost cause. She didn't remember closing her eyes, but the next thing she knew, George was driving over the Tacoma Narrows Bridge.

"Are you awake?" he asked in a whisper.

"Yes . . . I'm sorry, I didn't mean to be such poor company." It was barely after three in the afternoon and she could hardly keep her eyes open.

"Nonsense. You needed to sleep. Tell me the address of the inn."

"Pardon?"

"Rose Harbor? I'll put it in my GPS, and then you can rest and not worry about giving me directions."

"Oh, right, you haven't come in from this direction, have you?" She reached for her purse. "I have the address here."

"I could probably find it. I know the general direction, but this makes more sense."

Had that really been only yesterday morning that she was reluctant to divulge her whereabouts? It seemed silly now, in light of everything she'd told him since then.

Mary had never intended to tell George about Amanda. Seeing his reaction to the news made her realize how selfish she'd been. How cruel to keep this information to herself all these years. To be fair, she hadn't wanted to invade his life. He'd married, and it seemed grossly unfair to his wife.

"I'm sorry," she whispered.

"Do I wish that things had been different? Of course. But I'll always be grateful to you for giving birth to my child. For loving her enough to allow a loving family to adopt her and give her a good life. Don't apologize for that, Mary, but by all that is right, how could you not tell me? Didn't I have a right to know?" He paused, exhaled sharply, and added, his voice tight and controlled, "What's done is done, and considering the circumstances, you did what you thought was best."

He was far too good to her. That was his problem. He was simply too good to be believable. That he should still love her was a miracle she had never expected.

When they arrived in Cedar Cove, Mary was awake enough to give him directions. They found the waterfront, and once they did, Mary was on familiar ground and they easily made their way to the inn.

George turned off the engine and then in a firm voice instructed her, "Stay right where you are."

Mary hid a smile. At times he could be so bossy.

George ran around the car and opened the passenger door and helped her out. With his arm around her waist, he led her to the sidewalk leading to the front porch.

"For the last two days, I've sat outside and soaked in the sunshine." It was there that she'd napped in the warmth of the unexpected spring, with flowers blooming all around her, their sweet scent perfuming the air. Rose Harbor in bloom was a magical place.

"Shall we do the same?" he asked, patiently taking the porch steps one at a time, letting her set the pace. "I'd enjoy sitting in the sunshine with the woman I love."

"You have the time?"

"Mary, if you haven't figured it out by now, I'm savoring every minute we're together."

"Then yes, let's sit out here awhile."

"You're not too tired?"

She was, but like George, she relished this time together and didn't want him to go.

George guided her around to the side of the porch, and she sat in the wooden chair. A dog barked from inside the house, and after a couple of minutes Jo Marie stepped outside with the short-haired dog at her side.

"You're back," she commented, and glanced toward George. "Can I get you anything?"

"George Hudson," he said, stepping forward to introduce himself. "I think Mary would appreciate a blanket."

"Right away," Jo Marie said, and disappeared. She was back in short order with a hand-knit afghan, the very one Mary had used previously.

George settled into the chair next to her, with a side table between them.

"The view here is lovely," she said, drinking in the beauty of the blue sky, the Olympic mountain peaks, and the shipyard in the distance.

"It is," he agreed, but he was looking at her.

Mary wasn't accustomed to compliments. They made her uncomfortable, especially now, when she was very nearly bald and so terribly thin and pale. She did her best to ignore him.

"The Olympic Mountains are stunning, aren't they?" she said, turning the subject away from herself.

"Beautiful," he said, turning his attention toward the view.

"Oh, yes," and then because she was curious she asked, "Have you ever been to Hurricane Ridge?"

"No. I've heard about it, though."

"Me, too," she said, a bit wistfully.

Mary had read about visiting the ridge in one of the travel brochures she'd picked up while waiting for the Bremerton ferry. Now the chance was taken from her. It wouldn't be possible to make the long trip. Hurricane Ridge was less than a two-hour drive from Seattle and offered amazing views of the Olympic mountain peaks, wildflower-filled meadows, and excellent hiking trails. She'd read about the park in the Olympic National Forest and wished, as she had so many other things lately, that she'd taken the time . . . that she'd made the effort.

Regrets. Full loads of those came as a side effect with the cancer.

For several minutes, Mary and George chatted back and forth. George had a quick wit and a dry sense of humor, and she enjoyed bantering with him.

After thirty minutes, he said, "You're tired."

She didn't argue with him. Once more, she found it difficult to keep her eyes open. She'd rested for only a few minutes during the drive, and her energy level was hovering near empty.

"Let me see you to your room."

She nodded, wondering if she could make it up the stairs on her own strength.

George lifted the blanket from her lap, folded it, and set it aside before he bent over and helped Mary to her feet. He seemed to sense that she needed more than his arm and brought her close to his side.

The stairs were the challenge she'd feared they might be. He was patient, waiting on each step as she took them slowly and carefully. Mary extracted the room key from her purse, and he took it from her and unlocked the door to her room.

"I can remember a time when you escorted me to my door and didn't leave until late the next morning," she whispered.

"Don't tempt me, Mary."

She laughed.

"Do you think I'm joking?" he demanded.

"Yes." She wouldn't lie.

"Then you'd be in for a shock."

"Oh, honestly, George, I . . ."

He pressed a finger to her lips before she could say another word. "You. Are. Beautiful. And I love you."

Emotion nearly overwhelmed her. "Thank you." Whether it was true or not, it was exactly what Mary needed to hear. She reached for him, and George hugged her, holding her close and tight. A deep breath shuddered through her as she fought back the effect his words had on her.

"I'm so tired," she whispered.

"I know. I'm sorry. I should have left you to sleep a long time ago."

"No . . ." She sank onto the edge of the bed and removed her jacket.

One by one, George took off her shoes and then lifted her feet onto the mattress and covered her with the quilt that was folded at the bottom of the bed. Bending down, he very gently kissed her forehead.

"I'll call you later, okay?" he said.

"Of course."

Exhausted as she was, Mary fell into a deep, restful sleep before George had even closed the door. She woke an hour later, feeling worlds better. A few minutes later, after she was back from using the restroom, someone tapped gently against her door.

"Who is it?" Mary asked.

"Jo Marie. I have a tray for you."

Mary blinked back her surprise. "I didn't order anything." As far as she knew, the inn didn't provide room service.

Mary opened the door, and the innkeeper walked in, carting a wooden tray. On it rested a large pot of tea with a cup and saucer, a plate of store-bought Fig Newtons, a bright shiny apple, and a Butterfinger, her favorite candy bar.

"Your friend asked me to bring this up to you as soon as you woke."

All her favorite snacks. George remembered even that, every detail.

"He also ordered your dinner to be delivered at seven tonight. I told him I'd be happy to cook for you, but he insisted on this."

"Chicken with spicy noodles," Mary whispered.

"Yes." Jo Marie sounded surprised that she'd know. They'd often shared a bowl. Their favorite restaurant had been in the international district in Seattle.

"I believe he intends to fatten me up," Mary said, and reached for the candy bar.

"Enjoy," Jo Marie told her. "Feel free to call me if you need anything."

"I'm good, thank you."

She walked the innkeeper to the door and watched Jo Marie walk down the stairs before turning back and pouring herself a cup of tea. Peppermint. That, too, was her favorite.

To her surprise, Mary managed to eat a cookie and half the candy bar, and take a bite from the apple along with half a pot of tea. It was the most she'd eaten at one sitting in weeks. Months. For George's sake she made a show of eating but had no real appetite.

At half past seven that evening, her cell phone chimed. Anticipating George's call, she'd set it on her nightstand.

"Mary? Did I wake you?"

"No, I've been up for hours, reading. Thank you for my afternoon snack and for dinner."

"How were the noodles?"

"Incredible. You ordered these locally?"

He chuckled softly. "What do you think?"

"George, don't tell me you had these sent all the way from Seattle."

"Okay, I won't tell you."

The man was unbelievable. She grew serious then, because his actions made her return to New York on Monday all the more difficult. She had no choice but to go back. "Don't spoil me." She was serious.

He hesitated. "I guess that means I shouldn't tell you that I managed to scrounge up two tickets to the high school graduation ceremony."

She was almost afraid to believe him. "You're not teasing me, are you?"

"No."

"How? Where?"

"I told you I had connections, remember?"

"Yes, but I didn't think it was possible . . . From everything I heard, there was no way to squeeze another person into that auditorium."

"Well, they managed to squeeze in two more. We're going to see our daughter graduate."

"Thank you," she whispered, so overwhelmed it was difficult to speak.

"I'll be there at one tomorrow to pick you up. Sleep well, my love."

"You, too," she managed, and then before he could hear the tears in her voice, she disconnected the phone call.

Chapter 28

The anniversary party was winding down, and Annie could see that after all the excitement of the day her grandparents were tired out. She found her mother, who was busily chatting with a cousin and her family, giving them directions for the dinner in Seattle the following day.

"I think it might be best if we took Grandma and Grandpa back to the inn," Annie said, once she had her mother's attention.

"Not to worry, honey. Oliver has already seen to that."

"Oh." Annie looked up, and sure enough, she found Oliver escorting the anniversary couple out the door.

She couldn't help being disappointed. Annie had hoped the two of them would have some time together alone. If he left the party, she might not see him again until morning.

"That's all right, isn't it?" her mother asked.

Her mother must have read her look of dismay.

"Oh, sure, that's great . . . not a problem."

"You did a truly wonderful job, Annie. Dad and I couldn't be more proud of you."

"Thanks, Mom." Her mother's praise warmed her heart.

Before her parents left, Annie and her mother briefly hugged. Most all of her out-of-town relatives would head back to the inn, but her parents would return to Seattle.

Annie stuck around to write out the final checks to the caterer and the band. She sat at the head table while the crew dismantled the room, folding up the chairs and tearing down the tables. The door to the yacht club opened, and bright sunshine flooded the room.

Annie looked up as Oliver walked in. He'd changed into casual clothes and wore slacks and a light jacket. Her heart reacted immediately. This strong attraction caught her unaware. She wasn't prepared to deal with it, and try as she might, she couldn't hide her smile.

"You didn't really think I'd leave you here alone to deal with all this, did you?"

Instead of answering his question, she asked one of her own: "How are my grandparents?"

"Exhausted, excited, grateful, happy. They couldn't stop talking about the friends they saw and all the people who came."

"That's great." It was exactly the way Annie had hoped they'd feel.

"They couldn't stop talking about you, either, how wonderfully planned the party was and on and on and on."

Annie almost felt sorry for Oliver having to listen.

"It was a fabulous party, and I bet you're exhausted, too."

"It's not so bad." She could say that now that the grand affair was over. Her mother and aunt would take over from this point on. A big family dinner was planned for Sunday afternoon at Annie's parents' house.

Oliver picked up one of the checks she'd written. "Anything I can do to help?"

"I've got everything under control, but thanks. You were really helpful earlier."

"Glad to do what I could." He lifted himself up and sat on the table next to her, his feet dangling over the edge.

"You'll be with the family tomorrow for dinner, won't you?" she asked, although she assumed he would be.

"Actually, no."

Annie's head shot up. She'd naturally assumed that Oliver would be joining them. "But you drove my grandparents, and I thought . . ."

"Would you like me to come?"

"Yes," she said quickly, possibly too quickly, although the time for being coy had long passed.

A smile all but exploded across his face. "Then I'll see what I can do to make that happen. I would hate to disappoint you."

"Well, it isn't only me. I mean, I'm sure my parents would want you to join the family, not to mention Grandma and Grandpa." In retrospect, Annie didn't want to appear overly eager.

Tearing out the last check, she delivered it to the appropriate person while Oliver made a phone call. He didn't mention who was on the other end of the line, and she didn't ask, but from bits of the conversation it appeared to be one of his traveling buddies.

Oliver followed her out of the hall and into the sunshine. Although it was after seven, it wouldn't grow dark until eight-thirty or nine.

"Where to now?" he asked, matching his steps to hers.

"I left my car parked down by the gazebo."

"I'll walk with you."

"I'd like that," she admitted. Only a short while ago she would have strenuously objected to his company. So much had changed and so quickly. Everything she'd learned about him in the last few hours left her head spinning with unanswered questions.

"Would you like to sit on the dock for a while?" he asked, as they neared the marina.

He hadn't noticed that the marina was accessible only to those who moored boats there. "Yes, but how would we get inside . . ."

"There's another dock a short distance from here," he said, interrupting her. "We could sit and talk there."

"I'd like that." Her head was swimming from the events of the day. She was tired but happy and anxious to be with Oliver, to talk and examine these feelings they shared.

Oliver drove them along the waterfront to a space about two miles from the downtown area. It was near Cranberry Point. The dock was open to the public, just as Oliver had promised, and with the tide out it stood several feet above the water. A sign posted explained that it was used by the mosquito fleet to ferry the shipyard workers across the cove on weekdays.

Holding her hand, Oliver walked with her over the freshly painted gray dock. He shrugged off his jacket and spread it out for them to sit on. Annie removed her shoes and dangled her bare feet over the side. Oliver joined her, sitting so close their shoulders touched.

Not knowing where to start, she thought to let him speak first. With her hands braced against the dock at her sides, she leaned back and gently kicked her feet back and forth.

"This has been a big day for you."

"And you," she returned.

"Me?" he asked.

"Yes, you. I think I lost count of all the ladies who wanted you to dance with them," she teased. "I don't imagine that happens every day."

"I'd be more excited if they were a bit older than thirteen."

Annie laughed and turned her face up to catch the sunlight. It felt good on her skin, warming her. The weather couldn't have been more perfect. It was as if God had smiled down on her grandparents and blessed their special day.

"Are you jealous?"

"Of thirteen-year-olds?" she joked.

"Good point."

She supposed they could banter back and forth like this all evening, but this could well be the only opportunity they might have to talk, really talk.

"You're quiet all of a sudden."

"I know," she said. "Sorry. It's just that I have so much to ask you, and I'm not sure where to start."

"Do you want to go back to the time we were kids?"

"I don't know," she said thoughtfully. "It immediately brings up a lot of bad memories, and I'm not sure that's a good place to begin this conversation." Then, because it was the question that seemed to burn inside of her, she blurted out, "Is it really true you've liked me all these years?"

"Liked you is putting it mildly. I panted after you."

"Oliver, that can't be true, it just can't."

"I'm serious. If you think you were the brunt of the teasing after our kiss, you're wrong. Your brother didn't let up with me for years. Peter was unmerciful, taunting me with news about all your boyfriends, knowing how much it distressed me."

"You never said a word."

"I couldn't get close to you. You were like a wire scrub brush."

Annie didn't bother to deny it.

"I did everything I could think of to get you to notice me."

He hadn't tried that hard; otherwise, she would have seen more of him, especially in the last few years.

"The truth is, Annie, I had to accept the fact you weren't ever going to get over what happened after our kiss, and I decided to forget about you and get on with my life." ·

She looked at him and frowned.

"Then I heard you'd broken the engagement, and I knew I had to give it one last try."

His eyes focused solely on her, full of sincerity and warmth.

"I knew you'd need time to get over Lenny, and so I waited. I knew if I left for a year without letting you know how I felt that I would always regret it, so I made sure I was here this weekend."

"What about your trip? You're leaving, aren't you?"

He nodded. "The truth is I booked the trip when I heard about your engagement, and then after you broke it off, it was too late to back out. The anniversary party was perfect timing. I came to see you, one last time. I guess you could say it was a swan song on a teenage fantasy that refused to die a natural death."

"You're still going, aren't you?"

He hesitated and then nodded. "Yeah, my friends are relying on me, and we've already made plans, purchased our tickets, and have other arrangements." He stared at her for a long moment. "Are you asking me to stay?"

"No . . . no, I wouldn't want you to do that."

"I would, you know, if you asked."

Annie was speechless. He was sincere.

"When I learned you'd broken off the engagement, Annie, you don't know how excited I was."

Annie looked down at her feet, which had taken to kicking at a much faster rate.

"I realized I had to think this through carefully. My big fear was that I might say or do something that would make matters worse between us rather than better."

"My grandfather was advising you, wasn't he?"

"Yes, but that started long before anything came up about this party. He was the one who encouraged me to try again."

"The whole thing with him forgetting his glasses was a hoax, then, so you would drive them up?"

"No. I intended on driving up on my own anyway, but Julie phoned and asked if I'd drive, and seeing that I was headed to Cedar Cove, I thought, why not?"

So it wasn't as much of a conspiracy as she'd assumed.

"I have a question for you now. A serious question," he said.

"Okay, ask away."

"Be honest, Annie, because I need to know. Do I have a chance with you?"

She touched his face, and her hand lingered there. "Before I answer, I need you to do something first."

"Okay."

"Kiss me again."

His smile reached far beyond his eyes. "With pleasure."

He changed position, getting on his knees. They'd kissed more than once over the course of this weekend, and each kiss affected her in a different way. She couldn't deny that she liked it, but she resented the fact that she'd enjoyed their exchange. Her second kiss had been offered to him less grudgingly. Still, she'd enjoyed it far more than made her comfortable. This third kiss was a test for them both.

Oliver couldn't be sure of his feelings. They were adults now, and he might have built up a memory that would be impossible to live up to. Feelings change. Things change.

Slowly, he lowered his mouth to hers. He splayed his fingers and buried them deep in her hair, and angled her head in a way that gave him free access to her mouth. The kiss was sweet and gentle, moist and warm, and quickly changed to one filled with longing and passion. Annie didn't know how much time elapsed, but when he went to pull away, she let out a small cry of protest.

Oliver brushed his lips down her jaw and spread nibbling kisses along the side of her neck. By the time he broke away and leaned back on his haunches, Annie was grateful he'd kept his hands on her shoulders; otherwise, she might have toppled off the dock.

It took her several seconds to find the resolve to open her eyes.

"Does that answer your question?" he asked.

She blinked several times.

"Would you like another kiss? I'm willing, although much more of this and we might get arrested for where it could lead."

Annie grinned. "Thanks, but I think I have my answer."

"Can I ask what the question was?" he pried.

"I wanted to make sure what I felt was real and not . . . something I had enjoyed on the rebound."

"Ah." He hesitated, then asked, "And what's the verdict?"

Oh, yes, this was real. Very real. "I believe we're onto something," she said, not wanting to appear overly eager. He was leaving, after all, and planned to be away for an entire year. Besides, he lived in Portland and she lived in Seattle.

Oliver sat down next to her again and placed his hand over hers, wrapping his fingers around hers. "Now that we've got that settled, what are we going to do about it?"

That was exactly the question Annie had been asking herself. She met his gaze and then propped her head against his shoulder. "Honestly, Oliver, I don't have a clue."

"Me neither."

She smiled, happy, surprisingly so for a woman who only a few months ago had been engaged to be married to another man. With the way she felt right then, she couldn't be more pleased than to be exactly where she was with Oliver.

Chapter 29

I'd been unable to sleep more than an hour or two at a time and was up before dawn. My eyes burned and my head throbbed. How I would make it through this day was a mystery to me. I had guests to serve, and the open house was set for later this afternoon.

Dressed in my housecoat, I sat on a stool in the kitchen with Rover at my feet. Cupping a mug of steaming coffee, I stared sightlessly into the distance, doing my best to think positively. It didn't help. Not when this dark mood weighed so heavily on my shoulders. This had been one of my worst nights since I'd gotten word that my husband's helicopter had gone down.

Yet there was a possibility, however slight, that Paul might be alive. It was useless to believe it, and rationally I owned up to the truth, but I couldn't make my heart let go of the dream. Because I so badly wanted to believe Paul had somehow managed to survive, I clung to the improbable.

It went without saying that Paul wouldn't want this. Even without reading his last letter, I could guess what he had written.

Get on with your life.
Hold on to the memories.
Don't grieve.

Did he think I wasn't trying? Didn't he realize he was asking for the impossible? Here I was refuting his words before I'd even read through his letter.

My guests would be leaving soon, with the exception of Mary Smith, who would be spending the night and leaving sometime Monday morning. The Shivers, Oliver Sutton, and Annie Newton were scheduled to depart this morning, along with a variety of other relatives who'd come to share in the anniversary celebration.

As it was, my morning was sure to be hectic. In addition to serving breakfast and dealing with getting their sheets changed, rooms cleared and spiffed up, I had the open house to worry about. It felt as if the weight of the world had descended on me. I couldn't imagine what craziness had made me think I could pull this off when the yard was torn apart and I had a house full of guests. What was I? Nuts?

Rover placed his paw on my foot. Either it was an effort to comfort me or he was telling me he wanted to go outside. I slid off the stool and opened the back door off the kitchen to let him out.

He meandered outside, stood on the top step, and looked out over the yard as though checking over his property. Then he turned around and looked square at me. He seemed to want me to follow him.

"Do your business, Rover," I said, standing on the porch landing with my coffee mug in my hand.

Rover slowly descended the stairs and walked over to his favorite corner of the lawn. He sniffed around and then looked up at me as though I needed to confirm that this was a perfectly good location to be watered.

"That's it," I said, doing my best to sound encouraging.

My constant companion seemed to be in a disgruntled mood himself. He took his own sweet time and refused to be rushed before coming back into the house. He acted as if I'd done something to offend him, and retreated to his bed, curling up into a tight ball.

"So you're going to ignore me now?" I muttered.

Rover pretended to be asleep.

"Traitor," I whispered. I finished my coffee, placed the mug in the sink, and then returned to my room to dress for the day. I didn't have time to waste if I intended to have breakfast on the table when my guests woke.

Although my heart wasn't into being the perfect hostess, I was determined to do my best. I dressed casually, in jeans and a bright yellow long-sleeved blouse, thinking the color would help boost my spirits. I generally wore a bib apron and chose one of the more festive ones, again hoping my choice would help me out of this blue funk.

Annie was the first one down the stairs. She bounced her way into the dining room as if it was Christmas morning. I'd already determined she was a morning person.

"You're in a good mood this morning," I said, doing my best to sound positive and inviting.

"I am," she returned in such a bright, cheerful manner that I couldn't help being inspired. "The party went off without a hitch. Everything worked out beautifully. The food was great, the cakes were delicious, and the music was wonderful. It couldn't have turned out better."

"Fabulous." I was pleased for her, knowing how hard she'd worked to make this event a success.

Annie pulled out a chair at the dining room table, took her place, and sighed. "I'm still on an emotional high."

"I'm pleased everything went so well."

"More than well." She reached for a muffin from the plate in the center of the table. "It was . . . romantic." A dreamy look came over her, and she paused, deep in thought, holding the muffin over her plate.

"I know how important it was for you to make your grand-parents' anniversary special," I added conversationally. "It must be rewarding to have everything come together like that."

"I'm sorry?" she said, looking up at me expectantly. "Did you say something?"

"It wasn't anything important." I automatically poured her a glass of orange juice, seeing that her head was elsewhere.

"Have you seen Oliver this morning?" she asked.

"Not yet."

"Oh." She sounded disappointed.

That was a switch. From all appearances, the two had reached some sort of understanding. Earlier, I remembered watching her tense up at the mere mention of his name. I suspected she wanted nothing to do with the man, although I'd picked up on the fact Oliver hadn't been able to keep his eyes off her. If Annie noticed, she certainly hadn't indicated as much.

"What about my grandparents? Are they up yet?"

"I haven't heard a peep."

She looked up at me a second time with the same blank look, as if she'd lost track of the conversation.

I laughed. Clearly, this was a woman with her head in the clouds. I'd seen that look before and had to smile.

"He's leaving, you know."

"You mean Oliver, right?"

"Oh, yes, sorry, I must have been thinking out loud." She sipped her orange juice and set down the glass.

"Yes, I have him scheduled to depart this morning."

"Not from here," Annie clarified. "I mean he's leaving as in leaving the country."

"Oh, I didn't know that."

"He plans to be away for an entire year."

This sounded like more of an adventure than a vacation. "Where is he headed?"

"Away . . . for a long time, with two other friends. No girls, though." She frowned as she said it. "That makes it impossible."

"Makes what impossible?"

She was saved from responding when Kent and Julie Shivers came into the dining room. They wore twin shirts. They seemed to have declared a truce when it came to the squabbling. I'd wondered how long that would last. Just yesterday it seemed they couldn't go more than a few minutes without bickering with each other over one thing or another.

Kent pulled out Julie's chair, and she looked up at him with adoring eyes as she took her seat at the table.

"We'll want to check out as soon as we're finished with our breakfast," Kent told me.

I nodded, acknowledging his request.

I brought a platter of bacon into the dining room and set it on the table. I'd cooked it crisp, as I'd discovered that was the way most of my guests preferred it. I followed it up with thick slices of spinach-and-mushroom quiche still warm from the oven. The melted cheese oozed from the sides.

I heard Oliver's footsteps pounding down the stairs. A few seconds later, he appeared in the dining room.

"Good morning," he greeted cheerfully.

"Morning," Kent said, as he reached for three pieces of bacon.

I held my breath, half expecting Julie to remind him of his cholesterol levels. She surprised me and didn't say a word.

As if expecting to be chastised, Kent glanced at his wife, grinned, and replaced two of the bacon strips.

"I'll take those," Oliver said, raising his plate, and then, looking over at Julie, added, "It's a beautiful morning, isn't it?"

I glanced out the window and noticed that the weather was overcast and muggy, with gray skies. But in his present mood, which surprisingly matched Annie's, this was a beautiful day.

"You still up to driving to Seattle?" Oliver asked Kent.

"You're driving?" Julie asked, looking surprised. She directed the question to her husband.

"I'll do fine, don't you worry," Kent said, and patted Julie's knee. "Oliver and I have this all sorted out."

"You'll be taking Oliver's car?" Annie asked.

"Yup."

Annie's head swiveled to look at her grandfather, then at Oliver, and then back again.

"When did you decide this?"

"Earlier." Oliver reached for a muffin, four pieces of bacon, and two huge wedges of the quiche.

Apparently, he was famished.

"But how will you get to my parents' house?" Annie asked, looking at Oliver.

"Can't I ride with you?" He glanced up, his eyes full of question.

"Sure, but . . . this is all kind of sudden, isn't it?"

"I should say," Julie added. "Not that I don't think it's a good idea. Oh, my, that was a double negative, wasn't it?"

"I thought it was a fine idea myself," Kent agreed. "Annie and Oliver need to spend more time alone—right, kids?"

"And whose idea was this?" Annie asked.

To her credit, she didn't sound the least bit distressed by the sudden switch in plans.

"Mine," Oliver said.

"Mine," Kent echoed, and then chuckled. "Both of us thought of it at the same time."

"That way, I can help Annie in case there are any last-minute details she needs to handle here."

"I took care of everything yesterday."

"That way," Oliver corrected, "you can show me your apartment in Seattle."

"I am not taking you to my apartment," Annie insisted, and laughed. "You're impossible."

"Kent was like that," Julie said.

"But you tamed him, Grandma."

"Yes, but it took me nearly fifty years."

While the couples bantered back and forth, I returned to the kitchen to serve the rest of the anniversary party guests. The only person who wasn't down for breakfast was Mary.

Mary had been up in her room since yesterday afternoon, and frankly, I was worried about her. Every other morning of her stay, she'd been downstairs before now. A while passed, and soon I'd fed all the guests except Mary. I knew she hadn't been well, and so I risked going up the stairs and timidly knocking against her door.

"Who is it?" Her voice was weak, shaky.

"It's Jo Marie. I was just checking to be sure you're doing okay."

"I'm fine, thank you."

"Are you up and about?" Before she could answer, I qualified the question. "Breakfast is being served."

"Oh . . . that's okay. I'm not hungry this morning."

"Would you like me to bring you a tray?"

"No, thank you."

I hesitated, because I'd heard the tremble in her voice, and while she might claim she was perfectly fine, I had my fears. At the same time, I didn't want her to think I was prying into her private life. "Will you be down soon?" I asked.

"In a bit," she said through the door.

That was as comfortable as I got in questioning one of my guests. Never having run into a situation like this before, I turned back toward the stairwell. I would be patient.

By the time I returned to the kitchen, the only two people in the dining room were Annie and Oliver. They sat on opposite sides of the long table and were deeply involved in conversation. When Annie saw me, she blushed slightly and sat up straighter.

Seeing Annie's reaction, Oliver looked over his shoulder and smiled when he saw it was me.

I didn't know what they were discussing, but it appeared to be intimate. I didn't want to interrupt. But I didn't dare fall behind on my schedule. Not today, of all days.

Making myself scarce, I returned to the kitchen and made up a plate for Mary, whether she wanted it or not. Then I packed up the leftovers as best I could to store in the large refrigerator. I peeked out once to find Annie and Oliver in some kind of debate. I didn't want either of them to think I was eavesdropping, so once again I retreated to the kitchen.

Rover continued to nap contentedly in his bed, barely aware of my uneasiness. I wanted to grumble at him, but it wasn't his fault that I was having such a horrific morning.

When I heard the chairs scrape against the floor, I knew the two had finished their conversation. I practically leapt into the dining room to remove the last of the dirty dishes. The dishwasher was already open and ready for the plates, which I rinsed and set inside.

I was moving as quickly as I could when I heard a voice from behind me.

"Jo Marie, has something happened?"

Whirling around, I found Mary standing in the doorway, closely watching my erratic moves about the room. I'd been working in a frenzy, thinking, I suppose, that if I kept up this frantic pace, my mind would rest and I would have the answers I needed.

I froze at the sound of her voice. "Nothing's wrong," I assured her as calmly as I could. "Really." Because I was more than eager to change the subject, I had a question of my own. "Are you ready for your breakfast?"

"I'll just have juice."

"Just juice?" I repeated. Thin as she was, Mary could stand to eat something more.

"As I've explained before, I don't have much of an appetite these days."

I thought to offer her a bit of an incentive. "I've gotten raves over this quiche."

"I'm sure it's delicious, but I've got a big event to attend this afternoon, and I don't want an upset stomach."

I didn't argue with her. I reached for a glass and filled it with orange juice before handing it to her.

I, too, had a big event this afternoon.

Chapter 30

Annie had her suitcase all packed and ready to load into her car. She set it along with her garment bag in the hallway and went to check the room one last time to be sure she hadn't left anything behind. Her grandparents had driven off a few minutes earlier.

As best she could see, her room was clear. When she turned around, she discovered her luggage and garment bag were missing. That was odd. She hadn't heard anyone. Hurrying down the stairs, she saw her missing items were in the foyer next to Oliver's overnight satchel. He must have carried hers down with his own.

She hardly knew what to think about the events of the night before. Frankly, her feelings for him set her off balance. What astonished her most was what a quick turnaround they had made. When he'd arrived on Friday she could barely tolerate the sight of him. And now . . . well, now just thinking about him caused her heart rate to accelerate to an alarming level. He was the same Oliver she'd known most of her life, and yet he was completely different. He hadn't changed, but her view of him had. He'd gone from pest to prince in the blink of an eye. Amazing, really. And a bit overwhelming, too.

Oliver came out from the kitchen area folding a sheet of paper; apparently, it was the receipt for his stay at the inn. Annie had taken care of her bill earlier.

"You ready?" he asked.

She nodded. Although she'd pretended otherwise, she welcomed this time with Oliver. Her brain swarmed with questions. He'd already set his plans to travel to the South Pacific in motion.

A year could be a very long time. Circumstances could change. They often did. Last Thanksgiving, she'd been set to marry Lenny. Thankfully, she'd come to her senses in time. Marriage to the handsome car salesman would have been a disaster, and apparently everyone had known that but her.

"You look like you're deep in thought," Oliver said. "Are you still mulling over what I suggested this morning?"

"No. I meant what I said. I refuse to let you back out of this trip, Oliver. It's the adventure of a lifetime." They'd sat at the breakfast table, arguing about his trip. He was willing to put it off, but Annie refused to let him.

"Come with me, then?"

"I can't." Annie wished she could, but it was impossible. "I've got commitments and responsibilities. Perhaps I could leave in a few months, but not now. Besides, I think we both need time."

He contradicted her by rolling his eyes.

Annie playfully elbowed him in the ribs. "Okay, maybe you don't need time, but I do. You seem to forget that I just broke off an engagement."

His eyes grew dark and serious. "Any regrets?"

"None about us, but I'm not ready to leap into another committed relationship just yet."

He frowned as though her words alarmed him.

"You don't need to worry. Nothing is going to change between you and me."

"Okay." He accepted her word without question.

"Besides, you could meet some island girl and fall head over heels in love with her."

"Yeah, right. You think I haven't tried falling for someone else? It doesn't work—I'm all yours."

"Really?" He said the most romantic things.

He chuckled, reached for their suitcases, and together they walked out of the inn. Oliver carted their bags to the car.

Annie unlocked the driver's-side door and then pushed the release that would open the trunk, which popped up automatically.

She set her purse on the floor and heard a car drive into the parking area. It seemed Jo Marie was about to get another guest. When she turned around, she saw a fancy red sports car that reminded her of something Lenny would drive.

Then it hit her. That was Lenny behind the wheel.

Annie froze; the oxygen in her lungs seemed to solidify on the spot. Instantaneously, her mouth went dry.

Oliver closed the trunk, glanced at her, and immediately realized something was wrong.

"Annie?"

For the life of her, she couldn't speak.

Lenny climbed out of the car and slammed the door. "Well, well, well, what do we have here?" His eyes narrowed accusingly on Annie and then Oliver. "It seems my sweet, innocent bride-to-be isn't so innocent after all. It seems you like a bit of action on the side yourself."

"If you're who I think you are, then perhaps it would be best for you and I to talk this out man to man." Oliver stepped next to Annie.

She had yet to recover her wits. "I'm not your bride-to-be," she reminded him. "And, Oliver, stay out of this."

Lenny ignored Oliver and directed his comments to Annie. "I have a couple of minor slips and you're outraged; you're so appalled that you break off our engagement. You broke my heart and my mother's heart, and all the while you're sleeping with some . . . some bean counter."

Oliver laughed outright. "Bean counter?"

"All right. Some nerd."

"Annie, let me put this jackass in his place," Oliver said, clenching his fists.

"No," she shouted. The last thing she wanted was for these two to slug it out. How ridiculous that would be. She didn't need Oliver defending her honor.

"I'd like to see you try to put me in my place," Lenny challenged.

"Stop it, both of you," she cried. "This is ridiculous. Lenny, this is Oliver. Oliver, Lenny, my ex-fiancé. I realize it might look a bit suspicious, but rest assured, Oliver isn't my lover."

"At least not yet," Oliver added.

Annie glared at him and continued: "Oliver was helping me with my grandparents' anniversary party. He stayed at the inn after driving my grandparents up from Portland."

One look told her Lenny didn't believe a word of it.

He ignored her, his eyes glaring menacingly at Oliver. "If you want to fight, then let's have at it. But before we do, by law I am required to tell you I've had judo lessons."

"You have?" Annie didn't know that. "You're making this up, aren't you? This is just another one of your lies!" This was the man she had been about to marry, and it seemed every minute she discovered something else she didn't know about him.

"You're required by law?" Oliver echoed disdainfully, shaking his head. "That's a new one."

"How'd you find me?" she asked, wanting to distract Lenny.

"How else? I called your boss."

Annie groaned. This was getting worse every second.

"Well, what did you expect me to do? You wouldn't answer my phone calls. You ignored my text messages, and then you blocked my number. I had something important I needed to say."

Knowing Lenny, it was probably another plea, another meaningless apology.

"What could be so important that you contacted my boss?" Annie hated the thought of showing up for work Monday morning and having to explain this awkward situation.

"My mother wants to talk to you."

"That's your important message?" she cried. Oh, boy, had she hit the nail on the head with that one. "Did you tell your mother about your little slip with that cupcake?"

Lenny blinked, which was answer enough.

"You didn't." It was a statement instead of a question. "You placed the blame for the broken engagement on my shoulders."

"What did you expect? Well, if you hadn't broken off the engagement earlier, then it's over for sure now."

"Then there's no problem," she said, glad they could agree on the subject.

"You leave me no choice, especially in light of what I just witnessed between you and what's-his-name."

"Oliver," he said, answering for her.

Annie stepped forward. "I've already explained who Oliver is."

"Annie." Oliver placed his hand on her shoulder in an effort to silence her.

"Let me talk to him myself," she said, wanting this break with Lenny to be clean and final. It went without saying that it was difficult for Oliver to stand back and let her deal with her former fiancé. She placed a restraining hand on his forearm.

"All weekend I've been sick with worry because I haven't been able to reach you," Lenny continued, sounding sad and broken. "I was frantic. I didn't sell a single car. You know what that does to my monthly average. I could lose the top salesman award this month, and it would be all your fault."

"Really?" she asked, trying hard to hide her sarcasm. "And you didn't have a clue where I might be?"

"No. And it wasn't like I didn't try to find you, either," he argued. "I called all your friends."

"Who?" Any friend of hers would know exactly where she was, seeing how she'd worked tirelessly for this anniversary party.

"Elle, for one."

Elle, Annie's onetime friend, who Lenny had flirted with endlessly. Annie hadn't spoken to Elle in weeks—months, actually—now that she thought about it. "Anyone else?"

Lenny frowned and looked down. "There were others."

"Who?"

"What does it matter? The point is I was beside myself, sick with worry."

She didn't believe that for a moment. "You should have been able to figure it out for yourself, Lenny," she said, unwilling to listen to his excuses any longer.

"How was I supposed to know this was the weekend of your parents' big shindig?"

"Grandparents'."

"Whatever," he muttered.

"You should have known because it was important to me."

"Okay, I get it now. You're pissed because all those months ago I told you I couldn't come. I get it. This is what it's all about. But like I told you way back then, weekends are when I get my sales. I can't take off on a Saturday because a bunch of old people managed to stay married."

"Lenny, oh, Lenny, I made such a terrible mistake."

He looked up, and his eyes brightened. "I know, but I'm willing to put all this behind us. You're the first girl my mother ever liked, and she was really upset when I told her the wedding was off."

"Annie?" Oliver whispered.

"It's all right," she whispered back. Returning her attention to Lenny, she straightened her shoulders. "You're a handsome, charismatic man, with huge potential."

He smiled, and his eyes warmed as he shrugged.

"The thing is, I fell in love with being in love. I felt the need to have someone special in my life, and there you were—handsome and funny and successful."

Again he shrugged. "Some people claim I'm the life of the party."

"You are," she agreed. "But you don't know the meaning of being faithful or honorable . . ."

"Oh, come on, Annie, you aren't going back to that again, are you? Okay, you're right, I screwed up a second time, but I did end up selling her a car."

"Fidelity is important," she insisted.

Lenny glared at Oliver. "Well, isn't that a little like the pot calling the kettle black? It seems you had a cozy weekend yourself with an old family friend."

Right away, Oliver stepped forward and stood toe to toe with Lenny. They were so close their noses almost touched.

"You've got a pretty face, just the way Annie mentioned," Oliver said between clenched teeth. "I'd hate to break it, but you're making it extremely difficult to hold back."

"Stop it, both of you," Annie insisted.

Both men ignored her, staring each other down.

"A broken nose would likely ruin your looks," Oliver muttered.

"Do you seriously think you could take me?" Lenny challenged. "Remember, I've had judo classes."

"Oh, yes, I forgot. Well, guess what, lover boy, so have I."

Lenny blinked.

Annie wasn't about to idly stand by and let these two men with overactive testosterone make fools of themselves. She grabbed hold of each by the shoulder and attempted to separate them.

"This is crazy," she shouted. "I told you before, Lenny, it's over. There's no going back, so kindly leave. You're missing sales being here."

He dropped his arms and stepped back. "My mother . . ."

"You'll find someone else she approves of before you know it."

He sighed, and with a pained look said, "It isn't going to be that easy."

"Good-bye, Lenny."

He nodded, conceding that it was a lost cause. With his head down and his shoulders hunched, he climbed back into the red sports car and started the engine.

Annie faced Oliver. "Have you really had judo lessons?"

"Yes. Do you honestly think I'd lie in the face of such danger?"

Annie wasn't sure she should believe either man.

"I was eight," he added.

"Eight?"

"Lenny was bluffing as well. He wouldn't do anything that would mess up that face, and we both knew it."

He was probably right. If Lenny had really had judo lessons, he would have bragged about it long before now.

"There's something else."

"Oh, and what's that?"

"My mother likes you, too. She's been telling me for years I needed to find a nice girl like the Shivers's oldest granddaughter."

"You're making that up."

"Am not."

Laughing, Annie opened the car door and climbed into the driver's seat. Oliver got in beside her.

"We were in the middle of an important discussion, if you remember, before we were so rudely interrupted," Annie reminded him. "I want you to go on your trip."

"And give you the time you need."

"Right."

He wasn't happy, but there wasn't anything he could do to change that.

"You'll join me in a few months, when you can arrange it?"

She glanced over at him, smiled, and said, "We'll see, but right now I'd say it's a distinct possibility."

Chapter 31

Mary's heart raced as they pulled into the parking lot of the Bremerton stadium, where the graduation exercises were taking place. George drove around until he found a parking spot close to the entrance so she wouldn't have far to walk. He turned off the engine, but before he could open his door, Mary stopped him.

He turned toward her, his look expectant.

"George, are we doing the right thing?" she asked, grabbing hold of his arm. It felt as though her heart was about to pound straight out of her chest. In all her life, she'd never been this anxious or nervous about anything. Over the years, Mary had faced many challenges in her career, but nothing, not even meetings with government officials or irate fund managers, had unnerved her this much. She'd sat in stockholder meetings and faced angry boards of directors, and nothing—absolutely nothing—terrified her as much as the realization she was about to see the child she had given up for adoption. The daughter she loved.

"What do you mean?" George asked. "I thought this was what you wanted."

"It is."

"Don't tell me you're getting cold feet now."

Mary didn't know what to tell him. "I'd barely grown comfortable with just being in the same city as Amanda," she whispered.

"Are you"—he hesitated as though he couldn't imagine that it was even possible—"afraid?"

Instinctively, Mary felt she should deny it, but the denial died on her lips. She would never be able to fool George. He would see through her bravado in a heartbeat. "I'm scared to death," she whispered, hardly able to find her voice. "My heart is racing . . . and look at me." She held out her hands so he could see how badly shaken she was.

"My love," George said, smiling with serene confidence. "She'll never know her birth parents are in the audience."

"But I'll know she's there," Mary cried.

"Do you think there's even the slightest possibility that she would recognize us?"

"No . . ." Naming her fear was as difficult as admitting it.

"Then what?"

Mary hung her head and fiddled with her hands, clasping and unclasping the opening to her purse. "My biggest fear is not her recognizing me but me being unable to hold back from telling her how proud I am that she's my child."

"In a graduating class of six hundred, let me assure you that there is very little chance we will even get close to Amanda."

While he made perfect sense, his reassurances didn't help. "Our blood flows through her veins." She choked up and bit into her lower lip. "This is our daughter."

"I won't let anything happen to upset you," George reassured her in gentle tones, as if he understood far better than she realized. "Amanda is part of us, but she belongs to another family that loves her."

Mary accepted that she had no claim on Amanda Palmer; still, she felt such a deep hesitation that she remained frozen inside the car.

"Come, now; it's time."

"I don't think I can."

"You can, and you will," George insisted. Not waiting for her, he climbed out of the car, came around to her side, and opened the passenger door.

Mary looked up at him, stiff with indecision.

"You haven't come this far to turn back now."

He was right, and in her heart Mary knew it. Inhaling deeply, she stepped out of the vehicle. George's hand was at her elbow, helping her. They were silent as they walked across the parking lot and joined the throng of family and friends entering the building. As they came into the large auditorium, George handed the attendant two tickets. They were then escorted to their assigned seats.

The level of excitement could be felt the moment Mary entered the room. She felt the anticipation of the other guests, mingled with joy and happiness. The noise level was high, which made it almost impossible to be heard. She stayed close to George's side.

Mary didn't know how George had managed to acquire tickets. Their seats were in the middle section and allowed them a good view of the stage. As soon as they sat down, George reached for her hand.

Mary was grateful he was with her, and she clung to him. After a while, she wrapped her arm around his elbow and leaned against him, needing his strength and reassurance. This behavior was so unlike her, she could only imagine what George must be thinking.

She reached for his hand and held on tight. She doubted she would be able to get through this event without him.

Before long the music sounded and the graduating class entered the auditorium in the formal procession. Mary immediately scanned the faces of teenagers as they marched into the room, seeking out the ones with the markings that indicated they were members of the National Honor Society. As valedictorian, Amanda would be wearing one of those. She didn't immediately find Amanda, but when she did, Mary's grip tightened on George in a punishing hold.

He understood immediately. "You see her?"

Mary nodded. "She's walking into the front row. Third one in on the right."

The second row moved into place, so all George was likely to see of Amanda now was the back of her head.

Mary hadn't attended any graduations other than her own, and that had been many years ago. Far too many years to count. The atmosphere was certainly different. Her own graduations from high school and college had been solemn affairs. Here the ambience was completely different—festive and jovial. In Mary's time, such disrespect would never have been tolerated. The crowd reacted with whistles and applause at the slightest provocation.

When the ceremony began, the school principal, Mr. LaCombe, spoke briefly and introduced the class president, who said a few words. Mary barely heard the speaker, a young man who greeted the family and friends who had come to share in this happy occasion. When it came time for the valedictorian's speech, George placed Mary's hand over his forearm. It seemed they both held their breath as Amanda walked across the stage.

As the eighteen-year-old stepped up to the lectern, Mary could sense how nervous Amanda was. She unfolded her speech and set it down and then held on to both sides of the lectern as she looked out over the crowd as though searching for a familiar face.

After a moment, she smiled and Mary realized she had found the one who gave her confidence. Mary's gaze followed Amanda's, and she saw the woman, who gave her a thumbs-up. Amanda's mother.

Amanda started her speech by thanking the school principal and her fellow graduates.

Mary leaned forward, listening intently. The teenager spoke of her experiences as a student and of the others with whom she had spent the last twelve years.

This told Mary that Amanda had lived in Cedar Cove nearly all her life. She wondered when and how the family had moved into the area, but the answer was one she would probably never know.

"And now we're all on the brink of starting a new life," Amanda continued. "For some of us, that will mean college or trade school. For others, it might mean joining the armed forces. This will likely be the last time the entire senior class will ever be together again."

From life experience, Mary knew that was true. She'd never returned to her hometown for high school reunions, or for that matter college reunions. All the reunions had come at especially busy times, and she simply hadn't been able to get away. She would have liked to reconnect with some of her friends, although they were precious few, because she was so desperately needed at home. She could reach out, Mary realized, which was something she'd always meant to do and hadn't. And now it was probably too late.

When Amanda spoke of her parents, thanking them for their love and support, Mary looked to George and relaxed enough to smile.

"What most of you don't know," Amanda continued, "is that I have a second set of parents. My birth parents."

Mary sucked in her breath and held it. George's hand tightened around hers to the point of causing her pain.

"They are the ones responsible for giving me life," she continued. "They chose, for whatever reasons, to put me up for adoption. I was placed in a loving home with a family that nurtured and treasured me. Although I don't know my birth parents or why they chose not to raise me themselves, I will forever be grateful for being adopted by the Palmers."

The speech ended with a huge round of applause. Mary dabbed at the tears that leaked from the corners of her eyes, hoping she wasn't being obvious. When she dared to sneak a look at George, she saw that he, too, had tears.

The names of the students were recited one by one, and although the audience was instructed to wait until all the names were read and all the graduation certificates were given out before applauding, few heeded the request. Parents and friends whistled or called out the names of their loved ones almost routinely.

Surprisingly, it didn't take long to announce the names of all six hundred graduates. The line moved efficiently and effectively. And when the ceremony was over, tradition was followed and the students hurled their caps into the air. The closing music started as the class filed out.

As soon as the last graduate had left the auditorium, family and friends stood to leave. A mad tangle of people made their way to the exits, mingling with students who stood outside the doors waiting to meet their loved ones.

Mary and George moved at a snail's pace toward the exit. The entire time, George kept Mary protectively close to his side. Once out of the building, it seemed everyone moved in opposite directions. Parents searched for their graduating seniors, and graduating seniors searched for their parents.

"Beth," someone shouted right next to Mary, practically yelling in her ear, "wait up."

"Grad party starts at seven," an adult shouted out the reminder to someone else.

"Excuse me, excuse me." A student tried to finagle her way past

George, and in her rush nearly stumbled. George caught her arm, preventing her from falling.

It was Amanda.

"Oh, I'm sorry, did I step on your foot?" she asked George apologetically.

For one horrible moment, Mary thought she would burst into tears.

The three of them stood, facing one another like rocks in the middle of a river with the crowd flowing around and past them.

Mary's tongue felt glued to the roof of her mouth. She couldn't have managed to squeeze out a single syllable had her future depended on it.

"No," George said, and then quickly added, "That was a wonderful speech." He glanced toward Mary. "Wasn't it?"

Mary was too badly shaken to answer the question.

"Thank you." Amanda beamed at his praise, smiling at them both. "I rewrote it several times. I couldn't decide which version to use until the last minute. Even my mom didn't know which one I would choose."

The spell broke, and Mary smiled. "It was perfect, well thought out; you said what your family and friends most needed to hear."

"Oh, thank you." Her eyes left Mary's and searched the crowd. "Excuse me. I think I see my parents."

"Of course." Mary scooted aside just in time to see the Palmer family making its way toward Amanda.

The parents were nearly shoved into Mary and George as people rushed past.

"Hello," Amanda's mother said. "Sorry to steal her away, but we have a family party planned."

"Oh, no, we just wanted to tell her what a wonderful talk she gave."

"Amanda gave us far too much credit," Mrs. Palmer continued. "She worked hard for her grades. We're so very proud of her."

"As you should be," George said.

"Do you have a child graduating?" Mrs. Palmer asked.

Mary and George glanced at each other and George smiled. "Yes, we do, and we're very proud of her, too."

"Who is it?" Amanda asked.

"Honey, we need to go," Mr. Palmer said before George could answer. Almost right away, the Palmers left and George carefully steered Mary through the throng and into the parking lot. They found their car and then spent the next forty minutes waiting for their turn to exit.

For the entire length of time, neither spoke. For her part, Mary needed time to absorb what had happened.

She had spoken to her daughter. Face-to-face.

Without even knowing it, Amanda had just met her birth parents.

When George pulled into the turn that would take them to Rose Harbor Inn, he said, "She's petite, like my mother."

"And mine."

"And beautiful, so beautiful, just like her mother."

He pulled into the parking space at the inn and turned off the engine. Neither moved.

"Thank you," Mary whispered.

George reached for her hand. "It wasn't a problem getting the tickets. All I had to do was . . ."

"I'm not thanking you for that. I'm thanking you for loving me, for being a part of my life, for standing by my side these last few days. I have treasured every minute of our time together."

"It doesn't have to end . . ."

"It does."

"I want you to stay in Seattle. Move in with me; I'll make sure you get in to all the right doctors, and—"

"No," she said sharply, cutting him off. "I can't, George. My home is in New York." Mary refused to saddle him with what she would face in the future. Perhaps she might return if she were fortunate enough to go into remission. But she ardently refused to subject George to what lay ahead for her, not knowing if her treatments would be successful.

"So you're shoving me out of your life again. Is that what you want, Mary? After everything we've shared, this is what you honestly want?"

She hesitated and then nodded. "I'm sorry, but yes."

"So this is good-bye, just like that?"

"Yes," she whispered brokenly. "This is good-bye."

"I don't think so."

"George, please . . ."

"Do you love me?" he asked her point-blank.

She looked away. "You know I do."

"Then tell me why you can't put me first for once and give me what I have always wanted, and that's you."

"George, please." She hated that he made this so difficult. "I could be dying."

"Even if you are terminal, are you telling me you'd rather die alone than be with me?"

She didn't answer him, because she couldn't. She had cancer, and as much as she loved him and wanted to be with him, she refused to subject him to this ordeal.

They argued a bit more, and she made one small concession. He could drive her to the airport. They set a time to meet.

At the inn now, he helped her out of the car, but she didn't take his hand. Instead, she got out under her own power, collected her shawl and purse, and then, with her head held high and her heart breaking, walked away without looking back.

Chapter 32

I had been in a mad rush, getting all the sheets changed and the rooms cleaned before the open house. With my mind going in five different directions, it was a wonder I'd managed to do it all, and in record time. Normally, I'd have Hailey's help, but her graduation from high school was scheduled for this afternoon, and I knew she'd be too busy with visiting relatives. I didn't feel I could ask her for help.

The cookies I'd baked over the better part of a week were artfully arranged on colorful ceramic plates around a large white vase filled with budding red roses. I set everything out on the dining room table. On the sideboard I'd placed pitchers of iced tea and large urns of both coffee and tea alongside plates and cups and utensils. Stepping back, I surveyed the arrangement and felt a sense of satisfaction. The table looked just as I'd hoped it would, simple and stylish.

I wished dressing myself had been as easy as decorating the table. The business suits I'd worn while working for the bank were too dressy, too off-putting for someone who owned a B&B. But my usual jeans and bib apron were too casual. I was going for a look that was professional but at the same time welcoming. After changing clothes two or three times, I'd finally settled on a white skirt with a matching jacket. The blouse was pink silk, with pearl buttons. Rover had watched me quizzically when I asked him for his opinion. Frankly, he was no help whatsoever.

Rover was napping in the laundry room, the refreshments were out, and the drinks were ready to be poured. All I had to do now was wait for my guests to arrive. I nervously paced from room to room, checking and rechecking to be sure all was in order. Oh, how I wished I had scheduled this for later in the year, summertime or even autumn. Peggy Beldon from The Thyme and Tide had encouraged me not to wait, though, claiming that if I put it off until I was satisfied, then it would probably never happen. Instinctively, I knew she was right.

I'd made several small changes to the inn since taking it over from the Frelingers, the previous owners. Mark had built me a new oak mantel for the fireplace and done a lovely job. He'd replaced the railing on the front porch steps, too, and changed a couple of the light fixtures. He knew enough about electrical work and plumbing to make basic repairs, and I'd called on him a number of times.

I had come to love Cedar Cove. Although I'd lived in this town for only five months, it felt like home. I'd made friends and enjoyed becoming part of the business community. And I loved this inn. I'd found a certain measure of peace here.

A car rolled into the driveway, interrupting my thoughts. My first guest had arrived. Right away, I recognized Olivia Griffin, who had brought along her mother, Charlotte Jefferson Rhodes. I had to smile. I'd met Charlotte twice now, and both times she'd carried her knitting with her. She had it with her now, too.

Charlotte and her husband, Ben, had stopped by to introduce themselves shortly after I'd moved into the inn. We'd shared tea and the special scones she'd baked. While we chatted, she brought out her knitting and barely looked down as her fingers wove the yarn around the needles. As I recalled, she'd been working on a pair of socks for her son, Will.

I opened the door to welcome my friends.

"Are we the first ones here?" Olivia asked, looking very much the distinguished judge that she was. I hadn't gotten to know her as well as her friend Grace, but I hoped we would have the opportunity, given time. She possessed the grace and style of a Jacqueline Kennedy or an Audrey Hepburn. I imagined she made a striking presence in the courtroom.

"I'm pleased you could make it," I said, as I held open the door. Thankfully, the overcast skies from that morning had cleared, and the day, while cool, was sunny and bright. We'd had several days of sunshine, which wasn't the norm, and I was grateful.

"Mom and I were looking forward to seeing the inn. Church got out a bit early, so we went to brunch at Justine's restaurant. It seemed silly to take Mom back just to turn around a few minutes later to pick her up again."

"Please, don't worry. Your timing is perfect."

"I've come to see what you've done with the place," Charlotte said, looking around and nodding with approval. "I like the new sign and the name you chose: Rose Harbor Inn. Clever, seeing that your surname is Rose. Heard Mark Taylor made it for you."

"Yes, he did. He's done quite a bit of work for me."

Charlotte looked over the table and fingered the crocheted lace tablecloth I used. "Good man, Mark. He's done work for Ben and me, and always charged us a fair price."

Talking about Mark gave me a twinge of guilt. I'd meant to check up on him this morning, not that he'd appreciate it, but time had gotten away from me and it had slipped my mind.

"I see you changed the pillows in the living room," Olivia commented, glancing into the room.

"I rearranged several of the guest rooms, too." Mark had helped me with moving furniture as well. As we spoke, I realized how big a role Mark had played in my life and that of the inn.

"I'm looking forward to seeing the rooms," Charlotte commented.

Right away, Olivia glanced at the staircase. "Mom, you need an elevator. You shouldn't be climbing stairs at your age."

"Fiddlesticks. I can take the stairs."

"Mom."

Charlotte raised her hand in protest. "I'll take them one at a time and go slow. I didn't come to inspect the kitchen; I want to see what Jo Marie has done upstairs."

Seeing that her mother was determined, Olivia capitulated. She took her mother's arm and led her toward the staircase.

Sheriff Troy Davis and his wife, Faith, were the next to arrive. Sheriff Davis and I had both attended a charity auction and had bid against each other for a blue vase I thought would go perfectly in one of the guest rooms. He won, and later thanked me for bowing out. The vase was a gift for Faith. I hadn't met Faith, so we took a few moments to chat and exchange pleasantries.

Jack Griffin, the judge's husband, showed up in a battered fifteen-year-old Ford. He took the porch stairs two at a time and seemed to be in something of a rush. He wore a long raincoat and looked every inch the small-town newspaper editor he was. To complete the picture, all he needed was a felt hat and a pen and pad, which no doubt he had tucked away inside one of his coat pockets.

"Olivia here?" he asked, even before I had time to greet him.

"She's upstairs with her mother."

"Thanks." He started toward the stairs, stopped, and looked back at me. "By the way, you've done a great job with the place." His eyes fell on the table and the display of cookies.

"Those cookies look great," he said, as if he was a man lost in a desert who spied an oasis.

"Help yourself."

He shook his head, although clearly tempted. "Olivia will have my hide if I break this diet. She's on this healthy-eating kick." He walked over to the table in order to get a better look. "Peanut butter is healthy, isn't it?"

"Of course."

"According to Olivia, oatmeal is high in fiber," he added.

"Right again."

He chuckled, took one of each, and set them on a plate. "You can't eat much healthier than this."

"No, you can't," I agreed, enjoying his reasoning process.

Just as he was about to eat the first of the cookies, Olivia came down the stairwell. "Jack Griffin, what are you doing?" she asked.

He looked terribly guilty. "It's peanut butter, and the other one is oatmeal." He hesitated and glanced down longingly at the plate with the two cookies. "That's good fiber, right?"

"Go ahead," Olivia said, shaking her head in mock disgust. "I'm not your keeper. The choice is yours."

Jack sighed, and after a moment, he set the plate down with both cookies untouched. "You can't love a woman more than this," he told me.

I smiled and noticed a taxi pulling up to the front of the inn. A taxi? Oh, my, had I completely lost it and booked a guest who was due to arrive this Sunday? I'd purposely not accepted reservations for this date, but perhaps I'd overlooked one.

The cab door opened, but I didn't recognize the occupant right

away. When I did, I had to take a second look to be sure I was seeing right.

Mark Taylor.

I'd never seen him in anything but jeans or work clothes. This
afternoon, he wore slacks and a white shirt, and his hair was parted
on the side, wetted down, and combed. He appeared to have
shaved, too.

This was Mark? I stared at him, hardly knowing what to think.

He had some trouble getting his crutches out of the taxi. Once
he did, he leaned heavily on them as he made his way to the steps.
I held my breath as he started up them.

"Mark," I cried, slamming open the door and rushing to help
him. "What are you doing here?" That probably wasn't the best
question to ask coming out of the gate.

"I thought I was invited. You left an invitation."

"Of course you're welcome; it's just that I didn't expect you to
actually come." As I recalled, he'd made a rather brusque comment about the idea when I'd first mentioned holding an open
house.

"Let me help you," I said, my hand on his arm. I was afraid
he'd lose his balance on the steps with those crutches. He hadn't
had much time to get accustomed to using them.

"I don't need help."

"Of course you don't, but I'm here just in case you do."

He surprised me with how agile he was. Before I knew it, he
was up the steps and on the porch. I held the door open for him.
My mind stumbled over what to say. I'd been so stunned to see him
that I sounded as if he wasn't welcome. He was, of course.

He looked a bit wobbly by the time he was in the house.

"Would you like to sit down?" I asked.

"Might be a good idea."

I motioned toward the living room. He must have great upper-body strength, because he managed the crutches just fine. Sinking into the sofa, he parked the crutches down on the floor in front of him so they weren't a hazard to others.

More visitors arrived, and for the next two hours I was busy giving tours and answering questions. I'd put a guestbook out earlier, and by the end there were at least fifty names entered. Most visitors came and went within a few minutes.

I was exhausted when the second-to-last person left.

Only one person remained.

Mark.

He hadn't moved from the sofa, although I saw he was involved in conversation with a number of the townspeople.

"Any cookies left?" he asked, and while it was a casual question, I knew he was interested in the leftovers.

"A few. Want some?"

"I think I've already eaten more than my fair share."

"Would you like to take the rest home?"

His grin was huge. "I thought you'd never ask."

I started to package up the few remaining cookies, probably a dozen or so in three different varieties.

"Come sit," he ordered. "You've been on your feet for the last two hours without a break."

He was right. I didn't realize how exhausted I was until the open house was over. All at once it felt as if I'd run a marathon. I let Rover out of the laundry room, and he immediately wanted to go outside. Once he was back, I literally fell onto the sofa next to Mark.

"You did a good job. People were saying how much they liked what you've done with the inn."

"Thanks." I noticed that he didn't mention his own role in the changes I'd made. That was modest of him, seeing that he was the one responsible for the vast majority of the changes. I'd painted several of the guest rooms, rearranged furniture, purchased a few new things, but Mark was responsible for plenty, including the shutters I'd added to the windows.

"You clean up well," he said, looking over at me.

A compliment? From Mark? I hardly knew how to respond. "You, too."

He grinned and ran his hand over the top of his head and down his forehead. "Been a long time since I wore this shirt. Can't even remember when I last had it on. A wedding, I think."

I knew so little about him I found this a prime opportunity to ask him a few subtle questions. "Your wedding or someone else's?"

His eyes narrowed. "Someone else's." He looked away. "One of the reasons I decided to show was to find out if you're okay."

"What makes you think I might not be?"

He chuckled softly. "You mean other than the fact that you nearly bit my head off when I asked you a couple of innocent questions?"

"I did? When was that?"

"Yesterday afternoon. Told me to mind my own business and stalked off like someone had lit a fuse under you."

"Yeah, I guess I did. No offense meant."

He shrugged as if it wasn't any big deal, although he'd clearly been worried. "I don't have many friends, and I've sort of gotten accustomed to you."

I wasn't sure he meant that as a compliment, but I decided to take it as one. "Thanks. You, too."

"Anyone comment on the fact the yard is torn up?"

"No one." Although it was fairly obvious that work was being done in that area. "As a matter of course, I mentioned that I hoped to plant a rose garden with a gazebo."

"Did you happen to say that I was the one who got behind schedule and it's all my fault?"

"I wouldn't do that."

"Well, maybe not, but you sure came down hard on me."

I suppose I had. "I was disappointed, Mark."

"I know. I'll make it my top priority as soon as I'm back on my feet."

"I'd appreciate that."

Somewhat to my surprise, he didn't appear eager to be on his way. "Have you taken any pain pills lately?"

"No?" He made it a question, as if he wondered why I would be asking. "You have a reason for wanting to know?"

"I thought you might like to have a glass of wine."

"With you?"

"No," I teased. "With Rover."

He thought about it for a moment and then shrugged as if he didn't really care one way or the other. "I guess I could."

"Red or white?"

The decision appeared to be too much for him. "You choose."

I opened a bottle of pinot noir from the Willamette Valley in Oregon and poured us each a glass.

For the next half hour we sat and talked. Truth was, I did most of the talking. Mark never did have much to say. After a glass of wine, I was half tempted to tell him about the letter. Painful as the subject was, I decided against it.

Instead of having him call a cab, I drove Mark back to his house and got back in time to see that Mary Smith had returned to the inn. Without a word to me, she went straight to her room.

Chapter 33

Mary woke bright and early Monday morning. It was the best night's sleep she'd had in more weeks than she could remember. She sat up in bed and, yawning, raised her arms above her head. Looking out onto the cove, she noticed it had started to rain. After four glorious days of sunshine in a Pacific Northwest spring, a downpour should be expected.

A sense of contentment filled her. The opportunity to actually see the daughter she'd given birth to had been an unexpected gift. But to be able to speak to Amanda face-to-face had been above anything she had hoped for or imagined. She had George to thank for that.

At the thought of him, her spirits plummeted, and all the happiness drained from her. The joy diluted with the reality that once again she would be leaving him. As tempting as it was to remain in Seattle, that was impossible. Impractical. To do so would be completely and utterly selfish of her, and she couldn't do it, couldn't put him through this ordeal.

She loved him—yes, of course, how could she not?—but Mary wasn't about to saddle him with her health issues. He wanted her to stay, and they'd argued, but in the end she had succeeded in convincing him the only practical thing to do was for her to return to New York. Her doctors, medical records, and home were all there. To interrupt her treatment program now would be foolish and possibly dangerous.

George hadn't made the argument easy. When he'd grown weary, he'd requested one thing, that she let him drive her to the airport. She'd capitulated simply because the fight had gone out of her. With regret, she'd canceled the car service.

She was the only guest at the inn, and she'd warned Jo Marie she didn't have much appetite for breakfast. Toast and orange juice were all she requested. Even then, all she managed was a single slice of toast and a few sips of juice.

Now she waited for George to arrive. How foolish of him to drive all the way into Cedar Cove in order to drive her to Sea-Tac Airport. On a Monday, too, when traffic would be heavy in both directions. She could only imagine what that must have done to his appointment schedule. Nevertheless, she would be glad to see him one last time and would hold on to the memory for a very long while.

"Let me get your suitcase for you," Jo Marie offered when Mary came down the stairs. She'd taken care of her bill over breakfast. Her flight out wasn't scheduled until noon, so she had plenty of time.

"Thank you."

Jo Marie had been a good host. Mary had felt welcome and had been allowed to set her own boundaries. She valued her privacy and appreciated that the innkeeper hadn't been overly friendly or inquisitive.

Within a couple of minutes, Jo Marie came down the stairs with the suitcase as if it weighed next to nothing. Mary was glad for the assistance.

"Did you enjoy your stay?" Jo Marie asked.

"Oh, yes, very much." These few days in Cedar Cove would carry her the rest of her life. She'd had an opportunity she never expected to be repeated and would cherish the memories.

"I'm sure it will be good to get home, too," Jo Marie added. "There's something so comforting about returning home, isn't there? That sense of familiarity."

Mary smiled and didn't add a comment. Her New York condo was only a shell. Over the years she'd added a few decorative touches, but it'd never felt like a real home. It was where she slept and stored her things. Most of her meals were take-out or delivered; she never had been interested in cooking. Meals were a necessity but often rushed as she grabbed a bite between meetings. At night she was too worn out to enjoy her dinner.

George's vehicle pulled up in front of the inn, and her heart immediately gladdened at the sight of him. She watched as he climbed out of the car and made a dash for the porch, looking to avoid getting soaked. Knowing there was every likelihood she would encounter showers in Seattle, Mary had packed her raincoat. She put up the hood and walked onto the porch, pulling her suitcase behind her.

George raced up the few steps and automatically took the suitcase. "You ready?" he asked.

"Well, good morning to you, too."

He looked up and met her gaze and held it for a long moment. "It isn't a good morning for me."

"Oh, George, my darling, we've already been through this once."

He nodded and looked away.

Jo Marie joined them, with Rover at her side. "I hope you'll come back again sometime," she said.

It wasn't likely to happen, so Mary simply smiled. "Thank you for everything."

"My pleasure."

George took Mary's hand and guided her down the stairs and then saw her to the car, opening the door for her before tucking her lone piece of luggage into the trunk. By the time he joined her, he was soaked from the rain.

"Oh, George, you're drenched."

"I'll dry off in short order."

He looked miserable, shoulders hunched, eyes sad, as if she'd broken his heart all over again. He started the car, but before putting it in reverse, he stated casually, "I was thinking on the drive out here that I could take time off in a week or two and fly to New York." He hesitated as he awaited her reaction.

Already, Mary could see what he was doing. He was edging his way back into her life a little at a time. While she would love seeing him, living on two coasts would hurt his career. They'd tried that once, and it hadn't worked; she couldn't see doing it again. Still, the temptation to agree was so strong, she felt herself leaning toward him, the pull magnetic, electrifying.

The problem was the unknown future. Mary didn't know what life held in store for her, and if . . . if the chemo and radiation hadn't killed the cancer, then her options were limited. And it would kill him to watch her die in degrees, a little each day.

"What do you think?" he asked, his hands tight around the steering wheel.

"We'll see."

He released a heavy sigh. "Which is a polite way of telling me you aren't interested, right?"

She didn't answer him.

He sighed. "I've been fooling myself, haven't I?"

"About what?"

"I thought . . . this weekend. I'd hoped you might have come to the conclusion that you've never stopped loving me."

How could he believe otherwise? she wondered, and realized it was the hurt and disappointment talking. "I've always loved you, George. Always and forever."

"Even when you left me?"

More than he would ever know. "Even then."

"What about now?"

"Even now," she assured him softly.

He didn't say anything for a few moments, and then whispered, "You have a funny way of showing it."

In his eyes, she probably did. The real problem was she loved him too much to subject him to dealing with her cancer.

They didn't speak again until they reached Highway 16, which would eventually link up with the interstate in Tacoma. "Is there something you're not telling me?" he asked, carefully keeping his focus on the road.

"Like what?"

"Something having to do with the cancer?"

"No." She'd been completely honest from the first.

"You're sure?"

"George, of course I'm sure." Did he really think she would lie to him about a subject this serious? And then she realized he had every reason to doubt her after what he'd learned about her and Amanda these last few days.

"You're aware Seattle has one of the finest cancer research centers in the country, aren't you?"

"Yes." Fred Hutchinson Cancer Research Center was world-renowned.

Thinking she needed to change the subject completely, she said, "Let's not talk about my leaving, please. It's difficult for us both."

"What do you want to talk about, then?"

"Amanda."

Right away, she sensed the tension leaving his shoulders. "She's amazing."

Just mentioning their daughter brought a sense of lightness, and joy, to Mary, too. "I couldn't agree more. Seeing her, speaking to her one-on-one was so much more than I'd hoped for. I can't thank you enough."

"Did you find it hard not to touch her?" he asked.

"Yes, oh, yes. I had to clench my fists to remind myself not to reach out and cup her face. It was even harder not to hug her and explain that she was the one I carried beneath my heart for nine months."

"For a moment, I was afraid her parents might recognize the two of us," George said.

"How could they?"

"Mary, my goodness, she looks just like you; didn't you notice?"

She hadn't. "I thought she looked more like you."

For the first time that morning, George smiled. "You did the right thing by giving her up to the Palmers."

Mary had felt the same way, although over the course of the graduation, she'd been assaulted with regrets. Seeing her daughter stand up as valedictorian had filled Mary with doubts. She wanted everyone to know that this was her child, the fruit of her womb. That would have been completely unfair to the family that had raised her these last eighteen years. It had taken Mary several moments to realize it was too late for regrets now. As difficult as it was, she let those feelings go. Instead, she'd concentrated on her daughter's speech.

It was ironic, really. Seeing Amanda had produced profound joy and at the same time profound sadness. It was hard to explain, hard to understand how Mary could feel the mixture of the two emotions simultaneously.

The traffic was heavy as they merged with the interstate. Mary glanced at her watch. Because she moved slowly these days, she'd left herself plenty of time at the airport. At this rate, she would arrive two hours before her departure.

They rode in silence for the next several minutes, as if everything they wanted to say had already been said, in some cases multiple times.

George drove past the first exit to the airport.

"Shouldn't you have taken that exit?" she asked.

"There are two exits. I've always taken the other."

"Okay."

"Your flight isn't for another two hours," he reminded her.

"It takes awhile getting through security, and I walk slow." She might even need to stop and rest for a few minutes, depending on how far away the gate was. And she refused to be pushed in a wheelchair.

"Would you like me to see you to your gate? It doesn't take much to get a pass."

"No, but thanks." It would be difficult enough without prolonging the good-byes.

"You'll check your bag outside, won't you?"

"Yes. I've already printed out my boarding pass."

"Good idea. Jo Marie did that for you?"

"Yes. She was most helpful."

George changed lanes, getting into the far right-hand lane to exit. "I heard she's a widow."

"Yes." Getting this close to the airport, to leaving George, caused Mary's throat to tighten.

"Do you know her story?"

"I don't."

She mustn't have sounded like herself, because George glanced her way. "You okay?"

"Why wouldn't I be?" she asked, downplaying the dread that filled her.

The freeway sign indicating they were within one mile of the exit came into view. Her throat grew thicker. She wouldn't cry; she absolutely refused to let George see her weep.

After a few minutes, without warning, George changed lanes, swerving back into the heavy traffic heading north.

"What are you doing?" she demanded.

George didn't answer her.

"George, you just missed the exit."

"I know."

"But . . . George, I need to get to the airport. You said you would drive me to the airport."

"I lied," he said, as if this was a small thing.

"What do you mean you lied?" Mary was angry now.

"I'll explain everything once we're back at my condo."

"I am not going to your condo," she insisted.

"Oh, but you are. You have no other option."

He was right, but that didn't help matters any. "I insist you take the next exit and head back to the airport."

"Sorry, that isn't possible."

"Of course it's possible. Are you kidnapping me? Is that it?"

"I'll explain everything in a couple of minutes."

"Explain it now. This is the most ridiculous thing you've ever done."

"I thought you'd say that." He looked downright gleeful.

"George, for the love of heaven, what has gotten into you?"

He simply smiled and shook his head, refusing to answer her.

Demanding didn't work, and he ignored her pleas, so she sat back in the seat and crossed her arms, not knowing what else could be done.

He took one of the downtown Seattle exits and drove directly to his condo building. He pulled into the parking garage and into the space reserved for his vehicle.

After turning off the ignition, he climbed out of the car, walked around, and opened the passenger door. Mary refused to budge. If he could be stubborn, so could she. She had her arms crossed, and she looked straight ahead and refused to acknowledge the hand he held out to her.

"I let you walk away from me before," he said calmly, "and I decided I wasn't going to let you make the same mistake twice."

"Me?"

"I was a fool to let you go the first time. I'm not doing it again."

"George," she pleaded, squeezing her eyes closed with pain and frustration. "Don't you realize what you're doing? I have cancer. My doctors, my medical records, are in New York."

"Seattle has wonderful cancer doctors, too, and emailing records takes no time whatsoever."

"My home is in New York."

"No, it isn't," he challenged.

She sighed with annoyance.

"Your home is with me," he continued. "We've cheated each other out of nineteen years, and I'm unwilling to let one more unnecessary day go by without you in my life."

"Oh, George . . ."

"Do you love me or not?"

She bit down on her lip to keep from answering.

"You can't lie, Mary. I know you too well."

"Then why did you ask?" Tears crowded her eyes. Oh, dear heaven, here she was weeping again, weak as a newborn kitten.

"I refuse to give in. If I let you walk away from me again, I'll regret it the rest of my life."

"Don't you understand?" she whispered, her voice cracking. "I could be dying . . ."

"We're all dying."

She cupped her hand over her mouth.

George squatted down beside her. "You can fight me all you want, but this is a battle I intend to win. I'm not letting you leave me. You can argue until you're blue in the face, but the decision has been made."

"What do you mean?"

"I contacted a friend of mine who's getting me the name of the top cancer specialist in the country."

"He's in New York."

He laughed and shook his head. "Good try. I don't know where he practices; that isn't my concern. You are. No matter what the future holds, we're facing it together."

"Oh, George." It was impossible to hold back the tears any longer.

"We belong together. We always have. Just how long are you going to fight me on this?"

The will to leave him was gone. With a sob, she threw her arms around his neck and clung to him, nearly toppling him over. "I love you so much."

"I know . . . I love you, too. Whatever happens, Mary, I'll be at your side."

She nodded.

Mary didn't know what she'd done to deserve this man, but whatever it was, she would be forever grateful.

Chapter 34

I'd just finished the cleaning process in Mary Smith's room when the phone rang. I bebopped down the stairs to answer it, my mood lighter than it had been in the last couple of days. I felt good. As much as I'd fretted over the open house, everything had come together beautifully.

"Rose Harbor Inn," I greeted cheerfully.

"Jo Marie?" My name was followed by a slight hesitation.

Lieutenant Colonel Milford.

This was the call I'd been eagerly anticipating and dreading all at once. The conversation that would strengthen that slender thread of hope or sever it completely.

I collapsed into the desk chair. The phone was pressed hard against my ear, so hard that it hurt. "What did you find out?"

"I got word only a few minutes ago."

"The DNA tests are back?" Why couldn't he simply tell me rather than prolong my agony? Surely he knew the answer by now.

"It takes longer than a day or two to come up with that kind of information."

"So there's a chance—"

"No," he said, cutting me off. "There is no chance Paul survived the crash. None whatsoever."

"What do you mean?" I challenged.

"I'm sorry."

"But you said the DNA tests weren't back." I argued.

"They aren't."

"Then how can you be so sure Paul is dead? You told me yourself that—"

Again he interrupted me. "The remains of all six men have been accounted for now. I'm sorry. I wish I had better news."

His words knocked the breath right out of me. My lungs felt as if they had collapsed. A renewed sense of grief hit so hard it felt as if it had buried me.

The next sound frightened me. A wail of grief, of loss, of pain. All hope was gone now. It took me several moments to realize that cry had come from me. My husband was dead.

Instantly, Rover was at my side. He stood on his two hind legs and placed his front paws on my thigh as if to comfort me. My hand shook terribly as I set it on top of his head. My face burned hot, and the tears seared my cheeks as they squirted from my eyes.

"If you want Paul can be buried at Arlington National Cemetery," Milford continued. He told me again what a fine man Paul had been, but I already knew that. I listened but I barely heard his words.

After a few words of farewell, I replaced the phone.

It was over now.

For a long time I sat staring into the distance. Then I sucked in a deep breath and dried my tears. My heart felt like it had swollen to twice its normal size. All my options were gone, all the scenarios I'd built up in my mind dissolved into dust.

I was petting Rover's head, taking comfort in my special companion, when my hand froze. It was time to read Paul's letter.

Like a ghost walker, I made my way into my private quarters and sat on my bed. I opened my bedside drawer where I had tucked it away and pulled out the envelope.

I read it through twice, nonstop.

It didn't contain any surprises. He said exactly what I had expected.

He loved me.

He didn't want me to grieve.

He would meet me in heaven but he hoped that wouldn't be for a good many years because I had a great deal to offer to others.

When I finished, I folded it up and returned it to the envelope.

"Get on with your life," Paul wrote, and he was right. I had work to do.

I'd barely had time to recover when Rover barked and then raced frantically out of my room to the front door. I had company.

The doorbell rang a second time, and when I opened the door I immediately recognized the woman who stood on the other side.

"Michelle," I said. I'd met Michelle Nelson through Joshua Weaver, one of the very first guests to stay at Rose Harbor Inn. Joshua had come to visit his stepfather, who was dying and in fact did pass while Joshua was with him. Michelle had lived next door to Joshua's stepfather and had known Josh while she was in high school.

Michelle wasn't a member of the Chamber of Commerce. She worked for the state as a social worker, but she had many ties to the community. I'd invited her to the open house because I hadn't heard from him since he'd left town—not that I'd expected that I would. I'd sensed a romance brewing between him and Michelle, and wanted an update without appearing intrusive or overly inquisitive.

"I'm sorry I didn't make it to the open house," Michelle said by way of greeting.

To be honest, I hadn't noticed. With so many of my fellow business owners wandering in and out, I'd lost track of who had come and who hadn't.

"I bet you had a lot of people." Michelle stepped into the foyer, and Rover was right there, ready to greet her. She bent down and rubbed his ears while murmuring what a good dog he was. Rover reveled in her attention. It seemed men and dogs responded best to food, toys, and praise.

"Do you have time for coffee?" I asked, watching the interplay between Michelle and Rover.

"Do you?" she countered, glancing up at me.

"Sure." I could use a distraction. My one hope was that she wouldn't notice that I'd recently been crying. I'd move one foot forward, taking today one step at a time, while I dealt with the reality of what I'd just learned. Thankfully, my next set of guests wasn't scheduled to arrive until Tuesday, so I had a one-day break.

I led the way into the kitchen, and Michelle followed. While I reached for the coffeepot she took a chair at the small two-person table I had up against the wall.

"I'm due in court in a half hour," she explained. "I can only stay a few minutes."

"Not a problem. Is it for an adoption?"

"This is the best part of my job," Michelle said as she nodded. "This little boy is as cute as a button, and his new family is thrilled. His mom has gone through six IVF attempts without success. She was convinced she would never be a mother when they decided to apply for adoption. As most families do, they were looking to get an infant."

"That's perfectly understandable, isn't it?"

"Of course. Unfortunately, there are precious few newborns who come through the system."

"How old is the child they're adopting?"

"Three. He's the sweetest little boy you're likely to meet."

"What convinced them to adopt a three-year-old?" I asked, as I handed Michelle a steaming mug of coffee. I motioned toward the sugar bowl and she shook her head.

"I take it black, thanks." She sipped the coffee and then answered my question. "I told her about the boy and convinced her to take him as a foster child."

"The family fell in love with him?"

"I knew they would. This precious little boy is getting a family, and this husband and wife are seeing their dream of being parents become a reality. No wonder I love my job." Her eyes fairly sparkled. "I have a little girl in mind for them, too, but that's several months down the road."

Michelle was a little devil. Her smile was as big as any I've seen.

I decided the best way to learn about her and Josh was to ask her outright. Otherwise, I might never hear what was happening in his life.

"Tell me," I said, hoping to sound casual and nonchalant. "When was the last time you heard from Josh?"

I'd assumed her smile couldn't get any bigger, but it did. Her eyes brightened, and she quickly looked down at her coffee. "If you must know, we talk every day."

"Every day?" This was an interesting piece of news.

"He's involved in a huge construction project in North Dakota. It's demanding and exhausting, but he finds time for us to connect no matter what is happening on the site."

As I recalled, Josh was a project manager. When he'd come to the inn he'd just finished overseeing the construction of a strip mall, although for the life of me I couldn't remember in what state. I was sure he'd told me at one point or another.

"I'm glad to hear the two of you are staying in touch."

Michelle glanced up and met my gaze. "He recently asked me to marry him."

"Michelle, that's wonderful." I noticed right away that she hadn't said she'd accepted his proposal. "And what did you say?"

"I love Josh and I want to be his wife, but Cedar Cove is my home. I love living here. I have a job that's meaningful, and I don't want to give that up."

"Couldn't Josh move here?"

"He offered to do that, but his job takes him all over the country. He enjoys what he does and he's good at it, really good."

"Does this mean the two of you are deadlocked?"

Michelle shrugged. "You know that saying: Where there's a will there's a way?"

"I know it well."

"Josh and I have been negotiating back and forth. I think some union leaders could learn tricks from him. When he wants something, he makes it impossible to say no."

"And he wants you?"

Michelle blushed and nodded. "He talked to his company and got the CEO to agree to give him work somewhere in western Washington. That means he'll be working primarily in the Seattle/ Tacoma area. He gets first choice on those projects, and if there isn't a job site, then he'll take the ones that would require him staying away only two or three nights in a row."

"Did that satisfy you?"

"It did."

"So when's the wedding?"

"August, after this current project is finished, but then he's starting another one as soon as we're back from our honeymoon."

"A job close to home?"

"Very close. It's in Cedar Cove."

I frowned. I wasn't aware of any big construction project about to take place in the area. Surely the Chamber of Commerce and other local businesses would have been in the loop.

"It's a little ironic, really. Josh's stepfather put his house on the market with instructions that the funds be given to charity."

I'd heard that and felt bad for Josh, thinking as Richard's only surviving relative he should have inherited the house. Apparently not.

"Josh bought the house when it went on the market."

"His stepfather's house?"

"Yes. It's right next to my parents' home. He's going to do a major remodeling project on it, add a couple of bedrooms, and completely renovate the kitchen. Basically, it's going to be a brand-new house."

This was great news. "That's wonderful."

"We want to start a family, and Mom and Dad travel a lot and need someone close who can look after the house. It will be ideal for us all. Mom and Dad will give us our space and we'll be able to help them when they need it."

I could see that Josh had found the family he had always wanted with Michelle.

"I hope you'll make sure I get a wedding invitation."

"Not to worry; your name is already on the list."

"Give Josh my best when you speak with him later."

"I will." Michelle took one last sip of her coffee, stood, and set her mug in the sink. "Sorry to run off like this . . ."

"No problem. You've got important work to do." I followed her to the front door, and Rover did, too. The two of us stood in the doorway and watched Michelle leave. It'd been a good visit.

So Josh would be moving back to Cedar Cove. That was welcome news, and I was pleased for Michelle. We'd gotten to know each other a bit. I liked her and wished to know her better. She was a woman who knew what she wanted and wasn't willing to settle for second best. I admired that about her.

As she left I was reminded anew of the dream I'd had the first night I took over the inn, when Paul had come to me. He'd assured me this inn would be a healing place, for me and for others. I had seen the evidence of that twice over in the last couple of days. First with the wedding invitation from Abby Kincaid and now with Josh, finding love and a family.

I returned to the kitchen and had set the coffee mugs in the dishwasher when the phone rang.

"Rose Harbor Inn."

"This is Ms. Eleanor Reynolds. I'm inquiring about a room." Her voice was clipped and a bit stern. She asked about space for a weekend in late August and about the availability of a room for a few extra days if necessary after that specific weekend.

"As it happens, I have those days free," I assured her.

"Good. I'd like to place a reservation for that Friday, Saturday, and Sunday. I might stay on to Monday . . . and Tuesday. I just don't know yet."

"Certainly. Is it for a special occasion?"

"Yes. Well, we'll see if it is or not." She didn't elaborate.

I didn't inquire further. If she didn't want to volunteer the information, then I wasn't about to pry. Business had picked up considerably, with bookings for nearly every day starting in June. The cove was a popular boating area, and the farmers' market drew a crowd on the weekends. Weddings were big business, too, and if all went well my rose garden and gazebo would be completed by the end of summer.

"I have you down," I told her, repeating the August dates.

Rover barked, and I realized I had neglected to fill his water dish.

"You have animals?" She sounded quite prissy, as if she wasn't accustomed to being around animals.

"A dog," I told her. "I hope that isn't a problem." I knew some people were allergic. It was a risk I took bringing Rover into my business.

"I'm a cat person myself. I haven't been around dogs that much . . . I'm sure it will be fine."

"Not to worry. Rover's friendly."

"I'm sure he must be." Her tone defied her words.

I could see that my poor Rover had his work cut out for him, if he intended on winning Ms. Reynolds over.

Although I hadn't owned the inn long, I'd gotten quite good at making assumptions about guests when they booked their rooms. It surprised me how often I was right or nearly so. Time would tell with Ms. Eleanor Reynolds.

"I'll look forward to your visit, Ms. Reynolds."

"As I will to meeting you." After a brief farewell, she ended the call.

Prim and proper, a cat woman . . . Hmm, I was left to wonder. Possibly a librarian in her late forties or early fifties. In town for a special occasion? It certainly left me to ponder her story.

For whatever reason my eyes fell to the reservation book and on the two latest entries. Eleanor Reynolds and a young couple: Maggie and Roy Porter. Maggie had called a few days earlier to book a room for the same weekend as Eleanor. She sounded so young, as if she was barely out of her teens. She'd been talkative, telling me this was a getaway weekend she'd planned for her and her husband without the kids.

I would give anything to have issues to work out with Paul. Anything.

I continued about my morning, doing my best to follow my husband's advice and get on with life. I kept my cell phone in my pocket, and it thrummed, indicating I had a text. I reached for it and saw that the message was from Mark. Well, well, this was something new. Half the time he didn't even know where his cell phone was. Technology annoyed him. It appeared not having his cell phone with him when the table collapsed on his leg had taught him a lesson.

He wrote: I'm bored.

My fingers flew across the small keyboard. Read a book.

Very funny.

It isn't a joke. You need to stay off that leg.

Easy for you to say.

I grinned. Do you want me to bring you lunch?

What ya got?

Hey, this isn't a catering service. You take what you get and don't complain.

I don't have much choice, do I?

No choice whatsoever. I'll be by around noon. Count your blessings and show some gratitude.

Yes, ma'am.

Despite the news I had gotten earlier in the day, I glanced down at my phone and smiled.

I filled Rover's water dish and then made Mark lunch. Together Rover and I would personally deliver it to the prickly handyman who had become our friend.

ABOUT THE AUTHOR

DEBBIE MACOMBER, the author of *Starting Now, The Inn at Rose Harbor, Angels at the Table, A Turn in the Road, 1105 Yakima Street, Hannah's List,* and *Twenty Wishes,* is a leading voice in women's fiction. Seven of her novels have hit #1 on the *New York Times* bestseller list, with three debuting at #1 on the *New York Times, USA Today,* and *Publishers Weekly* lists. In 2009 and 2010, *Mrs. Miracle* and *Call Me Mrs. Miracle* were Hallmark Channel's top-watched movies for the year. Debbie Macomber has more than 160 million copies of her books in print worldwide.

www.debbiemacomber.com

ABOUT THE TYPE

This book was set in Sabon, a typeface designed by the well-known German typographer Jan Tschichold (1902–74). Sabon's design is based upon the original letter forms of Claude Garamond and was created specifically to be used for three sources: foundry type for hand composition, Linotype, and Monotype. Tschichold named his typeface for the famous Frankfurt typefounder Jacques Sabon, who died in 1580.